Thank
You!

whispers

J. Herman Kleiger

whispers

A Tale of Madness, Betrayal, and Revenge

Sequel to
Tears Are Only Water

J. HERMAN KLEIGER

WHISPERS

A TALE OF MADNESS, BETRAYAL, AND REVENGE

By J. Herman Kleiger

First Edition

Copyright © 2025 by J. Herman Kleiger

JAMES KLEIGER PC

The story, all names, characters, and incidents portrayed in this production are fictitious. No identification with actual persons (living or deceased), places, buildings, and products is intended or should be inferred.

Paperback ISBN# 978-1-960299-69-7
Hardcover ISBN: 978-1-960299-73-4

Printed in the United States of America

Dedication

To my loving family and to the majesty of birds

CONTENTS

Prologue

May 20, 2023,
Georgetown, Washington DC

Most people can't recall the smell of blood. Caralena couldn't until she walked into the doctor's office at 7 p.m. His was her last suite to clean, but the door to his waiting room was left ajar. No one entered without pressing the four-digit code into the keypad by the door. Curious, she scanned his waiting room. Everything was in place—dimly lit as usual, a shabby shrink décor with an eclectic mix of modern and ancient furniture. There were overstuffed IKEA faux leather chairs and a ratty end table with a towering stack of magazines, mostly with covers tattered and torn. Pictures of the seashore were strategically positioned on each wall to soothe those about to enter. Each time Caralena walked through the doorway with her vacuum, she couldn't help picturing the cramped examining rooms of the kind, old urologist who used to occupy Suite 44 before the psychiatrist took over the lease and reconfigured the spaces.

"Hellooo? Doctor? It's me, Cara, here to clean. Are you in there?" Recalling that he occasionally worked late, she called out, "I can come back later if you're still working."

His office door was cracked open, exposing the beige wall to his inner sanctum, where she believed important doctors healed their sick patients. As she approached, she was assaulted by a sickeningly sweet, metallic smell that no one should know, but everyone does. She had forgotten what her senses never had. Her mind in a jumble, she lightly tapped the door. "Doctor?"

Pushing it open, she looked inside and began to retch.

PART ONE

COMES THE WHISPERER

In the quiet of the night,
Silence prickles the skin and murmuring voices speak,
Telling stories in hushed tones of private lives and
Secrets buried so deeply that no one can hear,
Comes the Whisperer.
Tell me your secrets,
Speak to me of sin and shame,
And trust me with your soul.
—Anonymous

1

They're Killing All the Shrinks

The sirens were deafening, drowning out the heart-wrenching screams of frightened women and children. Around her lay the dead bodies of men from her platoon. Suddenly she was holding the limp body of her little brother Blue. The blaring sirens became the sound of her own scream. She awoke in a panic to the shrieking of her work phone.

Quickly orienting herself, she answered, "This is Kitts."

"Wakey, wakey Kitts. Rise and shine. Hope you're up. Doesn't matter because we've got another dead shrink. It's time to bring you in on this."

Special Agent Nicola Kitts immediately recognized the brassy voice of her boss, Executive Assistant Director Giancarlo Bozzio Baldazzar. Boz headed the FBI's Criminal, Cyber, Response, and Service Branch. Among his countless other jobs, he liked mentoring new agents. As a former Marine Captain, Boz had taken a shine to ex-gunnery sergeant Kitts. At 5'3," he chewed out anyone who looked down when talking to him. Although he downplayed their Marine Corps connection, Kitts felt the strength of their invisible *Semper Fi* bond.

She glanced at her clock: 4:30 a.m. With a rush of adrenalin, she sat up straight and said, "Yes, Sir. Copy that."

"Kitts, enough with the military, cop-speak bullshit. I've told you, we don't talk like that around here. But listen . . . we've got another one. This makes three—Tamerlane, Fortunato, and now this guy in his Georgetown office. Same MO and signature as the others. Also left another calling card—the same wacky quote and a bunch of those crazy equations, like before. Looks like we have a serial killer who loves math as much as he does butchering shrinks. Anyway, this will be your first rodeo, kid. BAU-4 is staffing this in two days, so you have time to get up to speed. They're a bunch of eggheaded profilers with egos to match, except for Sidd. He's good people. So, Kitts, you'll be there primarily to listen and learn. Their job is to profile. Yours is to keep a *low* profile."

"You said this is just like the other two? Same MO?"

"Yeah, Kitts, that's what I said. This last one was in DC. No suspects yet, but the local PD is working on this as a single homicide. They apparently don't know about the others. The vic's name is Linus Prokop. Maybe you've heard of him?"

"Yes, Sir. Isn't he the guy on the cable news? I remember that name. Didn't he do some kind of study on male adolescents?"

"That's right. He's a doozy. Been on the talk show circuit hawking his book about teenage boys and their hard-ons."

Kitts smiled at his raw and uncensored expressions. Suddenly, she felt as if she were back in bootcamp with Boz as her drill sergeant.

"DC Metro is still working the crime scene. Probably won't be too happy when we show up, but nothing new with that. So, get your rear in gear pronto and look at the files so you won't seem like Doby the village idiot when you meet with BAU Number 4. Got it?"

"Copy—I mean yes, Boz Sir. I'll be there by 7:00."

"Make it 6:30. Oh, and Kitts, leave your damn bird at home this time. Now fuck off."

She blushed as she remembered bringing Langston, her hyacinth macaw, to her office. He was not a hit since he wandered around, marked his territory, and chewed phone cords. Langston had been her sidekick for more than 15 years. If it hadn't been for Langston, her old boss, Sheriff Oliver Burwinkle, would have killed her too after he shot an agent point blank in her living room.

Nicola microwaved a cup of day-old coffee while scarfing down a banana. She pulled Langston's breakfast bowl out of the fridge, mixed in fresh fruit and vegetables, and topped it with large-shelled nuts.

The bird began to chatter and squawk to get her attention.

"Damn, cool it. Not in the mood this morning." She noticed he was picking at the feathers on his chest again. "Stop picking at yourself. I ain't got time for this shit now." She reached for the spray the vet had given her and gave him a couple of squirts.

Kitts rummaged through a pile of clothes on her chair and grabbed a wrinkled jacket from the floor. Life had been this way since moving to DC two years ago.

"Alexa, play some . . . Tracie Chapman music. No, cancel that. Play—"

Alexa cut her off and said, "Here is some music by Tracie Chapman on Amazon Music."

"Dammit, girl. Alexa, cancel that. Play music by Libba Cotton and turn up the volume by two." She felt there was something enchanting about Cotton, an obscure left-handed folk and blues musician who taught herself to play upside down on a right-handed guitar. That Cotton didn't begin recording until her 60s and won a Grammy at age 90 gave Kitts hope that people could successfully reinvent themselves in midlife.

She turned on the shower as Libba sang *Ain't Got No Honey Baby Now*. The water was cold, but she didn't have time for it to warm up. The chill jolted her senses. She threw on her clothes and hurried past Langston—*still* picking his chest feathers. "Langs! Stop that shit! I gotta cruise now. Won't be back until dark 'cause this is a big one. You got plenty to eat, so be cool and STOP doing that to yourself."

The thought of another dead therapist put her on full alert, especially with this last one being so close to home. On the way out the door, she stopped and reached out to Langston. "Damn boy, it looks like they're killing all the shrinks…. Betcha, you're glad I left shrink school, huh?"

* * *

It was still dark when she exited onto South Washington St. She opened the window, welcoming the chill of cool air on her face. She tried to focus on the killing of yet another psychiatrist, but the hangover from her nightmare was still taunting her. Her VA counselor told her that dreams about the war would never disappear entirely. He said she could learn to reprocess them to make them less frequent, vivid, and painful, but they would never disappear. *Fucking nightmares.*

In the darkness, surrounded by the hum of the tires, Kitts thought about the regular cast of characters who haunted her sleep. Her dreams were typically set in Afghanistan where her brother Blue, Burwinkle, or Pei would suddenly appear, always trying to speak to her in muffled voices. Desperate, she couldn't move. Her counselors told her she'd be dealing with the long reach of PTSD for the rest of her life. She should expect early and subsequent losses to merge with nightmares of her final bloody firefight in the Musa Qala District.

At times, she dreamed only of Blue and his death when they were kids. No matter how much Nicola tried to come to terms with what happened, the guilt never wore off. Paradoxically, there was something oddly comforting about her nighttime visits from Blue, as if he were trying to tell her something.

She hated how the traitorous bastard Oliver Burwinkle forced himself into her dreams. Her former boss and mentor back in Colorado continued to stalk her in her sleep after his final deceit. Now, Professor Omar Pei had become the latest cast member to appear uninvited in her dreams, whispering lustfully to her about their forbidden affair at Smith College.

Kitts checked her speed as a highway patrolman passed her on the right. *Cops.* The cruiser reminded her of the Ford Interceptor she used to drive when she was the only deputy of color in the sheriff's department in Colorado. She left law enforcement in 2014 after Burwinkle tried to kill her. Nicola's stomach churned when she thought of the impostor. Burwinkle turned out to be a serious bad guy. Fortunately, thanks to Langston's attacking him, Burwinkle dropped dead of a heart attack before pulling the trigger of the gun he had aimed at her head. *Fucking Burwinkle.*

Though she had long thought about leaving police work, the catastrophic events of 2014 and her subsequent treatment at the VA convinced her it was time to make a clean break and try something new, like becoming a social worker. Her decision to leave law enforcement always made her think of her quirky friend Carmine or "Books" as she called him. Nicola still felt embarrassed by his generous financial gift, which made it possible for her to go to Smith College of Social Work. She recalled their awkward conversation five years ago when she received a check from an anonymous donor that covered her tuition at Smith.

"I know it was you, Books. You're always up to something sneaky like this. I will pay you back. Got that? Been saving up my money."

But she hadn't paid him back.

She had been a rising star at Smith, earning her MSW in just under two years. Nicola had begun working on a PhD when she suddenly became the headliner in the campus rumor mill. She mistakenly thought her involvement with one of her professors was a private affair.

Thoughts about Pei always reminded Kitts of her misplaced trust in Burwinkle whose words she couldn't forget.

"Goddammit, Cole. You were like a daughter to me, girl."

Then he tried to kill her.

The relationship with Professor Omar Pei began innocently enough. He was struck by her intelligence, fascinating resume, dogged curiosity, and innate insight, and mentioned in passing her striking good looks.

Looking her up and down, he'd intoned, "You're special Nicola Kitts. I've had my eye on you. You have the intellectual gifts and instincts that most students can only dream of. I've taken a special interest in your academic development. Dine with me tonight so we can discuss your thesis."

And she did.

Kitts's internal signals told her she was straying into dangerous territory, but she ignored the warning lights. It felt good to be special.

Man, gotta figure out this shit with mentors, girl.

Their affair lasted less than three months but unleashed the hungry tabloid hounds within the small college community. Ultimately, the professor was dismissed, and his student branded with a scarlet letter. It didn't matter that no one formally blamed Nicola for her mammoth lapse in judgment. She heard the whispers and saw the looks wherever she went. It became too much to bear. One morning, she decided she'd had enough. She packed everything that would fit into her car and left with Langston.

Nicola knew that even before the Pei affair, she'd been questioning whether social work was her true calling. Maybe her embarrassment at Smith was just an excuse to leave social work. Part of her wanted to be done with policing but it wasn't done with her. Law enforcement was in her DNA. Her father and gramps had been Marines and then cops in the Wichita PD. Having no desire to return to the sheriff's department in Colorado, Kitts applied and was accepted to the FBI Academy.

The traffic was light. *Can't keep Boz waiting.* The final stretch of Richmond Highway reminded her of how she felt the first time she drove to Quantico. She had been filled with hopes about combining law enforcement with her curiosity about the workings of the mind. Even then, she aspired to someday become a profiler.

After completing the FBI Academy, Kitts worked as a junior agent before snagging an appointment to the BAU (Behavioral Assessment Unit). Only a year into her role as a special agent, Kitts felt she'd found a home where she could pursue criminals and discover the deep-seated pathologies that had turned them into killers and predators. She knew about the storied BAU-4 and its predecessor, the FBI's Elite Serial Crime Unit, popularized in one of her favorite books, *Mindhunter*. That someone at Boz's level would select her to shadow this celebrated team of profilers and analysts was a pulse-quickening honor. She thought of his words several months back.

"Kitts, I've been watching you. I think you got what it takes to work with the BAU. When the time is right, I'm going to bring you in. I got faith in you. Just don't try to act too much like a cop."

Kitts checked her watch as she flashed her ID to the Marine at the gate. Six twenty-seven—three minutes to spare. She sprinted to the building; Boz would be watching the clock. Kitts wanted to impress him but knew he would quickly pick up her efforts to curry favor. Boz had apparently seen something in her that she was not aware of. But hadn't Burwinkle and Pei? She was grateful that Boz was giving her a chance but determined not to make the same mistakes as before. All she needed to do was trust his judgment and not lose sight of hers. *Just be yourself, whoever that is, and steer clear of whatever's going on with mentors.* She speed-walked into his office and reminded herself not to speak like a cop and never look down at the top of his head.

2

THE WHISPERING WALL

Raevyn Nevenmoore awakened with a scream. The content of her nightmare became a watercolor mélange, images hidden behind terror. She oriented herself to her bed and her room. Frilly lace curtains lined windows overlooking the large river birch in the backyard. Her twin bed overflowed with stuffed animals, including Beanie Bear, her favorite. Piles of clothes and unopened boxes from her last spending spree in Georgetown lay strewn across the floor. The wall above her bed was still plastered with pictures of Olympic gymnasts Shannon Miller and Dominique Dawes. On an adjacent wall hung posters of *Blink-182* and *Alkaline Trio*, added during her punk rock craze when she was secretly fascinated by all things dark and wild. Trophies competed for space on her dresser, while medals and plaques spilled from boxes on the floor.

Someday, they would all be gone. The pictures and posters would all come down; the walls would be painted pink with rainbows and unicorns, and some sweet little girl would be nestled next to her own special stuffy. But for now, the room, like Raevyn, was stuck in time as if nothing had changed when in fact, everything had.

Linus Prokop suddenly entered her mind—*Well, hello there Linus*—followed quickly by uneasy thoughts of her twin brother Finch, who had recently wandered back into her life. But she knew Finch had never really left. Raevyn could keep secrets.

Thoughts about Finch released a flight of memories about the first time she saw Prokop five years earlier after a series of family tragedies and the debacle in St. Louis. She had just been released from the psych ward and was still feeling shaky, as the doctors struggled to find the right combination of medications to treat her unstable mood and paranoid thoughts.

As always, it had been her big sister Yeardley who had initially badgered her into seeing Prokop then, and again now. Yeardley had been the one to set up her 6:00 appointment yesterday and would be disappointed to learn about the cancellation. She was away at a conference and wouldn't be back for a few days, but Raevyn knew this wouldn't stop her from checking about her appointment.

Raevyn remembered that day in 2019 when Prokop first strutted out of his office to greet her. His thick head of salt and pepper hair sat atop a round face and pronounced cheekbones. He wore an expensive suit but looked like he needed to lose 20 pounds and trim the hairs peeking out from his jutting nostrils. More off-putting than his appearance were his grating words.

"Why, hello there Ms. Nevenmoore. Raevyn isn't it? What a pleasure, indeed. I'm Dr. Prokop. Let's go into my consultation room and find out how I can help you."

Raevyn burned as she recalled Prokop's pretense that he knew nothing about her past or her family, all of whom had previously been on his couch at one time or another. Seated across from him that day, she could not contain her wrath at his feigned sympathy for what had happened to her parents and then her brother. When he asked about her twin, she watched him wince as she let loose a manic fusillade laced with sarcasm and contempt. She remembered springing to her feet and pacing his office, hoping her unfiltered speech, dysregulated mood, and narcissistic snark would make him so uncomfortable that he would call her sister to say she was untreatable.

She remembered her words as if reading from a script. "Okay, I'll play along with your game that you don't know anything about Finch.

Let's just say he was everything I was not. I was always Corvie. I assume you already know that, but I'll humor you, Linus. Ravens are from the Corvidae family, right? Except Finch calls me Cobie because he couldn't pronounce his Rs when he was a kid. So, I was his Cobie, and he is my little Birdie. As kids, I was always taller, smarter, and more popular. He was a short nerd with coke bottle glasses that magnified his beady little eyes. I knew something about everything, just enough to dazzle people with the bullshit they mistakenly took as brilliance. Of course, you know about the selective growth restriction thing?"

Prokop listened intently without betraying his knowledge of her family history.

"I'm assuming you're pretending you don't know anything about my getting most of Mummie's intrauterine goodies, leaving poor Finchy with the poopies. You know that, right? Well, that was us. As babies, I was bigger and stronger. That's still the case, but when we were kids, I was confident and inquisitive, whereas Birdie was gripped by dullness and timidity. Honestly, if we were birds, Finch would have been the one you find on the sidewalk beneath the nest. Animals have a way of dealing with their genetic accidents. I could do any sport better than anyone at school, while he tripped over his shoelaces. I was always a first-team all-star until I fucked up in St. Louis...but he was a permanent backbencher, yada yada. No one could believe we were twins. As a kid, I pretended he wasn't my twin but just some annoying little kid who followed me around. Yep, I had all the accolades, top grades, scholarships to the best schools, and all the friends and attention that should make anyone happy. I think he still resents this."

Raevyn could still picture that odd look on Prokop's face when she said that Birdie still resented it.

"You said, *Still*?" Prokop had that look she would later recognize as doubt or skepticism when his nose hairs stood on end as if he'd seen through her smokescreen of targeted arrogance and callous disregard. But in their first session, he seemed more confused and alarmed.

"Yeah, I did."

"*Still* . . . You said Finch *still* resents this."

"I'm so happy your hearing is intact, Doctor."

He jotted a note on his pad and then asked about her parents.

"Okay, we're still pretending you don't know any of this. Raevyn told him that besides the intrauterine disparities, she'd inherited most of her gifts from their endlessly talented and celebrated mother, Dr. Abigail LeBlanc, a well-known thoracic surgeon at Georgetown Medical School. But I believe you already know my mother, Doctor."

Prokop asked about her bipolar disorder, which hadn't been diagnosed until it was on full display in St. Louis for the whole world to see. Before that, everyone had known about her moodiness, but they were more dazzled by her winning smile, academic excellence, and athletic accomplishments. Prokop had wondered about her decision in 2019 to begin medical school at Penn while also training for the Olympic trials. Hadn't she known that something was off when her mind raced and she was up all night?

She smiled as she recalled her cutting riposte. "You did study psychiatry, right Doctor? I guess you were absent when they taught about how self-awareness does not cohabitate with mania."

As if to halt her flood of memories about Prokop and soak up the bloody spillage from her nightmare, she closed her eyes. She reflexively turned toward the vent in her wall and did what she always had when she needed him. From the time they were kids and had moved into separate bedrooms, they whispered through the wall at night.

"Birdie?"

While in public, she acted as if she didn't know her awkward twin, but in the solitude of her room she depended on him. Late into the night, long past their 10 p.m. bedtime and lights out, she whispered to him, sometimes for hours, in hushed tones, confessing her worries and regrets, the *sturm* and *drang* in her life. She whispered about the distance between their parents, their mother's insufferable self-centeredness, and their father's icy indifference. Despite how she shunned him in public, he listened to her whispers and served not only as Echo to her Narcissus but also as humble confessor to sinful penitent. Within the sanctity of this intrauterine-like space, Raevyn unburdened herself while Finch listened and took mental notes.

But that morning, bloody images continued to seep into her consciousness. She whispered his name. No longer speaking in hushed tones, Raevyn grew more insistent. "We *have* to talk. Birdie. My God, Finch, what have you done!?"

3

COBIE & BIRDIE

March 1999

She couldn't recall when she first realized her brother was different. It might have been that morning in preschool when Finch was sent home for biting Annie Kim. Raevyn remembered her mother's loud fury and her father's quiet annoyance.

"You act like a little beast, Finch. Adolf, you need to deal with him because I can't!"

She remembered their mother's spittle spraying across the room as she shouted at her twin. Their father dragged a tearful Finch up from the basement and locked him in his room for three days for the unpardonable crime of biting another preschooler, which according to their mother, "No normal child would ever do!"

Although they were twins, Raevyn and Finch were opposites in every way. She was the rabbit to his tortoise. She was an early reader, he a "slow learner." Other parents wanted their children to play with Raevyn, but made excuses for excluding Finch from playdates, once he was labeled a biter.

Cartwheeling across the living room, Raevyn soon knew she was bigger, faster, quicker with her words and grasping new concepts.

"Watch, Mommy. See what I can do. Betcha Finch can't do this."

Raevyn knew in her bones she was the alpha and Finch the beta. She wore an invisible halo above her head and knew their mother viewed her as a talented and gifted child, while her twin brother was the developmental turd. Raevyn knew nothing about selective growth restriction until high school biology class when she first heard about intrauterine aberrations like vanishing twin syndrome. Until that time, all she knew was that whatever she could do easily was a struggle for Finch.

Their grandmother, Pansy, suggested the names Raevyn and Finch to their mother. She also gave them the nicknames Birdie and Corbie.

"Finch is like a little birdie, so delicate, and you, my dear Raevyn, are a powerful corvine. The Scots use the word "corbin" for Ravens. This is the family of strong, clever, and intelligent birds. Raven and Finch, Corbie and Birdie."

The names stuck, at least for Raevyn and Finch. Because Finch couldn't pronounce his Rs, all he could manage was *Cobie* and *Boodie*.

As with all siblings, especially twins, Cobie and Birdie had a complicated relationship. She cherished her preferred position and superior fitness while secretly relishing her brother's status as the family misfit. At the same time, she and Finch were deeply connected. How could she bask in her privilege and superiority while simultaneously loving and feeling protective of him? She rooted outwardly for him to succeed but secretly kept score of the countless times he failed, and she emerged the victor. Sadly, she had no one to help her make sense of this bundle of contradictions.

During preschool, their mother placed them in adjacent bedrooms. Because Raevyn could never fall asleep, she started whispering to Finch through the vent in their wall late into the night.

"Birdie? Birdieee. Are you awake? I'm scared. I can't sleep. Will you tell me a story?"

Everyone knew Finch idolized his sister, whom he clumsily tried to please. "What story do you want me to tell you, Cobie?"

"I like the one about the princess and her magical worm. Tell that one, Birdie."

4

BAU-4

At 6:30 a.m., Nicola sat in her cubical anxiously awaiting the Unit 4 staffing at 7:30. She had spent the past two days pouring over files of the dead shrinks. The MO was similar in each case: Three psychiatrists sitting in various states of nakedness at their desks with their throats cut. Each was holding a note with an obscure quote from someone called *The Whisperer* followed by cryptic mathematical equations that none of the analysts had so far been able to explain. She thought about Carmine Luedke, the awkward bookkeeper and mathematical savant from Colorado.

Nicola smiled as she thought about Carmine with his tortured speech, stooped posture, odd assortment of baggy clothes, shiny shoes, and brilliantly colored socks. First a suspect in an assault case, then a victim of a conspiracy, and eventually a friend and benefactor, Carmine, beyond anything else, was a mathematical wizard. She wondered what he would make of these formulas. Her reverie was interrupted by Boz's brusque greeting.

"Up and at 'em, Kitts. Time to put on your socks and drop your coc—. Shit, forget I said that. I don't need HR breathing down my neck again. I hope you've done your homework because they move fast in there. Remember you're in the F mother-bleeping BI, Kitts, and your job is to listen and learn. Here's a brief on the team."

Kitts nodded and took out her notebook and pen.

"BAU-4 is the real world, Kitts. It's not *Criminal Minds*. Most wannabe agents binge-watched that shit as kids. They don't have their own damn jet. The hours are long and the work tedious. Don't expect to have a social life. Team 4 is headed by three of our top profilers, Drs. Ramachandran, Saks, and De Vere. No doubt you've heard of them."

She widened her eyes at the third name, immediately aware that Boz had picked up on her reaction.

"Kitts, she's a hell of a lot smarter than you'll ever be, so don't stare when you're introduced."

Nicola nodded as she thought about Bernice De Vere, who was more than a curiosity. She briefly met De Vere two years ago when *he* was a guest lecturer on serial killers in a required course on criminology for new academy graduates. A striking figure with a jurisprudence doctorate and PhD in clinical psychology, De Vere had also received psychoanalytic training at the William Alanson White Institute. Best known for her profiling of Ted Bundy and John Wayne Gacy, De Vere's book *In the Shadows of Normalcy* was considered a companion piece to Cleckley's classic *The Mask of Sanity*. De Vere had a particular interest in the Jungian concept of the shadow self, hidden beneath the public persona.

When she first saw *him*, Bernard De Vere stood 6'6" and had the girth of a bear dressed in a gray three-piece suit. Kitts recalled his grim countenance and distant demeanor. She had heard the rumors but hadn't seen De Vere since she'd transitioned a year before.

Boz said, "Siddharth Ramachandran, the lead profiler who heads the team, goes by Sidd. He's a man of few words who has a sixth sense for this shit. Listen and learn, Kitts, but don't expect more than a formal greeting from him. He plays his cards close to his vest."

She nodded. Ramachandran was a legend at the FBI's Behavioral Science Units. The inscrutable profiler was a psychiatrist who had written *When Madness Turns Lethal*, the definitive textbook on criminality and psychosis. The ninja-like team leader was said to always dress in black and wear his long gray hair tied in a Samurai ponytail. Kitts had heard stories about his quiet demeanor and penetrating insight. She was proud of her fearlessness and determination not to let anything get to her—a remnant of her ex-Marine father's mantra, *It don't mean nuthin,'* which he drilled into her when she was a kid. As much as she tried to use this to silence fear and doubt, she felt intimidated by the thought of sitting around a conference table with the likes of Siddharth Ramachandran.

"You'll also have the pleasure—which is a much-overstated word in this case—of meeting the third profiler, Gideon Saks. Think boot camp, Kitts, when you had those sadistic noncoms sizing you up and trying to make you break. Saks is a card-carrying member of MENSA, but between us, he's a pencil-necked twit with an oversized ego. Remember to listen, learn, and keep your pie hole shut."

Everyone had heard of Gideon Saks, a DSc in neuroscience and PhD in English literature from Oxford, who was equally feared and admired. However, unlike Sidd Ramachandran, Saks's infamous arrogance and condescension made him easy to despise. Saks wore a perpetually bored look and had the kind of face that people wanted to smack. Kitts once heard how he reduced another faculty member to a quivering pool of pablum during a debate. He spoke in tome-length sentences and used obscure words to intimidate.

Someone once confronted him about his use of obscure words. He responded that imprecise words permanently eliminated crucial aspects of experience, so it was critical to capture reality as precisely as possible. He preached that words, even the most abstruse, brought us closer to our experiences in the real world. After becoming a senior behavioral analyst for the FBI, he authored two books on dissociation and violence.

The first time she saw Saks, he was with an entourage of students at a wine bar frequented by technical analysts and bureau consultants. He appeared to be holding court, as the others hung on his every word. His aquiline features, slicked-back hair, and thick eyebrows rose and fell like the Brooklyn Bridge when he spoke. He had a carefully manicured goatee and wore a drab-colored bowtie and wire-rimmed glasses attached to a gold chain around his neck. She had never imagined herself sitting in a room with him, let alone teaming up with someone like Gideon Saks.

Boz continued, "The other two special agents and our analyst techie, Patricia Smith, will introduce themselves when we get in there. They use Conference Room C-14. I'll introduce you but don't expect to get a warm introduction. They're all business and they stick to the script."

5

The How, What, Why, and Who

The building was a maze of white hallways lined with closed doors. Kitts followed Boz and avoided looking down at the top of his head.

"Here it is." He opened the door and nodded to the four people seated around a large conference table. Each was looking through a heavy binder. The room's perimeter was not well-lit, but several fluorescent fixtures illuminated the conference table. A video projector was centered on the table and a large screen stood at the end of the room.

Nicola had never seen three of them but immediately recognized the fourth as Gideon Saks, who looked up when they entered the room. The other three nodded and smiled, but Gideon lowered his head without acknowledgement and returned to the elaborate doodling on his Styrofoam coffee cup.

A dark-haired, mid-30s man looked up and said, "Hey, Boss."

Boz nodded and introduced Kitts. "Kitts, this is Special Agent Toby Potter, and next to him is Lenore Patterson, also Special Agent. They're our ground troops deployed to Unit 4. You'll be tagging along with them in the field."

Potter leaned over the desk, held out his hand, and placed Nicola's hand in a vice grip. She thought, *Okay, I see you and your play to establish a pecking order. That's cool.* Having worked in the male-dominated worlds of law enforcement and the military, she thought, *Man, this macho, little boy bullshit never goes away.*

Lenore Patterson stood up and said, "Hey, Executive Director Baldazzar, it's always great to see you, Boss." She held out her hand to Kitts. "Nice to meet you. You have probably heard a lot about BAU- 4. I hope it's everything you imagined."

Lenore looked slightly older than Potter. Her hair was closely cropped. Over-sized tortoise-shelled glasses framed striking blue eyes.

"Lenore's ex-Army intelligence, but we don't hold that against her," said Boz. "Kitts still whistles the Marine Hymn, but she's okay. And Potter over there, we're still trying to figure out where the hell he came from."

Potter gave a playful salute but did not smile.

Kitts heard stifled laughter about a private joke. She sat down next to Boz. Against the wall sat another woman who now stood and handed Nicola a binder.

"Hi, Agent Kitts, I'm Pat Smith, the technical analyst for Unit 4. You won't catch me in the field, but I'm your techie, always here for data searches and IT support. We have access to Radford's Serial Killer Database for researching victimology and multiple-murder methodology. Welcome aboard, Special Agent."

Pat looked as nondescript as her name. She could have passed for a shopper in any small-town Walmart. Dressed conservatively in gray slacks and a black sweater, Pat was pale with drab-colored shoulder-length hair. She wore no jewelry or a hint of makeup. Kitts caught sight of her gray roots peeking out along her part and profiled Pat as a single woman with no family, too many computers, too few friends, and a small house filled with too many cats and plants she had probably given individual names. Nicola inwardly cringed at having so quickly succumbed to the cat lady trope.

Boz spoke up. "Hey Patty, how are the kids and the pooches? Did you get Barney off to college?"

"Yeah, Boss. He's gone. Now, Davy and I have to get the other one ready next year. The dogs are eating us out of house and home. Where do the years go, huh?"

Missed that one by a sad mile. Kitts blushed, her profiling skills were still in their infancy.

The door opened, and all eyes fixed on the next team member to enter. Kitts told herself, *Don't stare, goddamit,* but she couldn't help it. Dr. Bernice De Vere filled the room with her striking and colorful appearance. She wore a midnight blue Ann Taylor plus-size suit with an apricot and ivory scarf. Her brown hair curled down her shoulders, flashing a few auburn highlights. Kitts remembered pictures she'd seen of the famous TV chef Julia Childs. De Vere had jeweled rings on several fingers and wore a large rainbow broach on her right lapel. Kitts spotted another pin on the left side resembling the Eagle, Globe, and Anchor.

She glanced at Boz, who winked and mouthed, "Oorah."

"Well, it's nice to see everyone," said De Vere. "Gio, it's always nice to see you, dear."

Kitts thought, *Who the hell is Gio?*

Boz nodded and said, "Thank you, Doctor. I appreciate that."

"And I'm delighted we're graced by the presence of a new member. Gio, this must be the young agent you told us about."

She turned to Kitts and held out her massive hand. "I'm Bernice De Vere. It's lovely to meet you."

Nicola stood and made eye contact with the woman she'd once known as someone else. When Bernice De Vere spoke, Kitts heard the same resonant voice from the lecture hall two years before. But apart from the obvious changes in her appearance, Nicola detected something more substantial—a liveliness and lightness in her ex-professor's expression, surely the result of having been liberated from her internal prison.

"Gio has told us of your curiosity and native instincts. Welcome, Agent Kitts. I think you'll bring a fresh perspective to our group, dear."

"It's an honor, Doctor. I'm—"

Up to that point, Gideon Saks hadn't said a word, much less looked up from the cup he was meticulously embroidering with his Monteblanc pen. When he finally spoke, his Queen's English was dry and crusty. "Greetings, Agent Kitts. I'm Dr. Gideon Saks, but I believe we have pressing business to attend to. We're here because our troubled world has offered up another taste of her infinite malevolence. So, now that our fearless leader has emerged from the ether, may we dispense with further formalities and begin?"

The group was startled to notice that Dr. Siddharth Ramachandran had stealthily entered the room and was already seated at the head of the table.

Boz spoke first. "And now the family is complete because our papa has arrived. This is Special Agent Kitts. She's just met the others. I have another meeting with the director to piss off to, but I wanted to make sure she settled in and met the team."

Sidd's penetrating look was unnerving. *Don't mean nuthin'*, she tried to tell herself, knowing that this actually meant a great deal. Kitts held his gaze until he formed a slight smile and said, "Ah, Nicola Kitts. I've been looking forward to meeting you."

Just as she'd heard, he was dressed in black with long gray hair. Kitts thought Ramachandran could have walked out of an ancient monastic order. He nodded to Boz, who said his goodbyes and exited the conference room.

Sidd began, "Let us start this consultation by reviewing the data. Remember, we have a series of *whats* and *hows*. In a few minutes, I'll have Special Agent Lenore Patterson walk us through *what* was found at the crime scenes and *how* each victim was killed. Our task is to understand the mindset of the unknown subject from what he has left for us. To paraphrase our original mind hunters, Douglas and Olshaker, understanding the artist means we must study his art. If we wish to decipher the criminal mind, we must learn to decode what he has left us, essentially a reflection of who he is. Observing the *what* and the *how* will lead to a discovery of the *why*, which will eventually reveal the *who*."

Gideon Saks added, "Your mention of John Douglas and Mark Olshaker should remind us that our UNSUB is likely compensating for his failings by assuming a sense of grandiosity. But like our forefathers in the profiling business said, in the end, such monsters end up being inadequate nobodies."

Sidd nodded and said, "You have all read the case file on these killings. Before we begin, I suggest we take a 10-minute break while I respond to an urgent message. Agent Kitts, there is a canteen down the hall if you'd like coffee or tea."

At that moment, Kitts had the sense that she'd come home and met for the first time the family she always sensed was out there. Smart and curious law enforcement professionals interested in the *whys*, not just the *hows* and *whats*. She was spellbound by the measured cadence of his speech. Sidd's words were crisp and sparse. Where it might have taken Saks 15 words to articulate a point, it took Sidd five.

She was about to stand up when Bernice De Vere surprised her with an invitation to have coffee together. Kitts agreed and followed the senior profiler down the narrow hallway to the canteen, taking note of the length of De Vere's stride and the lightness in her step. When they reached the coffee nook, De Vere doused a bag of Earl Grey in her cup while Kitts poured coffee into hers. They found a small table that all but disappeared beneath De Vere's large frame. Nicola wasn't sure what to expect. She felt flattered that someone with De Vere's status and reputation was reaching out but couldn't help having her radar attuned to what the storied profiler might have in mind. Was this a polite overture or was *she* being profiled?

6

LIVING IN THE SHADOWS

Kitts fiddled with her sugar packets, trying not to stare. De Vere sipped her tea. Her intense gaze was unnerving. Searching for what to say, Kitts blurted out, "Your book on the shadow selves in these killers got me pretty interested. Might have been one of the main things that got me interested in the BAU." She cringed at how she sounded like a high schooler at a career fair.

De Vere smiled. "I'm gratified that you found my work interesting. The Jungian concept of the shadow self has long intrigued me . . . I'm sure you won't be surprised to learn I've studied your personnel file, dear. We've all done that as a matter of routine, but let's say I've taken a special interest. It appears we share some things in common, Nicola Kitts."

Kitts was startled and felt uneasy. She suddenly felt transparent, a laboratory specimen on a slide to be studied and picked apart.

De Vere quickly caught Kitts's discomfort and said, "It's alright. That must have sounded like I was examining you like some type of rare sample in my lab. I didn't intend that. But what I meant is that we seem to have traveled down similar roads in our lives. Bundy, Gacy, and the lot aren't the only ones with shadow selves. We all have them. Although theirs were unspeakably evil and grotesque, for most of us, they harbor truths about ourselves that we cannot bring into the light of our public personas."

Uncertain of the latent meaning of the profiler's comments, Nicola nodded and listened uneasily.

"I suspect we may share some interesting similarities. You were a Marine Corps gunnery sergeant; I served the Corps as an intelligence officer. We both saw combat, though I imagine mine couldn't have compared to yours—a Silver Star for your heroic action in Musa Qala. Most importantly, I think we've both struggled to live our truths."

Nicola remained transfixed by the towering person across from her. Searching for the correct wavelength to decipher De Vere's message, she simply said, "Go on, Doctor. You got me interested."

"Well, first thing, please call me Bernice. We're colleagues now. And I *do* remember you from my lecture to your class a few years back. You can spot a Marine by the way they sit."

"You mean *ex,* ex-Marine," Kitts corrected her.

"We both know there really aren't ex-Marines, dear. Some chose service and sacrifice, and some did not. You had the same level of acuity and keen sense of purpose sitting upright in my class as I imagine you had in Afghanistan or when you served as a deputy in the Arapahoe County Sheriff's Office. Many things never change, but some things do. We all shed our old skins as we grow, don't we?"

Kitts nodded and sipped her coffee, wondering where this was leading.

"Back then, I was the one who looked a good deal different. You see, it took me most of my life to find my truth and the courage to live it. I know you've spent much of your life in the military and law enforcement but left all that to become a social worker. So, I don't know which is your true path. Maybe you've figured it all out. Maybe not.... What I'm trying to say is, I understand something about why you may have left Smith College. Rumors and whispers. I've lived in the shadows of whispers for a long time. Worse than those I heard from others were the ones inside. People still talk, but I breathe more easily now that I no longer listen to the murmurs inside myself. Anyway, welcome again to our team. I look forward to your contributions to the mission. I hope I haven't frightened you away, dear."

Kitts bristled at the mention of rumors and whispers at Smith. She forced a smile to mask her emotions, fearing she was revealing too much through her stiffness and tense facial expression. She felt unnerved yet oddly seen and accepted. Living in the shadows and hiding from parts of her past *had* dominated her life. Breathing and walking in the light were what mattered now.

They finished their coffee. De Vere made another cup of tea before they began walking back to the conference room. She walked ahead, then stopped and turned to Kitts. "After you, Gunny."

7

NAKED PERSONIFICATIONS

Kitts was unsettled by their conversation. She felt understood yet also outed and exposed; honored and respected but at the same time, stripped and placed on a phony pedestal. Back in the conference room, she inhaled deeply to silence her internal dissonance.

The team members opened their binders as Lenore Patterson turned on the projector, which flashed headshots of three men.

"This is what we know. Three shrinks ritualistically murdered in their offices. Seems they all had worked together on the ARES Project, a 10-year multisite research study on the sexual development of adolescent males. Last year, they released their book, *Masculīnus*, reviewing the study and its controversial conclusions."

With a click of her remote, she blew up each photo, then switched to vivid crime scene images of each victim. "The first, Dr. Arthur Tamerlanc, had been the head of the project. He was killed in Ann Arbor on February 16th. His body was discovered by the cleaning crew the next morning. Next, we have another psychiatrist, Julius Fortunato, MD, PhD, shown here at his desk. He was killed in Philadelphia on April 8th. The third, some of you may know from his lecture here last year on the hidden faces of psychopathy. He was also in the news recently after his book was released. Of course, I'm talking about Dr. Linus Prokop, who was found dead in his Georgetown office last Tuesday."

Gideon Saks cleared his throat and looked up from his cup. "Thank

you, Lenore, for setting the table and introducing our unfortunate fea-
tured players who met such grisly and ignominious fates. As our ill-fated
Hamlet put it, 'Foul deeds will arise, though all the earth o'erwhelm
them, to men's eyes.' And sadly, our friend Pinocchio should have satisfied himself with his timber head instead of questing to become a boy,
because only the human mind seeks such perverse and vicious abomina-
tions. And regarding Dr. Prokop, Siddharth and I knew him well, and
his death is a devastating loss for our behavioral forensic community."

All eyes shifted to Ramachandran, whose stoic expression remained
unchanged.

Putting down his pen and admiring his work, Saks continued,
"Let's take a moment, shall we, to discuss the tapestry that these crime
scene variables have woven into such savage, seemingly isolated killings,
keeping in mind the baser instincts that always underlie such obsceni-
ties: love, lust, jealousy, envy, betrayal, revenge, terror, and of course, the
hidden reservoirs of inadequacy and self-loathing that underpin them."

Kitts took an immediate dislike to this man, whom she sensed to
be a bully at heart, seeking to demonstrate his dominance. She tried to
side-step her feelings so she didn't miss what he was saying.

Saks scanned the room before landing on Toby Potter. "Ah, Special
Agent Potter, please enlighten us on what you've ascertained about the
linking factors, i.e., our killer's modus operandi, victimology, signature,
or these calling cards they've appeared to have left for us to see."

Potter stiffened and took the bait. "Sure, as we know, the victims
were all male mental health doctors somewhere between 45 and 65
years of age. Each was a famous professor at a major university and had
written lots of books and papers. All of them had traveled abroad to
lecture and present at international conferences. In discussing the MO,
both me and Lenore had—"

Saks sharpened his razor and interrupted with ruthless pedantry.
"God, deliver us from those intent on eviscerating the English language
and insisting on ignoring their grammar lessons from primary school.

Now, Tobias, you're obviously a bright and talented young man with a college degree, or you wouldn't be here. Still, I must insist that you speak like an educated adult, not some street ruffian. Let's try that again. From the top, please."

Kitts saw red blotches forming on Toby's neck and thought his voice had the quality of an injured tomcat. "Yes, Sir. Okay, where was I? Yeah, Lenore and I examined the MO in each case and noted some differences in all three crime scenes. At first, we weren't sure the cases were connected because of these differences."

Sidd made his first comment. "Tell us about the modus operandi and the variations you noticed. Remember, MO may evolve due to situational factors. They are not expected to remain immutable."

"That's right. All three victims were killed between the times of 5 and 8 p.m. They were each in their offices finishing up or waiting for a meeting or patient. There were no signs of forced entry. In Prokop's case, someone had to know the code on the keypad outside his door to get into his waiting room. Each of these guys had his throat cut by a scalpel-like blade. But Tamerlane, victim number one, was killed before his throat was cut. He was found seated at his desk, fully clothed. It looks like the UNSUB bashed his head in with a heavy object and then cut his throat. Forensics matched the wound to one of his cast iron bookends that sat on his desk. There were no prints."

Saks stood and turned to Lenore. "So, young Tobias has said the modus operandi changed in cases two and again in number three. Educate us, if you will."

Lenore projected the three crime scenes next to each other. She walked over to the screen, took out her laser pointer, and continued.

"Toby and *I* found distinct similarities, some of which were announced in the killer's MO. As Agent Potter said, Dr. Tamerlane died by blunt force trauma, and then his throat was cut. He bled out on his desk. The fact that he was fully clothed is a critical difference between the crime scenes. First, Fortunato, the second victim, was found with his wrists duct taped to the arms of his desk chair. He appears to have died of blood loss when his throat was cut. The other striking difference was that he was found with his shirt off. In each case, the killer positioned a piece of paper with—"

Sidd cut in with a Socratic reflection. "Special Agent, let us pause to process what we can all be sure of. If these are linked cases, and everything suggests they are, then we need to explain the change in modus operandi from scene one to two. Dr. Tamerlane was killed before the UNSUB cut his throat. Again, he was fully clothed and there were no ligatures on his wrist, no taping to the chair. Why not? Or, more importantly, why was this not the case in the murder of Dr. Fortunato?"

De Vere responded, "This is the kind of evolution in methodology that Douglas wrote about in his classic 1992 piece on MO, signature, and staging, which, of course, we're all familiar with. Agent Potter, any thoughts as to why our killer pummeled to death his first victim and not his second or third?"

Kitts thought De Vere had given Potter a chance to redeem himself and salvage his bruised ego.

Toby answered, "Well, we figured the UNSUB killed Tamerlane because he could have lost control of the situation. Maybe it was not in his plan. Tamerlane could have tried to fight back or bolt, so the UNSUB cracked his skull. He went to school on this killing and came prepared with duct tape for the others."

Not to be upstaged by De Vere, Saks added, "Excellent, Special Agent. An A for you. Very good, indeed. As our friend Tobias has inferred, the killer had not planned to end Dr. Tamerlane's life with a blow to the head. Things may have gotten out of control, and the killer came prepared the next time. You see, both victims, two and three, died by exsanguination. Their jugulars were severed while they were alive. We can assume that this had been the killer's intent all along—to kill his victims while they were fully conscious of what he was doing to them. We are consentient of this fact, thus proving, once again, that MOs are fickle beasts. They'd rather change stripes than remain the same."

Lenore spoke up. "But there were some other differences in how the bodies were found. Another aspect of shifting MO, Doctor?"

Sidd fielded this one. "No, not modus operandi. Here, you're referring to the victims who were found in different stages of undress. Hmm? Dr. Tamerlane was fully clothed, and Fortunato was found shirtless, while our latest victim, Dr. Prokop, was left completely naked. The state of undress in each case may not be related to the method or modus in which the crimes were committed. No, the fact that two had his clothing removed means something different, something more personal to the UNSUB. So, what do we conclude about this person-ification or signature aspect? Remember, as Agent Potter implied and Dr. Saks so skillfully explained, MOs are malleable. Killers make mis-takes and learn from them, but some things don't change from scene to scene. Nakedness means something to our UNSUB. We need to decipher that."

De Vere said, "Yes, this killer has left us with a signature or behav-ioral expression of something unique to their psychology, and as we'll also see, a distinct calling card that I believe is meant for us. Nakedness? Anyone?"

Nicola leaned forward and raised her hand. "I know my role is to observe and learn. I am doing that for sure, but if I can say something, Dr. Ramachandran?"

Sidd gave a hint of a nod. "Sidd is fine. Yes, please go ahead."

"He—if it is he— stripped his victims. Stripped them to make them naked. The second was halfway naked, and the last one was all the way. Could the killer want them to feel their nakedness, maybe like a projec-tion or something like that? Did he—I keep saying he, sorry—did he or she want them to feel something they had felt?" She looked at De Vere. "When we're naked, you know, nothing's hidden. People are ashamed of their nakedness, right?"

De Vere responded, "Very insightful Agent Kitts. I'm glad you spoke up, dear. Yes, nakedness reveals our shame. And we want to comprehend its unique meaning to our killer, who I agree could be any sex or gender at this point. Very good, indeed."

Yes! Kitts straightened up and caught a smile and approving nod from Sidd.

Toby dipped his toe in again. "So, why the overkill with Prokop? What was he trying to prove by cutting this guy's throat and then completely stripping him?"

Sidd answered, "You're making assumptions. You see, we don't know when the clothes were removed. But forensics found no blood on Dr. Prokop's clothes, which tells us that he most likely was forced to disrobe before he was killed. So, we are back to our newest member's inferences regarding the personification of nakedness in the mind of our UNSUB. It is safe to assume, and I believe that Dr. De Vere will agree, that the UNSUB wanted his victims to experience the nakedness in death that he—and I'll explain later why I believe our killer is male— felt in life. I think shame is an important motivator. Feeling shame in life and wanting others to experience this in death."

Saks spoke without looking up from his masterpiece. "Once again, we are entirely in accord, Siddharth. We can tussle over the sex/gender issue later. For now, we are piecing together a profile for this killer— their modus operandi, shifting each time, and the seeds of a signature, perhaps having to do with the victim's shame and wish to inject this into his victims. But alas, we are not finished with our killer. Indeed, we've only scratched the surface. You see, our killer has a reason for butchering doctors and stripping them naked for the world to see that for which he may also feel ashamed. But pray tell.... Why these three ill-fated souls?"

Ready to offer himself up again, Toby raised his hand. "Childhood trauma, maybe. Maybe the UNSUB was a bed-wetter as a kid and got tons of grief at sleepovers."

"Oh, dear Tobias, the question at hand is *not* his motivation, but *why* he chose these three. But as to the motivational issue, please desist from these simplistic leaps into hackneyed conclusions. Nocturnal micturition has gotten an unearned reputation as the boogeyman in every serial killer's childhood. I'll have you know, I wet the bed until I was 12, and, like the vast majority who suffered from various forms of nocturnal emissions, I have never thought of hurting, much less killing anyone. I'm afraid we'll have to dig deeper, Tobias."

Ouch, Toby, man. Read the room, dude. Kitts saw the blotches reappear around his neck and tried to unsee the image of Saks peeing his bed as a teenager.

Bernice De Vere must have also noticed Toby's reaction and said, "I will say this, Toby, I like where your mind was going before you took the easy exit onto Boulevard Cliché."

Lenore spoke up. "I've been wracking my brain about the UNSUB'S calling cards. It's like the killer is toying with us with these quotes about whispering and these mathematical formulas."

Sidd responded, "Yes, the elephant in the room. Most serial killers take trophies, and some leave calling cards for various reasons, which is our job to understand. Our UNSUB has taken the lives of these men and accentuated their terror and shame. The notes he has staged in their hands are communications. What is he trying to communicate?" He signaled to Lenore who showed a slide of the *Comes the Whisperer* note and equation left on Prokop's desk.

$$\frac{1}{6162-t\sqrt{2\pi^c}}-\tfrac{1}{2}(bc-B09U)^2X[3]+\frac{1}{284-t\sqrt{2\pi^c}}-\tfrac{1}{2}(cb-L04H)^2X[2]+\frac{1}{5205-t\sqrt{2\pi^c}}-\tfrac{1}{2}(bc-O07S)^2X[1]$$

"That we must find out. Pat is working on these quotes, searching online databases that might help us understand his language."

Kitts asked, "But all that math . . . what do you think he's trying to tell us?"

De Vere answered, "Maybe nothing more than to show us how smart they are. Consider this: Most people have a visceral fear of mathematics, which is why so few people learn about its concepts, complexities, and tricks."

Sidd added, "Of course Dr. De Vere is correct. Higher mathematics intimidates many of us. The UNSUB may be trying to do to us what he did to his victims: control, intimidate, and make us face our shame." Glancing at Saks, he continued, "Many of us have developed ways to achieve such ends. What better way to compensate for underlying feelings of inadequacy, and possibly humiliation, than to intimidate others, including those of us for whom his messages are intended. Whether these equations have embedded messages, the UNSUB uses them to establish a power dynamic. He seeks to dominate us the same way he did the victims. Violence is his proof of power with his victims. Impenetrable mathematics formulas may be his way of asserting his power over us. We need to figure out why."

De Vere glanced at Nicola as she spoke. "The UNSUB's—he/she/them/or their—preoccupation with whispering is a communication about revealing secrets. In this context, whispering is a form of betrayal. In hushed tones, secrets are revealed and rumors are spread."

Sidd pronounced their time was up. "Pat will message you about our next meeting."

Kitts had been unaware of the passage of time. They'd begun at 7 a.m. and had only scratched the surface about the so-called calling cards the killer or UNSUB—*gotta learn the lingo*—had left.

The coroner placed the time of Prokop's death between 5:00 and 7:00. There were reports the police were looking into his patients, especially his final appointment of the day—a Raevyn Nevenmoore. She might have been the last person to have seen him alive. Kitts wondered if she could be involved or was merely an unfortunate woman whose shrink was about to be gutted.

8

Masculīnus

Raevyn had not left the house. Huddled in her room, she spent the next day on her computer, reading and writing. When she grew tired of her internet searches, she whispered to Finch. But all she heard through her vent were angry taunts, threats, and pleas. This became too much, and she returned to her desk, pushing aside piles of articles and books. Countless scraps of paper with notes—some crinkled up with illegible scribbles—fell to the floor and lay at her feet. She caught sight of an unopened bag from the pharmacy with stapled instructions about her lithium prescription. Tossing it aside, she switched on her computer and opened a file labeled *SupraSyncronicity,* the title of the book manuscript she'd been writing—more off than on—for the last three years.

Her relentless discursive tome concerned the unseen connections between things most people choose to ignore. Her sister and her friend Marney read portions of what she'd written, politely commenting that it sounded over the top and "a bit paranoid," but they didn't grasp the significance of all she saw. Her word count approached 350,000 and the end was nowhere in sight. Raevyn told herself she would trim the fat later, but right now, she had such important things to say. Not tonight, however. She couldn't ignite the creative spark to work on her manuscript.

Though it was well past 11 p.m., she wasn't tired. *Sleep is what the lazy and uncreative do,* is what she always told herself when beginning to cycle upward. Staying up writing, doing deep dives on the internet, or staying out until sunrise ignited her fire. She felt compelled to continue her research on Prokop. Preoccupied with her brother's whispered rants, coupled with her intrusive images and nightmares, she had started looking into Prokop's storied career. True, she'd known him off and on for years, but she needed to know if what Finch was telling her was true.

Raevyn entered his name in Google Scholars and up popped pages of listings. Linus Prokop MD, PhD had over 75 publications and had written seven books. He was a rare breed. Trained as a neurologist, Prokop completed his general psychiatry residency and child and adolescent fellowship at Boston General before entering a doctoral program in clinical psychology at the University of Maryland. Not content with accumulating doctorates, he did his psychoanalytic training at the Washington Psychoanalytic Center. From there, he served as Chief of Psychiatry at Georgetown Medical Center and later became a leading developmental researcher at NIMH, while maintaining a niche private practice in Georgetown.

Prokop's recently released book, *Masculīnus: The Path from Boy to Man. A Developmental Critique* was a coauthored summary of a longitudinal study of adolescent males. The book had sparked a great deal of media interest. In addition to touring the country for book signings, Prokop had been on several podcasts and talk shows. One host dubbed him "America's Shrink," replacing Dr. Phil, whose homespun, conservative folksiness was eclipsed by Linus' Slavic charisma and polished veneer.

Raevyn's search led to the names of other researchers on his team. She found articles on two others who had recently died. Bloody images from her nightmares imposed themselves and refused to leave her alone. It was well past midnight, and she needed an escape.

She looked around her room and spotted unopened boxes of clothes she'd recently purchased at her favorite boutique in Georgetown. She tore open the larger box and fingered the smooth leather shorts and black sequined top. *Perfect.*

Raevyn ordered an Uber to take her to *Flash*, her favorite after-hours club in DC. When the silver Camry arrived, she climbed into the backseat and inhaled the minty scent.

The driver, a sleepy looking man in his 30s asked, "Can't sleep, Miss?"

She was incapable of corraling her words once she began to speak. Her response to his innocent query lasted much of the 40-minute drive. Dimly aware that she couldn't stop herself, Raevyn ignored what little filter she had and willingly succumbed to the intoxication of her soaring mood.

9

NIGHTSCAPES

The Uber dropped her at the club just after 1 a.m. Loud music spilled onto the street.

"Take care Miss. Here is my number if you want me to pick up. I'm driving all night so.... And good luck with your book. Sorry to hear about what happened to your parents and brother, that dead doctor, the Olympic trials, and all that."

Raevyn nodded in appreciation with a fleeting sense of embarrassment at her nonexistent sister. Turning to face the bright lights flashing on the marquis, she felt the vibe and buzz moving from the sidewalk up through her legs.

The chisel-bodied bouncer she knew from high school smiled when he recognized her. "Raevyn the Maven. Looking hot, girlfriend. No charge for you tonight."

He stamped her hand and ushered her into the entry of the Flash Bar with its adjacent dance floor. Undulating bodies bobbed in the crowded space. She inhaled sweat mixed with perfume and alcohol vapors, while the ear-piercing music blew cocaine to her senses.

A bartender named Snooty mixed a Negroni and handed it to her. "On the house for the queen."

She shut her eyes and began to sway as the vibrations brought warmth to her core. Raevyn moved up the stairs to the Green Room on the roof where another DJ played a more mellow vibe. Surrounded by greenery, Raevyn continued to move to the beat, letting her mind soar freely into the black sky above. Sipping her drink, she made eye contact with a tall redhead whose shirt was opened to his waist. He looked about 10 years younger. He smiled, his hungry eyes locking onto hers. Raevyn stared back, coyly at first, thinking, *He'll do.* She winked to signal that she, like the club, was open for business and ready to party. With panther-like desire, he moved toward her.

"An angel's come down from heaven. You're looking too good to be alone. I'm—"

Pearson or Patrick; she didn't hear his name, but details didn't matter. Not now. He was what she needed, the scratch for an itch and another distraction from her unquiet mind and distressing preoccupation with Prokop and her brother. She finished her drink, ordered another, then danced with the red-haired man until the heat from their bodies ignited pleasure centers in their midbrains. He eyed the restroom and tugged her toward it. Tonight, Raevyn the Maven, Princess of Hedonism, allowed herself to be pulled by an anonymous Pearson or Patrick.

Though it was by no means her first time doing it in the bathroom of a crowded club, or airplane, for that matter, Raevyn needed the passion and mindless release with a stranger tonight—another offramp from her highway of pain. The fleeting pleasure of a bump of white powder and a chance hook-up was enhanced by the rush of pushing the limits of acceptable behavior. Raevyn had always been the daredevil. Twin brother Finch, by contrast, feared all things devilish. Where she had broken rules, he'd invented rules for rules. Until all that changed.

After her libidinous bathroom encounter, the redhead disappeared into the crowd. They'd just announced last call, and the club would be closing in another 30 minutes. It was about 3:20, and she felt ready to go home. Raevyn found the number of the Uber driver and pressed it into her phone. He picked her up outside. The early morning air was still warm. Late June in the city can be roasting.

"Nice evening, Miss?"

Raevyn nodded, suddenly in no mood for conversation. She was coming down from her buzz, and the droning from the club now pounded in her head. The smell of a stranger on her skin made her feel hollow and disgusted. She wanted to be left alone.

A faint pinkish glow illuminated the eastern sky as Raevyn quietly unlocked the back door to the house. Coming in through the garage and tiptoeing up the back stairs, as she had done countless times before, would provide the stealth and silence she needed in case her sister had come home late. She gently closed the back door and turned around to face Yeardley sitting somberly at the kitchen table. Like the proverbial guardian, waiting for her wayward child to sneak back into the house, she wore a look of outrage and disappointment.

"Seriously, Raevyn? You look like hell. Have you forgotten you're 30 years old, and not some irresponsible adolescent rebelling against her parents? *Really*? You're doing this crap again? You promised to stop acting like a juvenile delinquent, placing yourself at risk, and treating your body as lab equipment. You agreed to get back on your medication and start seeing a therapist again to get your life together. Honestly Raev, when will you stop doing this to both of us? Did you see Prokop?"

Raevyn saw a hint of sadness on her sister's face, but in that moment, her shame made it impossible for her to accept Yeardley's concern as anything more than the boomeranging of her own self-loathing. She bristled with defensiveness. "No, he canceled."

"He *canceled*? Did you reschedule?"

Raevyn snarled, "Leave me the hell alone and stop pretending like you're my parent! None of this can be fixed, Yeardley! You always think that's the answer—"You need to see someone Raevyn; find a new therapist Raevyn"—like any of that will make a difference after all the shit I've gone through! Finch predicted you'd act this way because you always have!"

In an instant, Yeardley's anger gave way to confusion and dread.

"*Finch*? No, Raevyn. No, honey."

Raevyn stormed past her sister and bounded up the stairs to her room, slamming the door behind her. In a fit, she tore off her clothes, ripping her new blouse and throwing it on the floor. She went into the bathroom and turned on the shower. She saw her face in the mirror. Her lipstick had faded and her mascara wase smeared, leaving inkblot smudges beneath her eyes. Yeardley's words were a gut punch and left her feeling queasy. She violently shook her head and slapped herself across the face. *Stop it. Stop it. Stop it!*

Raevyn turned around and stepped into the shower. The hot water streamed down her face washing away the grime but not the shame. She thought about unkept promises—how she swore she'd restart her medications and get back into therapy. Her thoughts flashed to Yeardley's begging her to see him again. But images of Prokop refused to leave her alone. She had seen him sitting beside her in the backseat of the Uber and looking down at her on the dance floor. She saw him in the mirror of the men's room, gazing disapprovingly as a stranger thrust his body against hers.

Suddenly, she vomited and watched the pinkish coloring of the Negronis swirl around the drain. She wanted to empty herself of herself, of all that had happened—the prison of her highs and lows, what had gone on in her childhood, what she had done to Finch, what happened in St. Louis, and all the drinking, drugs, and meaningless sex she had used to forget and wash away the stains of self-loathing.

Raevyn stepped out of the shower, dried herself, and returned to her room. She whispered for her brother, but there was no answer. Her mood quickly collapsed; she closed her eyes and passed out.

, , ,

Several hours later, Yeardley banged at her door. "Raevyn, you've *got* to get up. There are two detectives who want to talk to you about something you were involved in. What the *hell* is going on, Raev?" She entered the room and gently shook her little sister, repeating that the police were downstairs and wanted to see her.

Feeling more zombie than human, Raevyn put on a robe and robotically followed Yeardley down the stairs. There in the living room stood a rumpled-looking man and a younger Asian woman.

Raevyn was struck by the man's sallow skin and yellow, tobacco-stained teeth. She could smell the odor of stale cigarettes from across the room. His hair, a classic comb-over style with a distant part above his left ear, salted dandruff onto his lapel. The man placed an unlit cigarette between his bulbous lips and said they had some questions.

"Good morning, or should I say afternoon, Miss. Is it pronounced Neven...moore? Sorry to interrupt your beauty sleep. I'm Lieutenant Edgar Bilch." He spoke the lexicon of a cop from a cheap crime drama and flashed a badge the way cops always did on TV. "This is Sergeant Sadat. We're investigating the homicide of a Dr. Linus Prokop and—"

Yeardley gasped and fell back.

"So, I take it you didn't know. Oops.... We have some questions for your sister."

Yeardley nodded and looked wide-eyed and open-mouthed at Raevyn, who showed no reaction.

"Forensics is still processing the crime scene. We checked his patient list and saw that you were down for a 6 p.m. appointment two days ago. Did you—"

"He canceled . . . and said he wanted to reschedule," claimed Raevyn a bit too quickly.

"You seem a bit jumpy, Miss—"

Yeardley interrupted this time. "Her psychiatrist's been *murdered*. How would you expect her to react, Lieutenant?"

"So, you're saying you didn't see him then? That's funny because his appointment book didn't say anything about a cancelation or rescheduling. I think shrinks are supposed to make note of that kind of thing," muttered Bilch as the unlit cigarette dangled from his lips.

Raevyn looked at Yeardley, "No . . . I told him I had to check my schedule first."

Bilch glanced at his silent partner, who continued to scribble notes. "You're pretty busy huh? Okay then, we've got your statement, Miss Neverman. After the forensics go over the office and everything they collect there, I'm sure we can sort all this out with you and your cancelation. So, best you stay put, Raevyn. No flying away, you know. No leaving the area because we'll probably need you to come down to the station to get this mess sorted."

Yeardley watched them walk down the driveway. She looked at Raevyn who was sitting with her head in her hands. "Oh my God, Raevyn, you poor thing! Why didn't you tell me he canceled?"

10

THE SEARCH

Muffled whispers seeped through the closed bedroom door. "No . . . no. I told you . . . I won't.... Don't say that!" Raevyn's words were quickly silenced by Yeardley's tapping at her door.

"Raevyn honey? Who are you talking to? You've been holed up in there for 24 hours. You've got to be hungry."

Raevyn hadn't left her room since the detectives' visit. Yeardley had taken off work to keep an eye on her. Raevyn bristled whenever she knocked at the door, peeked in, and started interrogating her about Prokop's cancellation or not taking her lithium.

"Oh my God, I can't *believe* you haven't been taking your medication! You're cycling again and refusing to do anything about this. We have to find you a new psychiatrist, Raevyn."

Raevyn answered from under the covers, "I can't *believe* you're still standing there and would bring up a new therapist when the last one was murdered. And the pills turn me into a zombie. Ask Finch.... Now, let me say this politely, leave me the *fuck* alone."

"*Finch*? Raevyn, *please* stop saying this!"

. . .

That afternoon, Yeardley tapped at her door again. "Raevyn . . . I know you want to be left alone, but those detectives are back, and you need to come downstairs to talk with them. Now."

It took Raevyn 10 minutes to pull herself out of bed. Invisible lead weights gripped her legs as she put on her robe and shuffled down the stairs. There stood the cartoonish-looking Bilch and his silent sidekick, backed up by two uniformed officers. He smirked as he watched her lumber into the room.

"Ah, so sorry to disrupt your beauty sleep again, Cinderella, but we're here for a different reason today. I have a warrant to search your house, bedroom, clothes, and computer for any additional information that would help us make sense of all of this. There are some discrepancies in what you told us the other day that we'd like to clear up. In the meantime, I have a warrant to search the house." He reached his thin fingers into his pocket and pulled out the folded paper.

Yeardley shot up and took the warrant from his hand. "What are you saying? She's a suspect!? I don't know what you're referring to. I've been away, and she said her appointment was canceled." She looked toward her sister. "Raevyn, what is this about?"

Bilch said the cleaning lady thought she saw someone fitting Raevyn's description leaving Prokop's office somewhere around the time of his murder. He paused and said, "You said he canceled, but this woman says she might have seen you there."

Yeardley's tone was sharp. "*Might?* Because a random woman saw someone with long dark hair leave the building? That's it? That's the discrepancy that makes you think you can harass my sister!?"

"Harass is a strong word, Ma'am. Let's just say there's more we have that we can't discuss right now. Look, your sister's not a suspect, but we find her a very interesting person whom we think can help us sort out what happened." Turning to Raevyn, he said, "You're still saying you didn't see Prokop that day? That's your story, right?"

Raevyn nodded.

"Okay, in the meantime, we need to conduct a search of the house for any additional information. Like I said, we're not at liberty to discuss this, but I'm sure we'll get it cleared up."

The detectives left as three uniformed officers entered. The sisters watched as they went through bookcases and cabinets, leaving the contents on the floor. One went upstairs and later came down with several stuffed trash bags and her desktop computer. After two hours, they left.

Raevyn remained frozen on the sofa. Yeardley walked back into the living room and sat beside her. "I'm really worried about you. What aren't you telling me?"

11

WEB OF LIES

Detectives Bilch, Sadat, and the officers returned the next day and were standing in the living room when Yeardley brought Raevyn down.

"Hello, Cinderella. We're here for a different reason today. Raevyn Nevenmoore, we're arresting you for the murder of Linus Prokop. You have the right to remain silent. What you say can be used against you in court. You have the right to speak to an attorney." Bilch continued reading her Miranda Rights and nodded to the police officers who stepped forward to handcuff her.

It was all a blur. Raevyn dropped her head and heard Yeardley begin to cry. She looked up and saw the horror on her sister's face and felt the sharp edge of the handcuffs on her wrists. She lost her balance as the officers walked her to the squad car for all the neighbors to see. She inhaled Bilch's cigarette stench and felt his meaty hands push her head into the back seat of the car.

The mental fog continued as she shuffled through the station for processing and into the booking room for fingerprinting. It lifted when she found herself in an interview room sitting across from Bilch and Sadat. On her right sat their family attorney Brisco Hooks, whom Yeardley had called after the officers took Raevyn away. Hooks was a well-heeled, heavyset man with gray hair. Raevyn first met him when her mother lost her medical license and then again at the reading of her parents' wills six years ago.

Bilch coughed and began. "You remember Sergeant Sadat, and of course, we've had the pleasure of meeting before. Let me lay the cards on the table for you here, Miss Nevenmoore. It seems that you've been lying to us and left out some pretty important information, hmm? So, the way we figure it, Raevyn, we already know you lie; we just don't yet know how much. Like the stories you've been telling us that you never entered Prokop's office, right? Are you still sticking to that story?"

Raevyn shifted in her seat. She lifted her manacled hands to wipe her nose, nodded, and quietly said, "Sure."

Bilch took out a cigarette and placed it between his lips. He lit up and blew smoke toward her. "See, Nevenmoore, we got your prints all over the place. I thought you hadn't seen him for five years. But it looks like you were there the night he was killed. And what a busy beaver you were in there, touching Prokop's desk and that paper he was holding. Then, we got your prints on his file cabinet and found blood spatter on the clothes we took from your room. I wonder what you were up to and why you lied. Care to explain?"

Raevyn remained silent.

Bilch blurted, "This isn't a fairytale, Cinderella. I'm tired of your bullshit game playing!"

Brisco inserted himself. "Now, just a minute, Lieutenant. My client is willing to answer all your questions, but I need to remind you that she remains innocent, and you have no right to subject her to this kind of verbal abuse. So, I don't think Chief Rainey will be too pleased when I inform him about your egregious behavior on the first tee this Sunday."

Bilch didn't hide his contempt. "Well, you just go ahead and do that, counselor. But this woman is a prime suspect at the scene of a crime. Oh, and how do you explain the computer searches you did on Prokop before and after you murdered him? And what do you have to say about this?"

He pulled a photo of a wrinkled yellow sticky note they'd fished out of her trash can with the words, "They have to pay for their sins."

"So, what the hell does this mean, Nevenmoore? You've been spinning a web of lies from the start. You lied to us about not going into his office. Now there's this. We got you and are going to nail you to the wall." He shot Hooks a hostile look. "Tell that to your golf buddy, Counselor." He waved to the two police officers standing by the door. "Okay, Raevyn, let's see how a DC holding cell suits you. Get her out of here, Sergeant." Bilch stood up, stubbed out his cigarette, turned, and exited.

Hooks leaned close to Raevyn to offer reassurance about her arraignment tomorrow. "We'll ask for bail, honey. I know Judge Howard. She's quite reasonable. When she hears about the abuse you've been subjected to, I'm confident she'll agree to bail. Chin up, kiddo." He gave her a hug. Raevyn tried to stand but remained limp and buckled at the knee.

The two officers escorted her to a holding cell where 10 other women sat and stood around. Raevyn found a spot and sat on the hard bench, holding her head in her hands, visually tracing cracks on the cement floor. She felt the women's stares and heard a hum of meaningless chatter.

She felt numb. Nothing mattered. Maybe she *had* killed him, and her nightmares were flashbacks. She knew she was guilty of more significant crimes. *You get what you deserve.* She should have been scared but wasn't. If anything, Raevyn felt she was where she belonged. Guilt has a way of creating internal prisons, and when an external one presents itself, you jump at it.

A guard took her to another cell where she would spend the night. She didn't touch the brown-colored meal that was brought to her. She curled up on her cot and began to drift off but was awakened by his taunting whispers.

But now the Raven still beguiling makes your sad soul into smiling. You're a killer. You're worthless and should die. Be gone forever more.

She shuddered and clasped her hands over her ears. "Stop! Leave me alone.... *Please!*"

*   *   *

Thirty-six hours later, Raevyn sat in the courtroom, head down. Brisco sat at her side. She turned around and saw Yeardley sitting behind her. She also caught sight of Bilch and Sadat behind an attractive blonde prosecutor.

They all rose when Judge Howard entered the courtroom. The prosecutor read the charges and requested that bail be denied due to the violent nature of the crime. Hooks quickly objected, saying that Raevyn had no history of violence and was not dangerous to others.

It was all over in 20 minutes. The judge denied the bail petition, agreeing with the prosecutor that the charges of murder outweighed the request for bail.

Hooks stood up and spoke. "Your Honor, Ms. Nevenmoore has a history of severe mental illness. We're requesting a 24-531.03 competency evaluation. My client should not be held in the Central Detention Facility pending her evaluation by a court-appointed forensic evaluator."

Judge Howard responded dryly, "I'm sorry, Mr. Hooks, but your client is accused of murder. So, unfortunately, that makes her ineligible for an alternative placement. However, I will grant your request for a 24-531. Let's see what they find out, and then we can revisit the issue of pretrial confinement. But let me repeat, there will be no bail in this case. And that, ladies and gentlemen, brings this arraignment to a close." She turned to the clerk and asked for the next case.

Raevyn was led out of the courtroom in handcuffs. Brisco Hooks tried to console Yeardley. "We'll get her evaluated as soon as possible. Let me ask someone in the DA's office for a top-tier forensic psychologist to see Raevyn this week. I think we can eventually get all this cleared up. We know Raevyn's innocent, but I have to tell you, they have some pretty damning evidence against your sister."

12

UNHINGED SISTER

They met in his corner office at *Odenheimer, Hooks, and Monk* the next day. Yeardley sat in the Chesterfield tufted leather chair across from his desk. "You mean they can't schedule her evaluation any sooner than next week, and she'll have to remain in jail until *then*? Oh, Brisco." Her voice was strained by fear and fatigue. Brisco Hooks buzzed his secretary to bring in water.

He walked over to the bar in the corner of his office. "Maybe you'd prefer something a tad stronger, what with the shock of all this." He poured two fingers of Macallan 40 into a crystal glass and held it up.

"No thanks, Brisco. Water's fine."

Brisco nodded and kept the glass for himself, sipping it as he returned to his desk. "Sheila will bring in some water." He continued, "We'll get through this mess, Yeard. I can ride shotgun, but you'll no doubt need a top-notch criminal defense attorney. I've asked Scotti to put together a list."

Yeardley gave a tense smile as she took in the expanse of the room. She remembered this office from her first meeting with Brisco when she was applying to business school. Towering 15 stories above K Street NW, the plush suite of offices had initially struck her as a stereotypical and uninspired boutique firm that announced to clients, *We are that important, and you should feel privileged that we've agreed to represent you.* Her parents had been dazzled by the allure of such lavishness with its dark-paneled walls, plush, over-stuffed leather chairs, and a floor-to-ceiling view of the White House. They had the money to spend on prestige—all the "right" schools, clubs, vacation homes, and expensive law firms. Appearances of status and importance constantly enhanced their collective sense of self-worth.

Yeardley hadn't seen Brisco since their last meeting to finalize her parents' estate and then to settle Finch's affairs. That would have been four or five years ago when the tragedies began piling up. She still had Brisco's number on speed dial. Regardless of her feelings about his elitist proclivities and conservative politics, she appreciated Hooks' accessibility and readiness to help.

Brisco leaned across his massive Serpentine Mahogany desk and said, "Look, this court is so backed up, we're lucky to get Raevyn on the schedule. Believe me, and I know this is of little consolation, Yeard, but by conventional standards, this is amazingly quick. Judge Howard will appoint a court psychologist to conduct their evaluation in a secure interview room at the detention facility. They'll probably seek collateral information from you as well." He paused to choose his words. "I know this feels surreal, but I have to ask: Any chance Raevyn was involved in this? I mean—"

"Like, did she do it? *No*, Brisco. Raevyn's many things, but she's not a violent criminal. She's . . . sick."

"Right, but with her condition and all that's happened to your family, your sister could have become unhinged—isn't that how you put it?—and simply snapped. I haven't seen all the evidence they collected from her room and computer. Still, they have her fingerprints in Prokop's office and even on that note he was holding. This is all circumstantial, but it doesn't look good when she apparently lied to the detectives about her appointment being canceled."

"Brisco, stop! I know this. But I also know my sister. *Unhinged* is certainly not a word I remember using. She suffers from a lifetime of parental neglect and trauma on top of her manic depression, which has never been managed very well. Once again, my sister has many chal-lenges, Brisco, but she *is not* a murderer!"

"Okay, sorry. Look, I believe you. I've known your family for decades and had a front-row seat at all her performances, award ceremo-nies, valedictorian speeches, ad infinitum. You'll remember we attended her college graduation and even flew to Montreal in 2017 to see her win the gold medal. And of course, you know how we tried but couldn't get tickets to watch her compete in St. Louis. But, Yeardley, she is simply *not* the same girl she was back then. I agree with you. Your sister is a severely ill young woman. If nothing more, we need to ensure the court knows this so she can get the treatment she needs. I believe the forensic evaluation will show the court just how compromised Raevyn is. Then we can prove her innocence."

"Thank you, Brisco." She reached for her bottle of *Perrier* and filled her glass. "She's not been the same since St. Louis." Yeardley hesitated. "There is something else . . . I didn't mention this before, but I feel it's important to bring it up now."

Brisco leaned in. "By all means, please tell me."

Yeardley looked away, struggling to find the words for what she didn't want to say. Clearing her throat, she took a tissue and wiped a tear at the corner of her eye. "My sister says she's been talking to Finch again."

13

St. Louis

June 27, 2019,
Enterprise Center,
St. Louis

"It's all come down to this, and I must say the competition this week has been fantastic."

"Yes, Tim, US women's gymnastics has come so far with reigning Olympic champion Simone Biles and youngsters Sunisa Lee and Grace McCallum. But perhaps the biggest surprise during these trials was what happened to crowd favorite, 25-year-old Raevyn Nevenmoore, with her remarkable story and name to go with it. Yesterday, our own Nastia Liukin caught up with the irrepressible Ms. Nevenmoore, known fondly as Raevyn the Maven, after she failed to finish in the top three in the uneven parallel bars. Let's listen to what Raevyn told her about this week's lackluster performances."

The camera switched to Nastia standing with her microphone in hand. "Thanks, Andrea. I had the chance to sit down with Raevyn yesterday, and I use the term 'sit down' rather loosely because, as we all know, Raevyn is like the Energizer Bunny. She is always on the go and never seems to stop moving. Let's take a look at what Raevyn told me when I asked if it was a mistake for her to prepare for the trials while also in her first year of medical school, especially in light of all the tragedies she's endured."

The clip showed an agitated-looking Raevyn Nevenmoore in her fuchsia leotard standing beside Nastia. Her tightly braided hair was pulled back, stretching her already gaunt appearance. Makeup could not disguise her strained expression or hide the dark circles under her eyes.

"We're here with the always vibrant Raevyn Nevenmoore. Really, Raevyn medical school *and* the trials? Both are full-time jobs. Not to mention what you've been going through with your—"

Raevyn cut in, speaking rapidly and a little too loudly. She began to ramble. "I'm fine. Honestly, I don't think about that kind of thing. I mean, I think a lot about many things, but who doesn't because it would be abnormal not to think, right? You know, I think therefore I am."

Nastia tried to speak, but Raevyn talked over her. Raising her voice an octave, Nastia found an opening to ask Raevyn again whether it was a mistake to train for the trials at the same time she was a full-time medical student.

Raevyn answered, "I *love* your hair. It's so cute. Sure, Nastia, of course, medical school is demanding, and the trials are commanding but outstanding. You know all about that, of course; you nailed it in 2008 in Beijing to rock the world—"

Seizing another opening, Nastia asked how she felt about her performances that week.

"Yeah, well, my timing's been off, you know, with a different time zone, and I reset my clock, so I'm in the zone now. I wouldn't have come if I didn't think I could make this team like you did in '08. I feel fantastic. Really! I know I'll nail my routine on the balance beam tomorrow and stick my landing. It's just what I do! I'm feeling great and super happy to be here and confident that I will show the world what I can do."

Nastia was distracted by the producer's voice in her earpiece urging her to wrap things up. "Okay. Always the optimist, Raevyn. It looks like you have a lot of supporters here today. I think the whole town of Bethesda, Maryland must have come out to root for you and share their support after all you've been through."

Raevyn smiled and waved to the crowd. "It's all good." She giggled, gave a strained smile, nodded uncomfortably, and walked rapidly away while appearing to talk to herself.

Nastia looked toward the camera. "And there you have it, Tim and Andrea. Raevyn's saying all the right words—lots of words, for sure— but quite honestly, her words don't match her demeanor. Frankly, and I say this with concern and respect, she seems off her game. This is not the same girl we saw competing at the World Gymnastics Championships in Montreal in 2017, and how could we expect her to be after all that's happened? But as we all know, she's such a tough competitor. The proof will be in her performance on the balance beam tomorrow. Until then, we'll have to wait and see if Raevyn the Maven can deliver. Back to you, Tim."

The camera switched back to Tim Daggett, Terry Gannon, and Andrea Joyce, who huddled beside each other in their booth. Daggett spoke first.

"Well, that was an interesting interview yesterday . . . to say the least. She certainly does not seem like the same young lady who dazzled us all at the Worlds last year. As we heard from Nastia before the break, all eyes will be on Raevyn in a few moments. After what we saw yesterday, we'll be more curious to see what happens today. And it all comes down to the balance beam, doesn't it? Raevyn Nevenmoore's final chance to score high enough to stand any chance of making this team."

Andrea agreed. "This is not the same girl we saw last year, Tim. Her performance today *has* to be a Hail Mary pass, but she is such a gifted athlete that none of us should count out Raevyn the Maven, even with all she's been through."

"Okay," said Tim. "I agree, a very steep climb indeed. All eyes are on crowd-pleaser Raevyn Nevenmoore, next up on the balance beam.

Let's watch."

There was an awkward silence from the booth as cameras focused on Raevyn arguing with her coach. She clearly looked agitated, flailing her arms and raising her voice several decibels.

Tim spoke. "Well, there's clearly some kind of problem. Nastia's on the floor. Maybe she can tell us what's going on."

Cut to Nastia, standing about 30 feet from where Raevyn is arguing with her coach. "She really looks agitated, Tim. You can see she's pacing and . . . really looks upset. It's apparently something about the . . . temperature on the floor? She's complaining it's too hot and about a high-pitched tone disturbing her equilibrium. We're not noticing anything with the temperature or the background noise she's complaining of. Now, she seems to be pointing to something or someone in the stands. I see her coach, Terry Miller, reaching out and trying to calm her down, but . . . it looks like Raevyn is waving him off and continuing to point to the stands. She looks agitated and is not being calmed by anything he's telling her. She actually just pushed him away, Tim, and it looks like one of the officials has come down to talk with Terry, but Raevyn has already moved toward the balance beam, where it looks like she's about to begin her routine. But . . . she appears to be . . . oh Lord, something is terribly wrong. What is she *doing*? Wait . . . no. Oh my God!"

14

The Icarus File

The room quieted when Sidd entered. He directed team members to open their binders.

"The police have taken a 30-year-old woman into custody and charged her in the murder of Linus Prokop. The judge at her arraignment agreed to the defense counsel's request for a competency evaluation. He appointed our friend Dr. Solomon Mendelson to conduct the evaluation. I've contacted him to conference with us after he meets with her."

"So, who is this woman we're looking at?" asked Toby.

Sidd answered, "It is the last patient he was supposed to see that night, Raevyn Nevenmoore."

"You've got to be kidding." Lenore chimed in. "A hippy name from the '60s?"

"No," said Saks wryly. "Can't you see? Edgar Allen Poe is playing us for fools from beyond the grave."

Kitts had read Raevyn's file before coming to the meeting. There were things that made her look suspicious, but not everything added up. She watched video snippets of Raevyn from the 2019 trials that went viral at the time. Images of the gymnast's career-ending, tragic, and humiliating downfall replayed themselves in Nicola's mind.

Bernice De Vere stood and moved toward the projector. "Let me tell you about Raevyn Nevenmoore, our Icarus girl with unbounded talents who flew too close to the sun and crashed." She projected a picture of Raevyn on the screen. "She was on Prokop's schedule as his 6:00 appointment, but she lied to the police and said it had been canceled. The police arrested her because they found her fingerprints on his desk, his file cabinet, and on the message from the Whisperer. The fact that she lied to the police makes her look guilty of something. But what?"

Toby said, "She's not some regular Jane. Raevyn Nevenmoore is famous, right? I mean, who saw what happened in the Tokyo gymnastics trials?"

"Only the whole world witnessed what happened to that poor girl." De Vere advanced the slides to the five-minute clip from St. Louis.

Kitts was deeply disturbed by images of Raevyn feverishly pointing to the stands and storming away from the judges' table. The camera zoomed to her sweat-soaked face. She frantically chalked her hands, while muttering angrily to herself. When she tried to wipe the perspiration from her brow, the chalky residue made her face look ashen and cadaverous. Her brightly colored leotard was saturated with perspiration as she approached the balance beam.

Suddenly, she began to undress in front of the audience, the cameras, and the world. Unable to cool down, she stripped naked and attempted to mount the four-inch-wide beam. Her feet slipped as she began her routine. The coaches and judges rushed over to cover her with her team jacket and tried to remove her from the floor. But Raevyn put up a colossal fight, punching and kicking, until the security guards subdued her, and the network cut to a commercial.

No one spoke for a moment.

"Naked in front of the world," said Lenore. "She shamed herself for the whole world to see. How do you ever come back from that?"

Sidd spoke, his voice soft with sorrow and lament. "She was 25 at the time, a first-year medical student at Penn, and a World Gymnastic Champion from two years before. Then, in front of the eyes of the world, she suffered an ignominious manic episode, and her life has never been the same."

Lenore added, "Her life was full of tragedy before what we witnessed." She read from her binder, "Parents were high-powered physicians. The mother, Abigail LaBlanc, was a renowned thoracic surgeon and pioneer in robotic-assisted tissue sampling technology. The father, Adolf Nevenmoore, was a workaholic pathologist who was eclipsed by Mother's brilliance. Both parents appeared to prioritize their careers over childrearing and family life. Dr. LeBlanc was also reputed to have had a string of affairs during their marriage. An endless stream of nannies and au pairs raised Raevyn, her twin brother Finch, and older sister Yeardley. Mother lost her medical license after her second DUI. She had some type of mood disorder too, which Raevyn apparently inherited. It seems she had been treated by none other than Dr. Linus Prokop. The same was true for the twin brother."

"Aside from the nullities in parental involvement, the interesting thing about young Raevyn and her twin brother," said Saks, "was that they were products of selective fetal growth restriction."

"Meaning what?" asked Toby.

"Meaning, Tobias, that our Raevyn received a queen's share of the intrauterine nutrients. Sadly, fraternal twin Finch got the droppings. He was always smaller, had borderline osteogenesis imperfecta, and essentially lived in his sister's shadow. Raevyn was an extrovert and glowed like Sirius in the winter sky, only to explode like a supernova. Her brother, on the other hand, had always been a black dwarf. Although socially introverted and physically awkward, there are reports that he was actually quite brilliant—even more than his celebrated sister, I dare say, but his gifts went largely undetected."

Kitts spoke for the first time. "And Finch . . . what happened to him?"

"Suicide," answered Sidd. "The parents were killed in a home invasion at their vacation home in 2018, which is now a cold case. Her brother reportedly disappeared before that, whereabouts unknown.

Then, he returned to the family home in 2019 before taking his own life several months before Raevyn decompensated in St. Louis. He was also rumored to be involved with a group that sold drugs. We know he went to rehab more than once."

De Vere spoke. "Sidd, if I may. Regarding the exact details of the brother's death, it was classified as a suspected suicide after he reportedly jumped off the Bay Bridge. I realize they found his jacket, and a year later they pulled fragments of a badly decomposed body out of the water, but without DNA evidence, forensic experts couldn't agree with absolute certainty it was young Nevenmoore."

Pat responded, "With respect, Dr. D, in addition to finding his coat, they did a lot of testing to establish that the remains belonged to Finch Nevenmoore. The lead pathologist called in a renowned forensic anthropologist who by a variety of techniques analyzed bone density and the size and weight of the remains. He concluded that it was a male of Finch's physical size and age. His team also did microscopic testing of skin prints, blood type, and dental records which helped establish with a high degree of confidence that this was Finch. Additionally, the remains were recovered in an area consistent with the tidal patterns in the Chesapeake Bay."

Kitts observed a hint of skepticism on De Vere's face. The profiler looked like she was about to speak but sat back and remained quiet.

"Regarding Finch, he was also treated by Prokop, too, right?" Lenore asked, but before receiving an answer, she continued, "Yes, I've got it here. Seems the whole family saw Prokop at one time or another. Everyone except the father, who was said to be distant and emotionally aloof. Mother was Prokop's patient first, then the brother, and finally Raevyn. It says here that Raevyn started seeing him after her breakdown in St. Louis."

Toby leaned forward. "So Raevyn loses it, spends the next couple of years going from one looney bin to the next, then the parents get killed at their beach house, and twin brother does a Greg Louganis off the Bay

Bridge. That's dark."

On cue, Saks was ready to pounce. "My dear Tobias, first, your *rechcheré* Louganis diving reference is neither clever nor cute. Second, your term looney bin and its cousins, booby hatch, madhouse, cuckoo's nest, and funny farm are all terms we *could* use, but don't. Having said all this, I agree that Poe couldn't have written a darker story. Dark and immeasurably tragic. Layers of neglect and trauma, laden with a severe and unregulated Type I Bipolar Disorder and perhaps a dissociative spectrum illness as well. Peace has eluded this sad woman. She experienced a veritable cavalcade of treatments, therapies, hospitalizations, residential programs, and medications with far too little yield I'm afraid."

Kitts raised her hand. "So, are we thinking Raevyn could be our UNSUB? I mean, she's brilliant. It says here that she even minored in math in college. She's unstable, right? And may have resented all the shrinks for failing to help her and her brother and maybe her mother too. There was even something about her mom having an affair with Prokop, but that was never confirmed. We know she suffered unbelievable shame when she stripped naked in front of the world. Maybe Raevyn took her revenge on the victims by making them feel the shame and terror she'd felt. I realize this doesn't really add up 'cause I don't know what I'm about here. Remember, I'm the new kid. Boz said I should keep my mouth shut, listen, and learn. But I'm way past that now."

De Vere offered reassurance. "No, Nicola, you're raw, but you know more than you realize. Pat, didn't we have data on Raevyn's whereabouts at the time of each killing?"

Pat spoke from the corner of the room. "That's right, Dr. D. She seems to have been off the radar at the time of the second killing in Philadelphia. No credit card receipts or cell phone pings. Looks like her phone was left in her room. Of course, we know she was in Prokop's office the night he was killed. So, we can't rule her out based on travel patterns."

De Vere quickly followed up. "This is why I insisted we not prematurely assign a gender to our UNSUB. Her direct contact with Prokop might suggest she had a special vendetta toward him."

"This is a dialectical process," said Sidd. "Synthesis evolves from the thesis and antithesis. With respect, I do not believe that Raevyn Nevenmoore is our UNSUB. Maybe I will be proven wrong, but I don't think this will happen. Our UNSUB is a male. We know that female serial killers are exceedingly rare. This will take more research on all our parts. Although I do not believe she is the killer, the special agents will need to follow up with interviews."

De Vere smiled and said, "Yes, and I'm sure Lavinia Fisher, Aileen Wuornos, Belle Gunness, and the other black widows were all quite comforted by those statistics, Sidd."

Sidd nodded. "Yes, thank you, Bernie. Point well taken. It's important that we not foreclose prematurely. Regardless of gender, let us infer that our UNSUB is an organized killer, most likely intelligent with social and interpersonal skills. He fashions himself something of a poet, although his style is unnaturally stiff and repetitive. He speaks of retribution, so we are dealing with someone who feels wronged and shamed by the psychiatric profession and these practitioners in particular."

Toby asked, "So, what are we doing about the notes he's left for us and the ones with the equations? Shouldn't we be getting some math geeks to consult on this?"

Sidd responded, "Of course we are pursuing this. Pat has contacted our field offices in Boston and Palo Alto to liaise with the mathematics departments at MIT and Stanford. We've spoken with Ellison at MIT, but I sensed some reticence in deploying their resources. He said it was red tape; I suspect something more political."

Lenore said, "Yeah, I think the political climate has made the elites less enamored with the FBI than they were in the good old days."

Saks looked up from his doodling. "Ellison's resistance doesn't surprise me. He's the dust that blows in the political winds. What about the young chap from Wisconsin? I think it's Lawrence University."

Pat answered, "You mean Roderick Cummings? Yes, we reached out, but he's also unavailable. He's on sabbatical for the next few months. I asked about others in the Math Department there but haven't heard back."

"Pity. Roddy Cummings is top-notch, a real corker. He was helpful a few years back on the Bracken case."

Kitts raised her hand again. "I know someone who might be able to help. There's this guy in Colorado I met working on a case 10 years ago. He was a suspect in an assault and embezzlement scheme but ended up being framed for the whole thing."

De Vere asked, "And just where does he teach, dear? Can you direct us to his publications?"

Kitts demurred. "Well, that's the thing. He isn't an academic. I don't even think he has a degree, but he's a whiz at anything mathematical."

After a pause, Sidd said, "You're speaking of the bookkeeper, Carmine Luedke. The man was once hospitalized at the state hospital in Pueblo, Colorado. He later re-invented himself as an abstract artist. Yes, I know about him. We've also learned of your financial arrangement with the bookkeeper."

"Man, are there no secrets with you people? Is *nothin'* off base? Of course, y'all know about what happened in Afghanistan and Aurora, Colorado when the crazy sheriff tried to kill me, and how I lost my shit, sorry, after that. You probably know about my little brother Blue, who got paralyzed 'cause of me, too. What else have you all memorized about my personal life? Smith College? Omar Pei?"

Bernice De Vere turned to Kitts; her tone grew stern. "Everything! We know it all. There are no secrets among us. It's what we do, Nicola. You don't think we would have asked EAD Baldazzar to bring you here if we hadn't learned critical details about your past and potential entanglements that make you who you are?"

Saks spoke emphatically. "Knowing about this is vital! We don't traffic in secrets and whispered innuendos, Agent Kitts. We deal in facts. We work the puzzles. To do so, we must collect all the pieces. It's beyond proficuous that we know such things."

"I don't know what that word means, Doctor." Kitts exhaled. "Okay . . . Carmine, Mr. Luedke, the bookkeeper, came into a lot of money because of the shit, sorry again, stuff that happened at the hospital and this company that tried to frame him. He was thankful for my help and wanted to show his gratitude by helping with my tuition. I intend to pay him back, too, but all that has nothin' to do with why I'm bringing him up. He is an odd man, but he knows more about math than most professors at MIT or wherever. I think you'd call him a mathematical savant. But sorry for bringing him up."

Sidd sighed. "That will do it for now. Thank you everyone. We need to have one of our team coordinate with DC police and interview Ms. Nevenmoore at the DC jail, but let's wait for Sol Mendelson to complete his competency evaluation first. Toby and Lenore, you can work the timeline and learn more about this woman's whereabouts at the time of the first killing. She can't have disappeared. Bernice and I will delve into the messages left by the UNSUB and check our databases to see if anything glows red. We shall meet again after Dr. Mendelson completes his evaluation. That's it for now."

As the team members filed out, Nicola heard Sidd turn to Pat and say, "Oh, one more thing, Pat. Please find the contact information for Mr. Luedke to set up a preliminary conversation with him."

15

RAEVYN AND THE SEVEN SISTERS

"I don't need you to tell me how to do my job, Rita. She already *is* on suicide watch. So don't act so high and mighty. Just worry 'bout your own self."

"Oh, there'd be nothing to worry about if I knew you were doing your job, Clarice. I always need to triple-check when I'm working the shift with your sorry ass."

Raevyn listened to the bickering outside her cell, not attending to the words but only to the annoying drone of their voices. Someone came by every 15 minutes to check on her. They called her name, waited for her to answer, signed the check sheet, and moved on.

Alone in her tiny cell with only a mattress and steel toilet, she curled into a tight ball and tried to separate herself from the world. Her sister and the attorney had visited briefly, but their words were muffled and vacant.

She hadn't touched the tray they left for her: a cup of soup, a packet of saltines, and a few carrot sticks. There was no silverware. Even plastic cutlery could make a lethal weapon for the determined, but she was too tired. Raevyn thought about all her lies and deceits, things done, and actions not taken. She was where she deserved to be. If she did survive, she'd need to devise a plan to make it all stop. But she was too tired. For now, the only thing she wanted to do more than sleep was die. She thought of drowning herself in the cup of soup but couldn't imagine the logistics. Even if there was a more viable means, her arms and legs had become lead weights that kept her anchored to the mattress.

Raevyn was no stranger to this deadening and hated it more than she hated herself. She had given all her moods—and there were many—different names. They became her seven sisters, each the embodiment of a different state, some of which she loved and others not so much. Like Snow White, she was surrounded by a gaggle of dwarfian moods. There was *Happy* and her twin *Witty*, and of course *Grumpy*, who fueled her power and kept others away. Raevyn especially embraced *Doc*, who knew and could do everything, feeding her ambitions and keeping watch over the others. As *Doc*, she morphed into the Phi Beta Kappa, world champion, whose brilliance shined like a first-magnitude star. This sisterly triumvirate formed her public persona—happy, funny, and brilliant. But *Grumpy* was always at hand whenever she felt slighted or ignored.

Raevyn always felt the term bipolar did not adequately capture her lived experience. The curse of her mood disorder was its multipolarity. The other dwarf sisters waited impatiently for their turns, which appeared suddenly and without warning when *Sleepy or Bashful* took charge. *Sleepy* was more potent than she seemed because she could join forces with *Grumpy* to spawn other hybrid mood sisters. She had names for them too, like *Edgy* when she felt both sluggish and agitated, or *Angsty*, a cousin of *Bashful,* and *Pointless,* known for her emptiness and hollow feelings. But lurking behind her mask-like moods of *Happy*, *Doc*, and *Grumpy,* was the dreaded impostor *Dopey*, the mood she felt embodied her essence. *Dopey* summoned the triplets, *Worthless, Hopeless*, and *Rubbish,* who resembled a pile of shit. Lurking deeply within the caverns, *Dopey's* gang knew all the backroads and shortcuts in her mind.

Finch knew about her seven sisters. He said he had some, too, but they differed from hers. Once, he tried to describe the odd inhabitants of his mind, but she was too distracted to learn their names. Her used-to-be best friend Marney knew about her dwarf sisters but only *Happy, Grumpy,* and *Doc. Dopey* and her sisters of shame were Raevyn's alone to bear.

Surrounded by four gray walls and with *Dopey* and the triplets by her side, Raevyn's mind returned to the possibility of death by soup asphyxiation.

16

24-531.03

The next day, Raevyn felt herself emerging from a dark emotional coma and becoming more aware of her confinement in a six-by-eight-foot jail cell. A metal bedframe bolted to the concrete floor was draped with a flimsy, stained mattress that had nestled the bodies of countless hookers, drug addicts, and killers. Opposite the bed stood a single-piece steel toilet attached to a sink.

For the last several days, her attention had been drawn inward, centering on the hazy sense that she was where she belonged. Finch's nightly whispers made this clear. She was where all worthless people deserved to be—imprisoned for crimes real and imagined. In her personal prison, actual proof mattered less than the internal rantings of her grand inquisitor and accuser. But today, she felt a stirring of restless energy that welcomed *Witty* back and propelled her to take stock of her external prison.

The grim-looking officer, whom she'd quietly named "Reaper," appeared at her cell to inform her that she had an interview. She provided little else, only to "Get your ass moving, Nevenmoore. You gotta see someone, *now*."

"Who?" Raevyn was struck by the curious sound of her voice as she hadn't spoken for the last several days. When Hooks and Yeardley last visited, Raevyn remained mute with her head down, watching a lone ant wander aimlessly across the floor.

"Well, you'll soon find that out. My job is to get you there, pure and simple. Now, get moving, princess."

When Raevyn entered the interview room, she saw a man at a small table, a notebook in his hand and a briefcase at his feet. Reaper attached her handcuffs to the bolt on the table as she looked at the man and said, "Just let us know when you're done." Reaper exited with the indifference of an underpaid and overworked civil servant.

The man spoke. "Hello, Ms. Nevenmoore. I'm Dr. Mendelson. I've been asked by Judge Howard to speak with you about your situation."

Raevyn studied this man. His white hair suggested that he was older, but his dark beard and youthful face told a different story. He wore a corduroy sports jacket with a loosened tie and had a disarming smile with pale blue eyes that drew her in. Still, she had no idea who he was or why he needed to see her.

"I'd like to get a sense of your understanding about what's happening to you. Clearly, we're meeting in the DC Jail. Can you tell me what you think this is all about?"

Raevyn recalled a memory fragment from her appearance in court the previous week. She remembered Hooks' words, "a history of severe mental illness" and "competency evaluation." *One more shrink*, she thought. Raevyn gazed into the coolness of his eyes and spoke, her words sounding alien and mechanical. "I'm accused of stripping and butchering one of your colleagues, the preeminent Linus Prokop, PhD, MD."

"I see. Yes, you have been accused of his murder, but tell me, who is representing you?"

"Why, Brisco Hooks, Esquire."

"Yes, and what is your understanding of Mr. Hooks' role in all of this?"

"You're asking if I understand that I've been accused of murder and that I have a lawyer who is trying to get me off? Yeah, that's what my sister hired him for, to rescue poor dear Raevyn, who fucked up again."

"Ms. Nevenmoore, is it okay to call you Raevyn? I'm not here to explore your guilt or innocence in what you've been accused of, only to make—"

"Sure, it's okay, but I have two questions. What's *your* first name, Doctor, and are those blue eyes real?"

He shifted in his chair, but Mendelson was unrattled by such questions. "Solomon, but Sol is just fine, and the eyes, for better or worse, are real. As I said, I'm here to make sure you clearly understand the charges against you and that you can assist Mr. Hooks in his defense strategy."

Raevyn nodded vigorously, and her words picked up speed. "Alas, Sol, I'm afraid it's the bipolar thing. That label doesn't carry an expiration date. It follows you and always pops up as an explanation or excuse. Brisco's going to argue that poor Raevyn is mentally ill, *non compos mentis,* and shouldn't be found guilty because, lamentably, she's a loon. Yeah, I think he'll pull the bipolar card to try to get me out of this."

"If that is his approach, what will you do? I mean, will you cooperate if this is his strategy?"

"Well, fuck-a-doodle-do, Sol, let me put it this way. Would *you* want to be here? I don't, and even though I generally think I'm a piece of shit, I don't want to spend my life in this kind of prison when I can just as easily be crazy in my own. Plus, the food's not great."

"This is quite an indictment and statement about your personal prison, but let's suppose that your attorney argues that as a result of your bipolar disorder—your mental illness, as you put it—you are not criminally responsible. What will you do? Will you be able to aid him in his strategy?"

She paused, "Yes and . . . no. Even crazy people are not *that* insane, plus I don't want my story reduced to a soundbite as it always has been. Catching my drift, Sol?"

"There is more to Raevyn Nevenmoore than the diagnosis of

bipolar disorder. I see what you're saying. Sounds like you've faced this before; the diagnosis defines the person. But, again, the issue at hand is whether you see Mr. Hooks as an ally and will be able to work with him in his defense strategy. I'd like to review a couple of questionnaires with you now."

They sat together for the next 90 minutes, as Dr. Mendelson asked her a series of detailed questions about her understanding of the charges against her and her capacity to assist in her defense. Then, he brought out a set of inkblot cards and asked her what each might be.

"Really, the Rorschach in a competency evaluation? You're completely old school, aren't you, Solly boy." Raevyn was no stranger to the Rorschach, which she had taken during her numerous hospitalizations and treatment programs. She remembered the cards and some of the things she had previously seen. Taking the first card, she responded, "Oh, I remember this cute one. It always looked like a girl with wings trapped inside a wall. Have a field day with that one."

Her spurt of dark energy was waning, and *Witty's* act was almost over. The next set was *Sleepy's*. "Are we done yet, Dad? I'm pooped." She longed for her stained, threadbare mattress.

"Yes, Raevyn. We're done. I appreciate your meeting with me and answering all these questions. I know it's been a lot. Is there anything else you think I should know before we stop?"

"Uh, yes there is Sol. Could you please speak with the guards and tell them I need a pair of noise-cancelling headphones? The walls are thin and don't block out the voices I hear at night."

17

MITTENS AND TWINKLES

January 14, 2004

She couldn't recall when she first knew there was something wrong with her brother. It might have been around the time of their ninth birthday when their maternal grandparents, whom they inaptly called Pansy and Sunny, gave her and Finch kittens. Their mother was not pleased with having pets in the house, while their father, as with most things, felt indifferent. Pansy insisted they keep the kittens, and Sunny headed to the liquor cabinet in the den to fix himself a Jack and Coke. Pansy was the senior version of their mother, always needing to have the last word and final say. Even as children, the twins could see that Pansy wielded a cudgel that invariably led to their mother's resentful acquiescence.

Raevyn and Finch watched as Pansy raised her finger and chided their mother, "Abigail, do *not* impose your own miserable childhood on your children. They *need* a pet to keep them company while their parents work until God knows when. Sunny and I will not hear another word about these kittens! Isn't that right, Gerald . . . Gerald?"

Of course, Sunny wouldn't have been able to hear another word as he had already passed out on the couch after slamming down his second drink. Raevyn watched the rosy rash take shape on their mother's neck. She always knew when Mother was upset because this scarlet ink spot would suddenly appear.

"Fine!" Then turning to the twins, she added, "But those cats can *only* remain if you children accept responsibility for their care. Do you hear me, Raevyn? You too, Finch. These cats are *your* responsibility and can stay until the day comes that you neglect their caretaking. Do I make myself clear?"

Raevyn summoned her sweetest voice, "Yes, Mama," while Finch quietly nodded. It was settled then that the twins would keep their kittens.

Pansy opened the cat carrier and pulled out a sweet-looking tabby for Raevyn. "Here you go, sweetie pie. This cute one's for you." Then, she reached in for the other but quickly withdrew her hand after it bit her finger. "Damned cat. Here, Finch, this is yours."

As Raevyn hugged her kitten, which she'd already named Twinkles, Finch backed away from Pansy's offering. His was a tiny tuxedo cat with white front paws. "Come, Finch, don't be a baby. Take your kitten that Pansy and Sunny brought for you."

Finch didn't move or reach for his kitten. Pansy grabbed him by the arm and insisted he hold the cat that had just bitten her. He reluctantly tried to cradle the kitten before it squirmed and scooted away.

"Finch, you'll need to find a name for this little creature and care for him just like your sister is doing." Pansy reached around and grabbed his kitten as he was preparing to pee on the carpet. "We have a litter box in the car. Sunny? Gerald, get off your keister and bring in the litter box and show them how to set it up and clean the damn thing." Then stooping down to the children's level, she said, "Oh, and children, these are indoor kittens. They can *never* go outside."

"Why, Pansy?" asked the innocent-sounding Raevyn.

"Because they'll run away and get eaten by dogs or foxes. And you don't want to let them near your swimming pool. You see, cats can't swim and will drown."

"I won't *ever* let Twinkles go outside, Pansy, I promise," said Raevyn as she hugged her kitten.

By this time, Finch had moved a step closer to his cat but still hadn't picked him up.

Raevyn cooed, "Whatcha gonna call him, Birdie? He's really cute. See, it looks like he's wearing little white mittens."

Finch shrugged his shoulders when Pansy suggested that Mittens was a good name. After lunch and birthday cake, Pansy peeled Sunny off the couch and left.

"Thank you, Pansy and Sunny," called Raevyn as they walked to their car. "I love my Twinkles."

Their father had briefly appeared for the birthday lunch before returning to the county morgue. Mother had things to do as their au pair, Isabella, cleared the dishes and sat with the children and their cats. Raevyn hugged Twinkles tightly while Mittens wandered toward the sliding glass door to the patio.

"No, no, Mittens," said Isabella. You will not be going outside, you bad little boy.... Aww, they are so sweet. Do you like your little Mittens, Finch? He is a very handsome kitty cat."

Finch said, "I'm scared he'll bite me like he did to Pansy. I don't think he likes me as much as Cobie's likes her."

Raevyn goaded, "You've got to try to hold him, Birdie. Like I'm doing with Twinkles. Just pick him up like this." She placed Twinkles on Isabella's lap and went over to Mittens. "Come on, kitty." She scooped him up and stroked his head as she walked him over to her brother. "Here, Birdie, just hold him like this."

Finch reached out awkwardly, and the kitten swatted his hand and jumped down from his sister's arms.

"Ow!" Tears welled up. "He hates me."

"But Finch, honey, it will take some time for him to get used to you," said Isabella with a lilting tone. "Just give him some time."

The following morning, their mother gave them strict instructions before leaving for the hospital. "I want those cats fed and the litter box changed like Sunny showed you. And make sure the door to the back is kept closed."

"We will, Mother," answered Raevyn in a voice she knew others found adorable and alluring.

"And Raevyn, make sure your brother reads his book for at least an hour today. Isabella, see to it that Yeardley has them ready when Mr. David comes for their swim lesson at noon."

Raevyn spent the rest of the morning playing with Twinkles. Then, she heard a scream coming from Finch's room. She burst in to see Mittens run out the door as Finch cried in pain. "He bit me!"

Isabella rushed in and stood beside Raevyn as the two inspected the tiny bite mark. Finch crossed his arms and turned away. Raevyn tried to console him but also felt a secret glee that her Twinkles loved her, while Mittens seemed allergic to her twin.

Finch spent the rest of the day in his room playing video games. As usual, their parents worked late and missed dinner with the children. Finch picked at his food and didn't say much. Raevyn was chatty and held Twinkles on her lap as she talked sweetly to her kitty. She looked up to see her brother glaring at her.

That night, Raevyn lay awake. She always had trouble falling asleep as thoughts tumbled through her busy mind. She whispered for Finch but heard no answer. She thought she heard the patio door open before she finally drifted off.

The following day, she awakened to her mother's angry shouting.

"Which of you left this back door open! Isabella, I told you that this patio door needs to remain shut. What about this do you seem not to understand!"

Raevyn bounded down the stairs and into the backyard. She ran to where her mother and Isabella were standing by the pool.

"Raevyn, get inside!" Their mother blocked her path. "You don't need to see this."

Isabella reached out to her. "Honey, come here now! It's okay."

But it wasn't. Raevyn pushed past her mother and gazed wide-eyed into the pool where two tiny kittens floated on the surface.

PART TWO

SPEAKS THE WHISPERER

Mere stowaways on a ship of fools,
Scattered among the legion of dunces
Who posture under the pseudoscientific mantle of supreme Authority
and
Beckon to the defenseless:
Come share with me in confidence that which you can tell no other,
Knowing full well that your Truth is kept hidden under my trust-
worthy cloak,
For none 'cept me shall know the depths of your shame.
Speaks the Whisperer,
To which I answer,
And none 'cept me shall taste the blood of retribution."
—*Anonymous*

18

False Self

Frazzled by her tardiness, Nicola sprinted down the long hallway, spilling her coffee as she ran. She dropped her satchel and watched wide-eyed as loose papers popped from their binder and slid across the floor. She quickly stuffed them back into her satchel as she pushed open the conference room door. The spill left an unsightly stain on her white blouse for the world to interpret, as she interrupted the meeting in progress. Everyone looked toward the commotion. Nicola felt sure that all eyes were affixed on her coffee-spattered blouse. Sidd was in the middle of speaking and stopped as Kitts shuffled clumsily toward the empty seat. Lenore smiled sympathetically, and Toby smirked.

Mortified, Nicola uttered, "I'm so sorry. I just—"

Bernice De Vere cut her short. "Please remember, Agent Kitts, we need everyone here on time. We require punctuality, not apologies or justifications for your tardiness, dear."

She felt the heat of her embarrassment rise through her neck. Nicola was learning quickly that De Vere could extend the hand of friendship, then harshly take it away. Kitts nodded uncomfortably and glanced toward the man seated at the far end of the table. She recognized him from her first year in the academy. Dr. Solomon Mendelson had lectured more than once. Kitts remembered the first time she'd seen him—the handsome face of a man in his prime with a full head of white hair. She never understood the genetic chicanery that would cause a man, probably in his early 50s, to look so young while simultaneously having snow-white hair with an incongruous dark beard and eyebrows.

Nicola remembered their first encounter. As he was talking about the minds of killers like Charles Manson and Ted Bundy, Kitts raised her hand. When Mendelson turned his head to look at her, she felt drawn into the pools of blue that were his eyes and promptly forgot what she was going to ask. Nicola still cringed at this memory and chided herself for acting like a silly schoolgirl and not a hardened ex-gunnery sergeant and seasoned law enforcement officer.

Mendelson nodded toward Kitts, his eyes flashing a hint of recognition.

Sidd began again. "Before we hear from Dr. Mendelson about his competency evaluation, I mentioned that we received a message like the ones left at each crime site."

Saks interjected, "Not another equation, mind you, but yet one more blustery screed from this person claiming to be the Whisperer—more style than substance, actually—promising more retribution."

Sidd continued. "We don't know if he intends to kill again. It was sent anonymously to IT Management Division this time. Someone flagged it for us. Pat, please circulate copies of this note."

All eyes focused on the second message. Lenore said, "Looks like the same language and overblown style like the other one. If it is a guy, he thinks he's a poet. But not a very good one."

"I agree with both observations," pronounced Sidd. "We shall take a closer look and make sure there are no more messages on the server. But I'd like to segue to Dr. Mendelson's evaluation." Then turning to Nicola, he said, "I'm sure you're familiar with Dr. Solomon Mendelson, Agent Kitts. He was a frequent lecturer at the academy. He has completed his competency evaluation of Ms. Nevenmoore, and Judge Howard has allowed him to brief us about his findings. Sol, please go ahead."

Mendelson opened his notebook. "Thank you, Sidd. I saw Ms.

Nevenmoore two days ago. Let's just say I found her to be a sorrowful and troubled soul."

Nicola recalled how Sheriff Burwinkle, her personal Judas, once used those words to describe Carmine Luedke when he labeled his actions the "misdeeds of a troubled soul." She wondered if her life's calling was to become entangled in the misdeeds of these sad and troubled souls. *Maybe it takes one to know one,* she thought. This idea disturbed her, and she shook off the intrusion and forced herself to refocus on Dr. Mendelson.

Mendelson looked down at his notes and began. "As to the question of whether Ms. Nevenmoore is competent to stand trial, there's no question. She is. Raevyn had no problem understanding the charges. She is aware of her circumstances and seems perfectly able to assist in her defense if she chooses to do so."

Toby co-opted the silence and interjected, "Slam dunk, right? So, they'll proceed with a trial. Easy peasy."

Sidd held up his hand. "Well, I think Dr. Mendelson has more to say." He nodded to the doctor.

"While she *is* competent and can assist in her defense, she can easily become hypomanic. But I have to say she made a rather strange request as I prepared to leave. She asked if I could arrange to get her some noise-canceling headphones because she hears voices that keep her up at night. Given her extensive psychiatric history, I think she may be psychotic. Her chart shows no indication that she has been taking medication. She apparently has a standing prescription for lithium and Vraylar, but pharmacy records show they haven't been filled for months."

"Or she just can't take the noise from the cells around her. Maybe that's all it is," said Toby, setting himself up for a predictable smackdown.

Saks stopped his doodling and shook his head. "Dear Tobias, you have the patience of a pup at dinner. It is true; our esteemed Solomon is not only a wise fellow, but in this case, he happens to be entirely spot-on.

There is no way to discount what she's communicating. From what you're telling us, her counsel will surely adduce an NGRI defense."

"That's not guilty by reason of insanity, Toby." Lenore seemed pleased to spell this out for her perplexed-looking counterpart.

"I know what NRGI means, Lenore. Chrissake. Just because you have a psych degree, you think—"

Sidd silenced the banter by raising his hand again. "Is there more, Sol?"

"She was calmer at the end of our appointment and asked to see me again. When we met the next day, she seemed hungry to talk. I'm not attributing it to me. I just happened to be a stranger with no baggage who seemed interested in her life. There was a loneliness that went beyond being isolated in a jail cell."

Kitts spoke for the first time. "I got that sense, too, from what I read. This is a rich kid who grew up in a high-achieving family that seemed to value the stuff she did over who she was. Looks like she had everything going for her on the outside. She was Icarus, like Dr. D said."

Saks looked up and smiled faintly. "Yes, the empty little rich girl who looked like a star from the outside. Taught to believe that her worth was tied to her boundless talents. Yes, quite a bit of poignancy there, indeed."

Directing his comments to Sol, De Vere said, "No doubt you are familiar with Alice Miller's *Drama of the Gifted Child*?"

Gideon Saks put down his cup and added, "Miller's eloquent little treatise was based on the work of Winnicott, Mahler, and Kohut and weaved a cautionary tale of the consequences for Icari like our Raevyn Nevenmoore."

"Yes Gid," responded De Vere. "Of course, she's a classic example of Miller's, or Winnicott's, concept of the true and false self."

Toby furrowed his brow, "This is the cop in me talking. I guess this psychology stuff and these people and books are interesting and all that, but I'm not sure it's gonna help us catch our killer. Sorry, just had to say it."

All heads turned to Kitts as she spoke. "Yeah, I hear you, Toby. Those are a lot of names, but I think what they're saying is every kid has a basic need to be noticed and seen for who they are, not just what they're supposed to be according to what their folks need them to be."

Sol smiled and looked at Nicola. "Exactly, Agent Kitts. That's a good summary of what Winnicott meant by the true self. The problem is what happens when that need is squashed by parental expectations."

De Vere said, "From what we've been able to deduce, the mother, a pioneering, rather self-absorbed surgeon, only saw her youngest daughter when her brilliance was burning brightest.

Not to be outdone, Saks interjected, "That's correct, Bernie, but when the penumbra was showing, Mother went dark. Abigail feasted off her daughter's successes—internationally renowned gymnast and medical student following in mother's footsteps."

Lenore added, "What if all she was remembered for was the worst day of her life in St Louis? Wasn't Bryan Stevenson the guy who said something like, 'People are only remembered for the worst thing they've done'?"

Saks answered, "Good girl, Lenore, and quite fitting. A social activist, Stevenson stated, 'Every person in our society is more than the worst thing they've ever done.' So, you're bringing that up is apropos to the profile we're beginning to construct."

Sidd said, "I believe the parents' brittle egos were shattered by the normal imperfections and foibles that all children manifest. It seems the parents' collective shame was projected onto their daughter. It is very tragic to see what happened to this family. The mother lost her license following a second charge of driving while intoxicated. I believe there is some evidence of a troubled marriage. Lenore, can you tell us more about the father?"

"Yes, Sidd. As I said before, he was a pathologist who seemed to fit everyone's worst stereotypes about that specialty. He worked in the county morgue and was overshadowed by his famous wife."

"Father was essentially a colorless figure, who faded to gray," said De Vere. "He was said to be somewhat melancholic. I believe we also have a composite of the mother's psychiatric diagnosis, true?"

"Yes," answered Sidd, pulling a report from the folder before him. "She was treated for an unspecified mood disorder in her early 30s. She took a leave of absence from her practice, during which her whereabouts were not known. But we were able to discover the treatment records from McLean Hospital documenting several trials of ECT."

Sol was quick to add, "Mother was, as Kay Jamison would say, 'touched by fire.' She was a brilliant, witty, charming, and seductive woman suffering from alcoholism and a narcissistic disorder, but she also had one hell of a temper."

Toby dove in headfirst. "Some family, huh? Temperamental doctors, self-absorbed manic-depressives, and drunks to boot. Then Mom and Pops get killed in their beach house in 2017. Parents both dead, boom. Then, the brother offs himself two years later, boom, boom; then Raevyn loses it in St. Louis, boom, boom, boom."

On cue, Saks quickly responded, "That's quite a barrage, Tobias. An interesting synthesis, so colorfully expressed indeed. The amassing of trauma upon trauma is tragic, but what is the nexus between this and the murderous mayhem she's been alleged to have perpetrated? Why target a gaggle of esteemed psychiatrists?"

Sol raised his hand. "To your point, Gideon, let's talk about her twin brother, Finch. I think he's a big part of this. Much of what she told me during our second meeting concerned their relationship. I think this weighs heavily on her. I know he also suddenly exited from her life. Their parents are tragically murdered at their beach house, and two years later her twin brother jumps off the Bay Bridge. When we talked again, Raevyn told me what a genius she thought Finch was with math and computers. She said she relied on him throughout her life and regrets how she treated him."

Kitts spoke up. "Excuse me, Doctor, but back to Dr. De Vere's question about the shrinks, I mean the mental health—"

"That's okay, Agent, 'shrinks' is a fine term," interjected Sol.

"Gotcha. Shrinks then. Didn't it say that the brother had lots of contact with psychiatrists? Y'all said he saw Prokop too, right?"

Sidd responded, "Finch had an extensive history of treatment and was a patient of Dr. Prokop's well before his sister ever saw him. We've already noted the mother had seen Dr. Prokop as well."

Lenore agreed, "Yes, that's right. Prokop saw them all. The family was a poster child for the DSM, right? I mean, there was a lot going on in that family, right?"

"Indeed, to say the least," said Saks. "Mental health professionals, Dr. Prokop in particular, occupied an outsized role in the family's psyche. But was this sufficient for Raevyn to begin targeting prominent psychiatrists en masse? I think we need to delve further and learn more about the dead brother. If it's true that his genius was in mathematics, this makes the calling cards left at each murder site even more compelling."

Kitts interjected, "Y'all thinking what I'm thinking? Makes me wonder whose voice she's hearing. His, maybe?"

Sol replied, "I was wondering the same thing, Agent Kitts. When I asked her whose voice she heard, she pulled back and ended the interview. I think there's something there."

Sidd stood, signaling their time was up. "Thank you, Solomon. As always, we are grateful for your insights. I believe we should schedule our own interviews with Ms. Nevenmoore. So as not to overwhelm her, I wonder whether you, Agent Kitts, would be someone she might find easy to speak with. Dr. De Vere can prep you for that interview, but I think a one-on-one is the way to approach her."

Putting papers back in his satchel, Sol said, "I agree, Sidd. I think Agent Kitts may be the perfect fit. She can approach her in a way that I couldn't. If this woman does harbor animosity toward us shrinks, then I'm probably not going to get much further with her. But aside from the investigative needs, Raevyn absolutely needs to get back on her medication. And regardless of how this goes, she needs to talk to someone. But medication should come first."

"Are you volunteering to become her therapist, Sol?" Bernice asked wryly.

"No, as I said, I think she and I have gone about as far as we can. Raevyn will be a handful, but I'm thinking of a person who would be a good fit with this troubled young woman."

Saks raised his brow. "Oh my, dear Solomon. It's not who I'm thinking, I hope. If you're referring to Idina Madrigal, then that would be a mistake. I didn't think she was fit to practice."

"Sol shrugged. "I understand your concerns, Gideon. But she has resumed her practice. I'll reach out to her to see if she's accepting new patients."

As the team filed out of the conference room, Sidd signaled Nicola. "Good comments, Agent Kitts. I want to inform you that we reached Mr. Luedke. He has agreed to offer his help and will be here by the end of the week. Given your history, I would like you to act as our liaison with your old friend the bookkeeper."

19

NICOLA MINEOLA

I should be happy, right? Nicola dusted off her gratitude journal and began to make entries about her gifts and blessings—her health, education, and a dream job. She had what she wanted, yes indeed. But her journal remained understocked, filled with trite-sounding affirmations and repetitive entries that rang hollow. She was grateful for Langston, who though a faithful companion and more intelligent than many people she knew, was, after all, a bird. She felt a bond but realized this was not enough.

When she went to Smith College, she hoped to find it all—a new career and exciting path that would take her beyond the narrow confines of her old life. It did that, but not in the ways she'd hoped. Her exciting path led straight to the bed of Omar Pei. Their brief affair led to his dismissal and her humiliation. Whatever they say about teachers violating boundaries with their students, victims *do* get blamed. Maybe not overtly like receiving a formal censure or, worse, being booted from the program, but she heard the whispers behind her back. She'd spent much of her life honing her skills at ignoring such things. She was as tough as they came, a Silver Star combat-hardened ex-grunt, but she couldn't tune out the constant chatter and innuendos. Even more upsetting, she couldn't hide from her shame.

Kitts thought her new assignment to the BAU would wash away more than a coffee stain. Surely working shoulder to shoulder with brilliant forensic specialists would offer, if not redemption, then at least a distraction from the noise inside.

She was surprised that her thoughts turned to Sol Mendelson, another unexpected but welcome diversion. She remembered her initial attraction when he walked into the auditorium for his introductory lecture on serial killers. Something about his soft smile and deep blue eyes. But an infatuation with another older instructor felt dangerously familiar. She realized that fantasizing about Sol Mendelson, if it could be contained, provided at best a momentary refuge. At the end of the day, she would still return to an empty apartment and a hungry bird. Langston had recently begun picking feathers from his chest, nape, and thighs, a sure sign that whatever was gnawing at her had also affected him.

This morning felt slightly different. She managed to distract herself by burrowing into Raevyn Nevenmoore's file. Since her arrest, cable news had played nonstop footage of the St. Louis Olympic trials. Nicola couldn't stop thinking about Raevyn's wild rant by the balance beam and the throng of officials and coaches trying to cover up her madness.

Sidd had put his faith in her to interview Raevyn, an assignment that felt both exciting and daunting. She had memorized details from her life and spoken to De Vere about how she should approach someone like Raevyn. Nicola reminded herself of the patients she had interviewed during her graduate school externships, though none as troubled as the young woman she was about to encounter. She told herself that she had walked point and witnessed the horrors of war. Surely she was ready for this.

, *,* *,*

Before going to the Central Detention Facility—commonly known as the DC Jail—Agent Kitts would check in with Lt. Edgar Bilch, the DC detective in charge of the case. Though not a requirement—after all, she *was* a federal agent—meeting with Bilch was a courtesy. Local police often resented the feds intruding into their domain, co-opting their responsibilities, and questioning their authority, so she wanted to avoid needlessly ruffling feathers. She called ahead to meet up with Bilch. Kitts would greet him as a colleague with appropriate clarity and firmness, one professional to another.

Bilch kept her waiting 20 minutes. He greeted her dismissively and led her to his desk. The detective appeared rumpled, grim, and grumpy. He reeked of cigarettes, and his teeth were the color of creamed corn. Nicola quickly knew that there would be little collegiality.

"I have no idea why the FBI needs to poke its damn nose into this case. The evidence against this girl is solid. I don't have time to babysit junior agents."

His eyebrow-singeing comments threw her off. This was not how she thought it would go.

"Um, yeah, I feel ya, Lieutenant. You don't want us nosey feds butting in. I get it. I'm not here to take over and push y'all aside. But we've got our job to do, too. See, it's not just this case with the dead doctor in Georgetown. We're tracking several similar murders of shrinks. So, we can't be too sure here, but it looks like we could have a serial killer on our hands. I can't say much more, but I need to get in and talk with your suspect today. We've got a rapidly developing situation, so I appreciate your help."

Bilch aggressively exhaled a malodorous cloud. "Serial killer, huh? I can't stop you, but it's best not to forget this is *our* case. If we need to widen our investigation, we'll do just that. So have at it, Agent."

With that, Bilch got up from his desk, leaving Kitts wondering if he was coming back. She waited a few minutes and left when it was clear he was done with her.

When she walked through the doors of the DC Jail, she felt she'd been there before. *All jails look and smell the same.* The correctional officers looked like those she'd seen before—busy, bored, distracted, and dour. She showed her ID and clipped her visitor's badge onto her lapel as she followed a tall officer down the corridor to the detention cells.

"I don't think I'll be that long. Just wanna conduct an interview with Ms. Nevenmoore. You got any update about her condition?"

"What? Update? Um, don't know nothing about that, 'cept I heard she's being one crazy bitch today. Maybe Officer Rounds can tell you more. Here, you'll be in this interview room. They'll bring her down. She'll be cuffed, and guards will be outside 'til you're done."

Kitts sat in the same kind of room she'd been in a hundred times before. After all, she was the consummate law enforcement officer. She could handle this—just establish command of the suspect, direct the interview, and emerge with new bits of information to share with Unit 4. She pulled the file and notepad from her satchel. A low drone of voices was suddenly pierced by the shrieking voice of a woman. Her words were not clear; only that she was protesting something.

"FUCK . . . fuck, fuckity duck. I did not! Just tell me why sweetie pie, that's all I'm asking."

"You need to behave, Nevenmoore. There is someone who needs to talk to you. Any more crap like this morning, and you'll be back in your cell quick."

"Ah, come on, Roundy, you're no fun, but I can be good, promise."

The officer led Raevyn into the interview room. "Agent, here's Miss Nevenmoore. She's got a wild hair up her you know what this morning. Any trouble with her, just holler." The officer connected the prisoner's cuffs to the bolt on the table.

Kitts was immediately struck by Raevyn's appearance—long scraggly jet-black hair and a wild look in her eyes that would turn mere mortals to stone. The young woman flashed a friendly smile, both engaging and ominous.

"Well, hi there! Who the hell are you?"

Nicola pulled out her badge and said, "Agent Kitts, Ms. Nevenmoore. I'm here to—"

"But what's your name? Like I'm Raevyn the Maven."

"Agent Kitts."

"Agent Kitts with kibbles and bits. Your mama didn't give you a proper name?"

Kitts conceded, "It's Nicola, but that's—"

"Now we're cooking with grits, Nicola Kitts. Nicola, Nicola, the girl from Mineola, or is it Pensacola, whose shit's from Shinola when you dance the rock and rolla."

Raevyn's staccato clanging was punctuated by jagged shards of laughter. Her handcuffs were bolted to the table, but Raevyn was in constant motion. The speed of her speech was matched by the nonstop movements of her hands and arms.

Kitts felt rattled. Mendelson said she was slightly hypomanic when he interviewed her the other day, but now she was clearly in the midst of a full-blown manic episode. "Okay, Raevyn, I'd like to ask—"

"Ask, and you shall receive, young lady." Suddenly she started singing, 'Into the mist with a young lady on your arm looking for a kiss.' I love that old man, Neil Young."

Kitts repeated that she was with the FBI.

"OH, the FBI, well, this must be important, but I'll tell you what's important, and we'll be good friends if you do this for me. I need my computer but will settle for the files of my manuscript, which has some really important stuff that the world needs to hear. How much do you know about quantum physics and the simulation hypothesis? Well, I'm writing a book about the origins of life, and I need to have it because I'm behind on my schedule. So close to solving the riddle, which is hidden in the numbers. See, it's there, and no one else has been able to decipher this, and because—"

Nicola from Mineola forcefully interjected, "Hey, hey, Raevyn, I'm here to talk to you about Dr. Prokop and what you can tell me about—"

But Raevyn continued talking about her manuscript, which left Kitts outmaneuvered, frustrated, and confused. She felt she was losing command of an interview she had never controlled. Raevyn continued to dominate the space when Kitts stood up and raised her voice.

"Tell me about your brother. TELL ME ABOUT FINCH!"

Like a mic that's suddenly been cut, her torrential speech screeched to a halt. These words, these four words about Finch Nevenmoore, magically silenced Raevyn the Maven, who sat motionless and mute.

"I'd like to know more about your brother. Is it his the voice you've been hearing? Does he have some connection to Prokop's murder?"

Raevyn put her head in her hands and began to moan as if in severe pain. "No, no, no .... Please, Birdie. Bye, bye Birdie. No, please . . . I didn't. I did, I mean. No, I'm so, so sorry."

Kitts leaned in. "Raevyn, can you tell me—"

"SHUUSH YOU!" Raevyn made exaggerated, aggressive gestures to silence Kitts. "Shush . . . I'm so sorry . . . I didn't mean to do it. I didn't do it, but I'm sorry I did."

The tears began without warning. Raevyn's rapid-fire, incoherent banter and puzzling references to her manuscript disappeared as suddenly as they had emerged. What now sat before Kitts was a painfully diminished young woman, the woman Kitts had seen at the end of the video from the gymnastics trials in St. Louis.

"I'm sorry, Birdie. Please. I fucked up. I'm so sorry for what I did."

Kitts watched as the woman before her—10 minutes ago, so outlandishly confident and brazenly mad—was reduced to a heap of remorse, laden with difficult-to-follow contradictions and confessions.

Then, Raevyn raised her head and began wailing at the top of her lungs.

Kitts drew back and stood up. "Uh, I think we need some help here! Hey, we need help NOW!"

Two correctional officers rushed in. One unlocked Raevyn's cuffs, and the other pulled her up. "That's enough, baby girl. You're done here. It's okay, honey. We got you."

The so-called interview had lasted all of 15 minutes. It was done.

Kitts said, "Raevyn . . . I, I'm sorry. I . . . hope we can talk again."

Raevyn whispered, "Nooo, I'm dead now."

The guards guided this puddle of a woman out of the room, leaving Nicola alone. She felt her skin vibrating from what had just happened. The closest she had come to dealing with an acutely manic patient previously was the video she'd watched during her abnormal psych class at Smith. She was unglued by Raevyn's crazed bluster but more bothered by her sudden, nightmarish transformation. Scenes of St. Louis merged with what she had just witnessed—the sad and terrifying image of a woman in the grip of madness. As a combat veteran, Gunnery Sergeant Nicola Kitts had seen bleeding bodies in Musa Qala. As a deputy, she had studied gruesome crime scene photos. Still, it was unnerving to see this woman dramatically crash from the heights of maniacal grandiosity into a cesspool of self-loathing, panic, and fear. She slowly gathered her files and put them into her satchel.

The cool air helped ground Nicola's senses as she exited the facility and found her car in the parking garage. Her mind began to clear as she looked for the 395 South exit. Their meeting was off the rails from the minute Raevyn entered the room. Kitts felt anxious about her botched interview and what she would relay back to her new team. What cutting comments would Saks make? What would Sidd think of her and how would De Vere or Sol have handled Raevyn Nevenmoore? For sure they would have responded with more skill and expertise. Her fretful rumination and shame were interrupted by a ping on her phone. At the light, she looked at the message. It was from Boz.

"There's been another killing. Get here ASAP! Unit 4 meeting at 5:00."

20

THEY CALL YOU THE BOOKKEEPER

Once again, the team had already assembled when Kitts took her seat. Head down, she looked up to catch a wink from Sol.

Sidd began, "The latest victim is a Professor of Psychiatry at Hopkins. Auguste Pough was found by one of his students on Wednesday the third. Same MO and another note, but this one was only a single equation." He hesitated and looked around the room. "But before we talk about our latest victim, I need to alert you to something we've just received from the assistant director of the IT Branch." Sidd nodded to Pat who projected a series of equations on the screen.

$$\frac{1}{6162-t\sqrt{2\pi^c}} -\tfrac{1}{2}(bc-B09U)^2X[3]+ \frac{1}{284-t\sqrt{2\pi^c}} -\tfrac{1}{2}(cb-L04H)^2X[2]+ \frac{1}{5205-t\sqrt{2\pi^c}} -\tfrac{1}{2}(bc-O07S)^2X[1]$$

$$+ \frac{1}{437-t\sqrt{2\pi^c}} -\tfrac{1}{2}(bc-E05T)^2X[0]$$

Pat cleared her throat. "In mid-January, a month before the first killing, an anonymous source sent these equations to a server in IT Services Division. There was no message nor an intended recipient. Because no one had any idea what it meant or who it was intended for, it sat on their server for weeks until someone finally flagged it and sent it our way."

The team stared at the screen. Lenore asked, "There was no message accompanying this? It looks just like the ones left in each victim's office."

Adjusting his bowtie, Saks answered dismissively, "Of course it is. Darlings, close your mouths. We only just received this. No one knew what this was, its source, or its intended recipient. And, as with all such puzzles, no one asked questions, followed the thread, or thought to ask the big boys. So, now it looks like our UNSUB was playing a long game from the start, only he had no one to play with until the bodies began to drop."

Sidd concurred, "Yes, no doubt they're from the same hand and contain all the equations from each crime scene."

Saks added, "Suffice it to say, we can probably rule out our mad gymnast Nevenmoore, about whom I'll admit I had strong suspicions. Regarding the criminal mind, I'm afraid we're all perpetual students of its malevolent cleverness."

At the mention of Raevyn, all eyes shifted to Kitts, who responded self-consciously. "Yeah, I-I'd just left her when I got Sidd's text. She was . . . acutely manic and pretty psychotic. She lost it when I asked about her brother." She blushed when her eyes met Sol's.

Noticing their exchange of glances, Sidd announced, "Dr. Mendelson will be joining us on this one. Even though Ms. Nevenmoore is no longer our prime suspect, she will remain a person of interest. Sol's expertise in bipolar illness and ritual killings will be a valuable resource."

"Thank you, Sidd. Glad to be included, but before we move on from Raevyn, I would like to make sure she is being seen and medicated appropriately—a mood stabilizer and antipsychotic for starters. She sounds in great pain and should be treated immediately."

"Certainly, Sol. Pat, please contact the medical officer assigned to the DC jail and pass on Dr. Mendelson's recommendation. Now, regarding these equations, I'm afraid we encountered unfortunate delays with our academic contractors in the math and physics departments at Cal Poly and MIT. Pat, can you say more please?"

"Unfortunately, our in-house analysts have not provided much. The four equations would seem to refer to the four killings, one for each victim. Beyond that, they've not made much of the number and letter patterns, some of which are repeated. Our people have been unable to decipher the intended meaning of these abstruse communications. Some suggested that the message is more in the form and not so much the content of the equations."

De Vere picked at her nails. "In other words, we know nothing except our UNSUB is taunting us, delighting in the fact that they think they're smarter and know something we do not."

Toby spoke for the first time. "Bastard. He's toying with us."

Saks chided reflexively, "I beg your pardon, Tobias. Did you have something intelligent to contribute?"

"Sorry. Just pisses me off."

Sidd held up his hand before Saks could speak. "Yes, we're all frustrated. I'm not sure it is simply a matter of form over substance. Certainly, our UNSUB is trying to exhibit a superior intellect. Still, I'm not convinced the equations are gibberish, or merely hollow vessels for expressing his narcissistic contempt." He paused before continuing, "I authorized Pat to contact Mr. Luedke, the gentleman Agent Kitts mentioned last week. If for no other reason, it is important for us to expand our network of technical consultants. So, let us see what Mr. Luedke can offer."

Lenore spoke up, "I agree. There must be something the UNSUB is trying to tell us,—besides showing off that he's the smartest person in the room. When can we expect to meet this Mr. Luedke?"

Pat looked to Sidd. "Well, he's here now, waiting in Sidd's office. He was picked up at Dulles earlier this afternoon. I'll have someone bring him in."

Nicola was stunned. *Carmine, here, now?* Her heart quickened at the anticipation of seeing him. It had been five years. Though she would always feel indebted to his generosity, he remained an enigma.

When Carmine walked through the door, the room grew quiet. And there he was. All eyes fastened on the slightly built figure in a bright-colored aloha shirt—at least two sizes too big—with an unkempt reddish mane tied in a short ponytail. Nicola was struck by the changes in his appearance, which contrasted with all the ways he'd remained the same. He was thinner and more hunched over than she'd remembered. She recognized the tattoos on his left arm—an eagle feather on one side and that strange mathematical formula, $e^{i\pi} + 1 = 0$, the formula he used as a mantra of sorts, on the other—and she noticed a new tattoo running the length of his right forearm. It looked like a hawk in flight. Carmine wore the same drab-colored trousers, still baggy but pleated, with sharp crease lines standing at attention. Shiny shoes peeked out from beneath the cuffs of his pant legs. He no longer wore black horn-rimmed glasses. His frames now had a pinkish gloss but were still taped together at the bridge. The new version of Carmine was not so new after all. A few variables among a set of constants.

Carmine glanced around the room, his eyes settling on Kitts. After an awkward smile, he looked back to Sidd.

"Welcome, Mr. Luedke. I know you've had a long journey and must be tired. I'd like you to meet our team. I believe you know Agent Kitts."

Carmine nodded as Sidd introduced the others, but his eyes averted constantly to the equations on the screen.

After all members were introduced, Sidd continued. "Mr. Luedke, I believe they call you the bookkeeper. Agent Kitts has told us that you might be of help with evidence left at several recent crime scenes."

"I-I was . . . the bookkeeper once. Not now. Oh, and not Mr. Luedke. I'm C-C-Carmine. That's it." He continued to stare at the screen as his mechanical words hung in the air.

Saks spoke. "Yes, we all have proper names, do we not? Greetings, Carmine Luedke. I extend my welcome. You seem transfixed by the numbers on the screen. Is there something you can share with us? You see, our people seem convinced that the UNSUB, the killer that is, has left these strange statistical equations at the scene of each of his crimes to taunt and confound us with his insatiable appetite for killing and to keep us guessing and dazzled by his brilliance. Unfortunately, our overpriced consultants have offered us nothing more than this."

"They're Gaussian D-Distributions. Discovered by Carl Friedrich Gauss in 1809. They describe how data c-clusters around a core value. These are used in p-probability theory and modeling statistics. That's all."

Nicola recalled how Carmine's speech grew more halting and broken around unfamiliar people and how he had a way of ending sentences with a verbal tic."

"They're found in linear algebra, m-machine learning, signal p-processing, and physics. That's it. No, that's not right. Engineers use them t-too. Oh, and key features include symmetry, mean, mode, and m-medians...."

The room was silent as Carmine filled the void with more disconnected factoids. "All distributions like these are called normal because they're p-perfectly symmetrical and conform to the 68-95-99.7 rule. That's all. Oh, and the G-Gaussian distribution has a probability density function (pdf) of the normal distribution given by the formula: $f(x) = 1 \sigma 2 \pi e - 1 2 (x - \mu \sigma) 2$."

Kitts feared that Carmine, her so-called mathematical genius, was unable to read the room and was coming across as weird and remote. She spoke to throw him a line and try to reign him in. "Hey, Carmine, nice to see you. We'll catch up later, but we're most interested in your helping us make sense of all this for now."

Sidd interrupted, "Mr. Luedke, Carmine, has been briefed about these mathematical notes left at each crime scene." Pointing to the screen, "He also knows about this first set of four equations received at IT Services Division in January."

Carmine walked toward the screen. His voice was quiet and halting. "These tell a story about a progression of events over time. Four events. F-four killings. A distribution of k-killings. There are variables and constants. See these?" Pointing to the lowercase letters, "They are the constants that appear in each equation. See, *b-b*, and *c*, here, here, here, and here. The variables are the numbers and the capital letters that change in each. D-don't know what they represent, but there is a thing we know. He told you what he was g-going to do."

Tossing his decorated cup aside, Saks said, "Just dandy. How charitable that our maniac would be so considerate and our IT department so inept—present company excepted, Patricia. Our killer is entertained by our buffoonery and amateurish negligence. How the criminally deranged love to play with us as cat toys."

Carmine's pronouncement and Sak's acerbic words landed heavily. After a beat, Sidd said, "We don't know whether there will be more ritual killings, but we're all agreed that finding and stopping this UNSUB remains our top priority. I agree that there is more to the equations, or distributions, than posturing and intimidation. Mr. Luedke, er Carmine, has agreed to remain involved to help decipher the messages in these equations. Given the sensitivity and urgency of the matter, I think it best to have Carmine remain in the area. Pat has arranged lodging at one of our secure facilities." Turning to Pat, he continued, "Oh, and please make sure Mr. Luedke has a secure link to the formulas and access to whatever technical support he may need while working to determine if they contain coded information."

Nicola spoke as the others gathered their notebooks and prepared to leave. "Sidd, would it be okay if I drive Carmine to the facility? It's been quite some time since we've seen each other, and I'd welcome a chance to catch up."

Sidd studied her and said, "I can find nothing wrong with this, Agent Kitts. But I must stress that the mission preempts the social. We must remain on alert and focused. Pat, please text the agent the address and directions to the facility."

21

RUFFLED FEATHERS

After the others exited, Kitts turned to Carmine. "Man, Books, that's quite the fashion upgrade, dude. Look at you, got your nice little Hawaiian shirt. Very cool. I like your new glasses, man, and you let your hair grow out. Wow, nice to see you, Books."

He smiled when she called him Books. "Nice to see you too. It's been a long time. G-guess I could say, 'Look at you t-too. You got your nice little agent suit."

Kitts was surprised by his playful banter. His appearance was not the only thing that seemed different. "Yeah, well, let's get you settled in. Thanks so much, Books, for agreeing to do this for us. Been knee-deep in this shit case, and man, it's been wild." She stood and beckoned him to the door. "Let's find my car, and we'll head on over to your digs. Believe I just got the directions. But do you mind if we make a pit stop on the way? Gotta give Langston his medicine. You remember my bird Langston, right?"

Carmine nodded, followed her to the car, and put his small bag in the back seat. They sat in silence for a few moments. Nicola remembered their first trip together 10 years before when she drove him to the state hospital in Pueblo, Colorado. Thinking he was asleep in the back of her cruiser, she'd spilled her life story to reduce the tedium of the drive. But Carmine heard every word. More than her words, he had studied her face. Like a coded message for all to see if they could decipher the language, he read the story etched in the lines of her face. What would he see today? Would he notice her tense smile, the distractible look in her eyes?

The last time she saw Carmine was after he had started painting. She'd flown back from Smith to attend his art exhibition. Then, the tight lines around her eyes had softened, and a storm inside quieted. She'd felt something approaching contentment. Now, would he see the gathering storm clouds in her eyes? She tried to say the right things—a friendly greeting, chatter about her mission, how glad she was to see him—but she knew he was watching. At the stoplights, she felt his gaze while she was texting.

Nicola tried to make small talk. "This your first time to DC, Books? Man, it sure ain't Aurora, Colorado. I actually miss that place. Don't miss all the nonsense and shenanigans of the sheriff's department, but the air was cleaner there. And those Rockies. Man, I miss all that. Hey, do ya ever hear from your crazy sister? Hope you don't mind me saying that Books. Truth is, I really liked Annie, even though—"

"Anne . . . she's okay. She lives in Santa Barbara with her friend K-Katie. She started teaching at a c-community college."

"Cool, glad to hear that." Nicola's voice trailed off as she glanced at her phone again.

Always the man of silence, Carmine nodded but kept glancing at Kitts as she drove and texted. "No, I've never been in Washington DC before, but have read a lot about it. That's all."

After another awkward silence, Nicola put her phone down and said, "You know, Books, I felt bad about leaving Smith what with you being so generous in helping with tuition and all that. Man, I just feel like shit, wondering what you must think about me pulling up stakes and quitting like that."

"W-when I . . . when I gave you the money, it was because I had it, and you needed it. That's it. It didn't come with any c-conditions or attached s-strings. You needed it and had your reasons for leaving."

"Yeah, all that's true, but Books, I don't think I'll ever be able to thank you. I *will* pay you back. I promise you that, but I don't think I can say a proper thanks for what you did."

Carmine nodded. "I-it's okay. I'm sure you left . . . that you left for good reasons. That's it. No worries."

Her apartment in Adams Morgan was small. Carmine noted the pile of unfolded laundry on her couch. He could see into the kitchen, where dishes were piled high by the sink. Kitts disappeared and came back with Langston on her arm.

"I keep him in the back room. Too much noise and shit out front with all the traffic and stuff. Hey, boy, you remember Books, don't you? Good ol' Carmie?"

The enormous blue macaw tilted his head and lifted a foot toward Carmine's direction. "Braak."

Carmine was struck by the bare patches on Langston's breast and thighs. Kitts grabbed a bottle from the dining room table and began to spray a mist onto Langston's naked chest.

"W-what happened? Did he do that to himself?"

"Yeah, Books. Some birds just do that. Vet says it's stress. Maybe the move, my schedule, or hell, maybe he gets bored. Truth is, probably means nothin.' Really. He's fine."

"I g-guess birds are like some p-people. They show us what they can't tell us."

"Yeah, he's a righteous little dude—an old soul, like my dear auntie used to say. Not a problem with this one. Truth is, he's okay."

Carmine nodded as he looked at her.

But Nicola knew the difference between telling and showing. Carmine would hear the truth in her voice and read the code around her eyes. She suddenly felt exposed. What was she showing him?

22

NOT DEAD YET

Yeardley was waiting in her car when they wheeled her sister to the curb. The nurse's aide helped her crawl into the back seat as Raevyn muttered, "Fuck you very much" under her breath.

Yeardley said, "Buckle up, honey. You know I won't move an inch until your seat belt is on."

Holding her tongue, Raevyn begrudgingly complied, "Yes honey. Fully belted and ready to inch away."

The last month had been a blur. After leaving the jail, she was transported by ambulance to Georgetown Medical Center for admission to inpatient psychiatry. They stabilized her acute mania with 1200 mg of lithium and added 800 Seroquel to treat what were determined to be auditory hallucinations after she admitted hearing the voice of her dead brother Finch. She left the hospital three weeks later. Even though she was no longer a suspect, the police told her she still remained a person of interest.

The discharge plan was to live with Yeardley while receiving follow-up treatment at Georgetown pending a referral to a new therapist. Raevyn had protested loudly, but medication and psychotherapy were the conditions for discharge.

At breakfast the next day, Yeardley announced, "I've set up your appointment with the therapist they recommended. Her name is Idina Madrigal. That's a pretty name, don't you think? I asked Dorine, and she had terrific things to say about her. But she was surprised when I first mentioned her name. Apparently, Mrs. Madrigal had taken a leave of absence from her practice but is seeing patients again. I booked your appointment for today at 3:00."

Raevyn gagged on her toast. She shifted her position, leaned forward, and started to speak, but quickly retreated to her silent cocoon. Discussing this bullshit was useless. As a worthless loon whom others feared and pitied, she had no say in the matter. The last thing she wanted to do was step foot in another shrink's office. She'd tried playing the PTSD card at Georgetown when the doctor in charge mandated psychotherapy. *How could she be expected to set foot in another shrink's office after her beloved former psychiatrist was butchered?* She implored her doctor but concluded that loud protests and feigned tears had no impact on someone with the compassion of a housefly.

Raevyn finally spoke. "Today!? Geez Yeardley, I know you think this will help, but what I really need is time to clear the batshit from my brain and get used to the chemical restraints they've got me on. So, how about—"

"I know, honey. We'll try to go slow, but seeing Mrs. Madrigal *is* a condition for your release. The hospital was very clear about this. If you don't follow their recommendations, they'll send you to another treatment program. So, you need to see her today."

Raevyn stomped back upstairs. She'd forgotten to thank her sister for cleaning her room. The piles of clothes on the floor were put away. Her computer, which had been impounded by the police, sat neatly on her desk. She felt caught in a time warp, looking at her posters of gymnasts and boy bands and the stuffed animals on her bed, each like a museum exhibit cataloging epochs of her life. Entombed in the past, she felt unable to let go and move on. If the death of her parents and her brother's dark turn had crippled her, St. Louis had delivered the final blow. She thought about Finch, who'd fooled everyone with his suicide note, but she knew better. *Clever, shrewd Birdie.* Raevyn lay on her bed, turned toward the wall, and began to whisper.

, ,

The sisters sat in silence on the drive to the therapist's office. They climbed the stairs to the waiting room in its unadorned simplicity and thumbed through the two magazines on the end table.

The door from the office opened and a young woman emerged, quickly exiting, trying not to establish eye contact with her therapist's next patient. A moment later, Madrigal emerged, introduced herself, and invited Raevyn into her office.

Raevyn took the seat to the therapist's left. The office was small but warm, welcoming, and uncluttered by trappings of prestige and self-importance. It was the opposite of how she remembered Prokop's inner sanctum, which screamed of smugness and pomposity. She stared at the frail-looking woman beside her. Gaunt and pale, Idina Madrigal wore a brightly colored headscarf. Once youthful and pretty, her face was deeply lined, not so much by age but by the medical ordeal she had undoubtedly endured. Her appearance announced to all that she was being treated for cancer.

"So, Raevyn, is it okay to call you Raevyn? I'm Mrs. Madrigal. You may call me that or Idina if you wish. I see you're staring at my appearance. I—"

Raevyn cut her off. "Uh, *yeah*. I don't mean to be rude, but don't they have ethics about this sort of thing? I mean are you even allowed to see patients in your . . . condition?"

Idina Madrigal paused and smiled before responding. "You know, I can't help thinking of John Cleese's line from *Monty Python and the Holy Grail* when they're collecting all the bodies of those killed by the black plague. You know the movie? When they pile this one old guy onto the cart with all the dead people, and we hear this small voice, 'I'm not dead yet.'"

Raevyn was taken aback by the woman's dark and clever riposte.

"But—"

The therapist continued. "I have Stage 3 Hodgkins Disease. They've recently determined I'm in remission and cleared me to resume my practice. So, here we are. Will this," signaling to her scarf, "be a problem?"

"*Nooo*. Well, not for me, but I think it could be for you. Hey, I just got it. Your name is Madrigal, right? Wasn't that the name of the kid in the Disney movie *Encanto*—and between us, I *do* think we should talk about Bruno. So, in case you didn't get the memo, you're dealing with Raevyn, slayer of the high priests of Shrinkingdom. Maybe I didn't kill the last one I saw, but the correlation is 1.0. I show up and wambo, death follows. I'm just saying, Encanto, if you end up seeing me, I wouldn't recommend buying ripe bananas."

"Ha, thank you, Raevyn. It sounds like you're quite dangerous. I'll keep that in mind and take my chances. As for your advice about ripe bananas, I buy my produce at the farmer's market, where the fruit is always fresh and sweet. Dr. Mendelson told me about you. If you're comfortable seeing me, I'm interested in hearing your story to see if we can do some work together."

23

DANGEROUS LIAISONS

"Me too." Nicola's heart quickened as she put down her phone. She couldn't believe how quickly she'd fallen. Over the last two weeks, her days had been punctuated by sweet and affectionate calls, voicemails, and texts. Her once lonely evenings were now filled with drinks, dinners out, and late-night trysts. She wasn't sure when, or even how, it began. She had been attracted to Sol from the moment he appeared at the podium for his first lecture at the academy. She didn't think he recognized her. After his first meeting with Unit 4, she approached him and said, "Dr. Mendelson, you probably don't remember me. I attended your lecture on serial killers, and I just—"

"Oh, of course, I remember you. How could I possibly forget? You raised your hand to ask a question, Agent Kitts—"

"Nicola, Nicola is fine."

"Okay then, Nicola. You raised your hand, stood up, cleared your throat, and drew a blank."

She was embarrassed that what he remembered most was her bubble-headed lapse.

"That kind of thing happens to us all. Actually, I spotted you that. In fact, I was quite pleased to see you'd joined the BAU, and that we'd have the chance to work together. Can I call you Niki?" He didn't wait for an answer but said something about how she would bring freshness to Unit 4, "which can be a bit stuffy."

Marine gunnery sergeants and FBI agents don't swoon, but Niki did. In the moment their eyes met, she began to feel light-headed and warm. Groping for a vestige of professional cool, she said, "Yes, uh, this case, especially this woman, Raevyn . . . well, I haven't been able to get you, I mean *her*, out of my mind."

Sol smiled, winked at her slip, and asked if she would like to get lunch.

And so, it began—sitting next to each other in team meetings, trying to elude De Vere's sidewise glances and Gideon Saks's prying eyes, which he attempted to hide behind his cup doodling. Mostly, she hoped to evade Sidd's hawk-eyed vigilance and judgment. At least she imagined he'd disapprove. They inhaled the perfume of each other's presence. When they strolled down the hallway to get coffee, their fingers casually brushed against each other. Then, the texting began. Sol suggested dinner so they could discuss the case and the dynamics of Raevyn Nevenmoore's psychopathology. He chose a table at the Michelin-starred *Causa* for a Peruvian dinner and drinks; she chose to ignore the warning lights.

During dinner, Sol asked about her flip-flopping career path. "Weren't you in graduate school in social work or something? And now—"

"Yeah, and now a gig with the F-bleeping-BI. Wrap your head around that one. Story for another day."

Nicola wanted to hear Sol's take on Raevyn Nevenmoore. "Can we talk about her? She seems so damaged. Can someone like that ever be helped?"

"Honestly, I don't know. She has endured so much shit in her life, all while appearing to be Little Miss Perfect to the outside world. That's why I suggested she see Idina Madrigal, who's a whiz in working with complex trauma. I'm not sure what will happen with Raevyn, but Idina has as good a chance as anyone of reaching her. In the end, it really depends on the patient."

"Meaning?"

"Can she face all that she's gone through?"

With that, Nicola dropped further mention of the case. She wanted to be in the moment and focus only on those magnetic blue eyes and that mane of white hair. She found the man with those eyes to be kind, funny, deeply intelligent, and sexy. He had everything—a vast fund of knowledge, wit, charm . . . and a wife. Though she tried to resist, she felt herself succumbing to his spell. This was just how it started with her professor at Smith. Nicola vowed she would *never* again lower her guard and let herself be so vulnerable . . . and stupid. But Sol Mendelson was not Omar Pei. He didn't have Omar's coolness and arrogance. She felt a warmth with Sol that she'd never known with Pei.

Sol's demeanor grew serious while they picked at their desserts and sipped cognac. "You said you had been involved with your professor."

Kitts nodded.

"Well, I was your professor once, so to speak. Any misgivings about spending the evening with me? I don't mean to be a putz, but—"

She shook her head sharply and a bit too quickly. "No, you're far from a putz. I can maintain boundaries." But her assertion came too easily and silenced the little voice inside saying, "Stop."

When they finished dinner, Sol suggested an after-dinner drink at the *Eighteenth Street Lounge*. The wine and cognac made their conversation light and woozy as they side-stepped anything too serious or personal. Seated in the crowded bar with loud music, Sol reached for Nicola's hand and steered her toward the dance floor.

"I'm not a dancer, but—"

He either didn't hear or didn't heed her response. When the music slowed, Sol pulled her close. "God, you're so hot, Niki."

With the heat rising and her head spinning, she whispered, "But you're married."

Sol tried to explain in as few words as possible that "Things are complicated. We have an understanding, and in addition to a house and three children, we share a great distance in our relationship. *This*," pointing to himself and to her, "feels right. I'd like more."

They took an Uber to the Willard Hotel. Like passionate scenes from Hollywood movies, their bodies collided in a hot-blooded embrace. They groped one another and slow danced awkwardly toward the bed. His hands searched impatiently and pulled at her clothes. She felt his hips grinding against hers. Nicola tried to silence internal alarm bells and focus instead on his hands cupping her breasts. Sol fumbled with her buttons. Unrestrained, Nicola reached up and ripped open her blouse as they fell on the bed. They both giggled after Sol stood to pull his pants over his shoes, only to trip and fall to the floor.

"God, I'm such a putz!"

"Nooo...not a putz at all," Nicola cooed. "Come here."

Their laughter was silenced when he finished undressing her. Through it all, she tried to cancel the noise of her internal doubt, which told her to steer clear of dangerous liaisons with older married men. But none of that mattered. She was tired of being alone with only a blue bird as her companion. For the next several hours, the heat and grinding of their bodies filled her with rapture. With all her doubters silenced, she gave herself completely and took what he could offer.

The following morning, they lay in bed holding each other. Nicola rested her head on Sol's chest as he traced the eagle, globe, and anchor tattoo on her shoulder.

"You were hardcore," he said.

Nicola smiled faintly. "Seems like a lifetime ago. A lot of folks didn't make it home." Her thoughts turned to Langston—lonely and wondering where she was. *Don't mean nuthin,'* she told herself, *but this does.*

Surprisingly, she had neither a hangover nor regret. Something about last night felt right. But they would have to be discreet. For all she knew, this was nothing more than a thrilling one-night stand, which would be fine. But it was immediately clear that neither she nor Sol wanted to stop. They texted in the morning and continued through the day. They met up late at night. Nicola had always tried to keep her life in compartments. This would be no different: stay focused on the mission, keep Sol in one compartment, Raevyn and the BAU in another. This is how she survived, her life stuffed into little boxes, all clearly labeled, sealed, and stacked. But her compartments were beginning to leak. When she was away from him, she began to feel adrift.

Just a few nights later, Sol chose another restaurant in the District he promised her she'd like. As they drank cocktails and discussed his impressions of Raevyn and her embarrassing interview in the jail, he pulled out his phone and groped to take their selfie.

A small man suddenly appeared at the side of their table. Neither of them had seen him approaching. He wore a maroon fedora and a rumpled raincoat. The man had thick spectacles that magnified his dark eyes. "Excuse me, but perhaps I can be of help."

Surprised by this man's sudden appearance, they smiled and nodded, as Sol handed him his phone. The stranger took several photos, then handed the phone back.

"Thank you," both said, one after the other.

"Of course, but I must thank you. Even to a stranger, you are quite noticeable from across the room. You see, anonymity provides an open window for the observant. I can see you care a great deal for one another. But you shouldn't take that for granted. Life is so fragile, and time is always too short. Take heed." The man stared momentarily, tipped his hat, and disappeared into the crowd.

Most would have dismissed this as a harmless encounter with an odd-looking stranger who offered a gesture of kindness and a cryptic message. The city was full of eccentrics. But Kitts had walked point in the Helmond Province where too quickly dismissing seemingly harmless encounters could get you killed.

24

KILLING DISTRIBUTIONS

Sidd Ramachandran entered with Carmine a step behind. The appearance of either would have silenced the room. Together, the effect was deafening. Sidd's dark attire created shadows, while Carmine's garish colors made him an unwitting focal point. Kitts thought that for a man who had always wanted to disappear in a crowd, Carmine's vibrant ensemble had the opposite effect. His baggy gray pants were offset by an orange and blue cabana shirt, brilliantly shined shoes, and neon-colored green socks.

Kitts smiled at Carmine as he entered. He returned the smile and awkwardly waved a hand before shrinking into his seat like a child summoned to a parent-teacher conference. As much as she was drawn to his enigmatic nature, Nicola had been distracted over the last two weeks by the whirlwind in her personal life. The *first* thing she noticed was Sol's absence from the meeting.

"Dr. Mendelson will not be joining us today due to a prior teaching commitment," said Sidd as he called the meeting to order.

Kitts found this curious because Sol hadn't said anything about this the night before. In fact, when she said, "See you tomorrow after they kissed goodbye," he told her he'd be counting the minutes. She tried to ignore this deviation from the script and dial down her innate suspiciousness, but she worried he was having second thoughts about their affair.

Sidd continued, "Carmine wants to brief us about these Gaussian formulas. I think you'll find what he has to say illuminating."

Carmine walked to the screen, carrying an overstuffed notebook and laser pointer. He presented the slide with the distribution of all equations.

$$\frac{1}{6162-t\sqrt{2\pi^e}} -\tfrac{1}{2}(bc-B09U)^2X[3] + \frac{1}{284-t\sqrt{2\pi^e}} -\tfrac{1}{2}(cb-L04H)^2X[2] + \frac{1}{5205-t\sqrt{2\pi^e}} -\tfrac{1}{2}(bc-O07S)^2X[1]$$

$$+ \frac{1}{437-t\sqrt{2\pi^e}} -\tfrac{1}{2}(bc-E05T)^2X[0]$$

"Uh...okay. I see these equations as a m-map that shows how the k-killings were distributed over time and space. The first set told us what this murderer intended to do—who he planned to k-kill, when, and where. That's all."

"Oh I, for one, hope there is *much* more." Someone laughed. "Please enlighten us, Mr. Luedke," said Saks.

Carmine appeared confused by Saks's sarcasm. "Okay. I was g-given files on each of the dead victims with their names, when they got killed, and where it happened. That's it." He pointed to the first equation.

$$\frac{1}{6162-t\sqrt{2\pi^e}} -\tfrac{1}{2}(bc-B09U)^2X[3]$$

"Look. This first man was named Mr. Arthur T-Tamerlane, and his initials were *A* and *T*. B-but we see the cipher involves advancing each initial in his name one space because he was the first to be k-k-killed. So, you see *AT* becomes the letters *B* and *U*. One space in the alphabet for the number in the killing distribution. This is the cipher for Arthur Tamerlane."

Saks spoke up. "So, you're telling us that *LH* is our *numero dos* victim, AKA Julius Fortunato? His initials *JF* plus two gets us to *LH*? Really...such a juvenile riddle...but the simplicity is quite ingenious."

"Y-yes. You advance the initials of each dead person by the order that they were killed—1, 2, 3, and 4. So, *BU* for Mr. Tamerlane who was number one. *LH* is for J. Fortunato, number t-two. Then, there is *OS* for the third victim or *LP* for Linus P-Prokop. When you advance the letters by three you get *OS*. And the last—"

De Vere interrupted, "Our victim number four was *ET* for Auguste Pough, *AP* plus 4 . . . Gid is correct. The genius of this lies in its utter simplicity. Hidden in plain sight. But have you determined the significance of the lower-case *b's* and *c's*?"

"T-that's right!" exclaimed Carmine, answering a little too loudly. "You notice there are s-some things in each equation that don't change." He pointed to letters that were repeated in each equation across the distribution. "These are c-constants that appear in each iteration. You see how the variables *b* and *c* co-occur in the numerator of each one. Sometimes they appear as *bc* and other times as *cb*, but the letters remain constant. Changing ordinal p-positions may have meaning, but the values *b* and *c* are constant. C-could these initials be someone, besides the guys that got cut up, who was present at each murder? Reversing the order may mean something, or it c-could be a way to confuse."

"Or there could be two killers, a *bc* and a *cb*, maybe?" said Kitts.

Sidd responded, "Interesting, but we have no indication that there is more than one UNSUB. Let's not get ahead of ourselves, Agent Kitts. The letters *bc* or *cb*, like their capitalized counterparts, may well be initials. This is what you're suggesting, Carmine?"

The bookkeeper hesitated before responding. "I-I can't say, but their appearance in each set means something remained c-constant in each murder. So, maybe it was the k-killer. Maybe not. That's all."

"Oh, I think there is *much* more, Mr. Luedke. *Much* more to discern," chimed in Saks, who mistook Carmine's verbal tick *That's all* for a more substantive communication that there was nothing more to be said.

"N-no. There is more, Mr. Saks. W-what we see down here—" Carmine pointed to the series of numbers in the denominators. "I believe these first numbers represent the day of the week. See, they r-range from 1 to 7. Next are one or two digits r-representing dates in the month, 1 to 30. They are followed by the numbers 1 to 12 for the month he planned to k-kill these people." Directing his laser pointer to the final two numbers in the numerators, Carmine said, "These numbers . . . I'm not sure, b-but they may be the last two digits in a Zip Code. They c-correspond to the locations each person died. That's all."

Before Saks could interrupt, Carmine continued. "So, *BU*, for Arthur Tamerlane, who was killed on a F-Friday. The *6* stands for Friday, the sixth d-day of the week. That was the 16th of February, see *16*, here. Then, there is a *2*, for the month of F-February, the second month. Putting this together, it'd be *6162*. And the *09* could be the last t-two numerals of the Zip Code in Ann Arbor, Michigan where Mr. Tamerlane d-died."

Lenore spoke for the first time. "If I'm tracking this right, Tamerlane was killed on Friday, February 16 in Ann Arbor with a Zip of 48109, so *6162* down here and those digits *09* up there would fit. And Fortunato was found dead on Monday, April 8 at U Penn with a Zip of 19104. That would give us . . . *284* for time and the *04* for location, right?"

Sidd said, "I think you will find the same numbers corresponding to the names, dates, and locations of all four victims, whose initials have been altered."

De Vere added, "Mr. Carmine has provided more in a few short days than our consultants have in weeks. Sadly, had we received this in January, we may have prevented these needless killings."

Unusually quiet, Toby finally spoke up. "What about those numbers in the brackets at the end? Are they supposed to mean something?"

"Yes, all of this was his k-killing set from the start that got sent to the FBI building in January. He planned to murder four people. This was his announcement. One equation for each d-dead person. He t-told you who, when, and where. These n-numbers in the brackets show how many more guys were left to k-kill." Pointing to the numbers in the brackets, he added, "See, *3* more, then *2*, *1*, and. . . *0*."

Kitt's asked, "Zero . . . meaning?"

"His task is c-complete. He was saying he was d-done. That's all."

Ever the one to rain on a parade, Saks looked up and clapped slowly, "Well done, Sir. Well done. But that's *not all*, indeed, is it? Unfortunately, you've deciphered our maniac's plan *ex post facto*. As an academic exercise, this is all quite interesting; however, I detect an obvious flaw in your final conclusions. What your equations *don't* account for is the devilry in our criminal's mind and intent; in particular, this killer's thirst for some deluded form of retribution against the mental health profession. Can we assume, for the moment, that the UNSUB was simply perfecting his method with this initial trial set of four? Why stop there, when, in fact, this may only be the beginning? That our evil friend is done with his killing distribution, as you put it, is naïve and offers false reassurance that the boogeyman no longer poses a threat when, *in fact*, the wolf has *not* disappeared. He may alter his method to drive us mad, but he has not disappeared. Our perverse and twisted killer has tasted blood from brutally eviscerating four psychiatrists—a minuscule fraction of the broader psychiatric community, writ large. So, let us not be so quick to stand down. Mark my words, children, he *will* go rogue, and he *will* kill again."

25

Voices In the Wall

It was the kind of undisguised dream that quickly became a nightmare—he was on a family camping trip with a young woman, and his kids suddenly went missing. The dream father searched frantically, suffocating in guilt for having diverted his eyes away from them. The piercing ring of his phone jolted him from the netherworld of his perspiration-soaked night terror. Sol answered in a low voice trying not to disturb his softly snoring lover.

"Sol, sorry, It's Idina Madrigal. I hope this isn't too early to be calling."

Sol saw that it was 7:30. He rubbed his face and walked quietly from the bedroom. "Idina, no, I was just going to make some coffee. I worked late last night, but I'm up now. What's up? How are you?"

"Doing better every day, thanks for asking. Chemo's done and recent labs and scans look good. I'm still on a reduced caseload but am gaining strength and stamina. It feels good to be working again."

"I'm so glad to hear that. The world with all its messes is a little neater with you in it. I know the young woman we sent you last month is a good case in point. I told the FBI team that if there was anyone who could reach her it was you."

"That's very dear of you, Sol. Actually, she's the reason I'm calling. Some things have surfaced that I . . . well, I think might have some bearing on the investigation into those murders. I know it's a longshot and probably the product of an idle brain starved for intrigue and puzzles, but something doesn't feel right about this woman. I wasn't sure who else to call and was hoping we could meet for coffee so I could run all this by you."

"Um, sure. Sure. I can contact Special Agent Nicola Kitts. She's been at the forefront of this investigation. In fact, she's the one who interviewed Raevyn just before she was sent to Georgetown after the fourth killing."

"I'm sure that's okay. I told Raevyn I would need to talk with the FBI. Needless to say, she wasn't too happy and accused me of whispering to others. But this is something we can work on in our sessions. I told her I wouldn't talk to anyone without letting her know first, but I felt there were some issues that could possibly put people at risk. Anyway, I know I'm being a bit cryptic about this. That's why I wanted to meet to get your take on what's come up."

Nicola was quiet during the car ride to the Starbucks on 15th and Connecticut Ave. Nursing a hangover, her temples throbbed as she tried to tune into what Sol was saying about the therapist's concerns.

Things seemed stalled after Carmine talked to the team about the equations. She worried his explanations were the products of an eccentric mind and had come too late in the investigation to be of much help, especially if he was right about the killings being over. Saks and De Vere would eventually become skeptical and start to question whether it was wise to have brought in someone like Carmine.

Kitts wore her sunglasses into the Starbucks. Sol waved to a woman in the back. "I'll order us coffees and bring them over," she told him. "It looks like she's already drinking hers."

Although Sol had told her about Madrigal, Nicola had never met her. All she knew was that Madrigal was supposed to be some guru shrink with a long waiting list. And there was something about a cancer diagnosis and how she'd recently resumed her practice. Kitts walked over with the coffees and was immediately struck by the therapist's appearance, most notably her waxy, pale complexion and the gaunt look around her eyes, which were offset by a colorful headscarf.

"Idina, this is Agent Nicola Kitts. She's been heavily involved in this investigation and met with Ms. Nevenmoore a couple of months back. Nicola, I've already told you about Idina. She's a gifted therapist, and we're grateful she happily agreed to begin working with Raevyn."

Idina held out her hand. "Thank you for coming. I agreed to Sol's bringing you along because this may or may not have something to do with these killings you're investigating. I must say, I'm not privy to the details but only know that Raevyn was initially thought to be a suspect. In any event, some things have surfaced that have concerned me enough to reach out. I already mentioned to Sol that my clinical suspicions may be the residual result of chemo brain and that none of my concerns may hold water."

Sol sipped his coffee. "What you got, Idina? What's going on with Raevyn that's triggered your radar?"

"Raevyn has been on heavy doses of lithium and lumateperone to treat her manic and psychotic symptoms for about two months. On the one hand, she does seem more grounded—her speech is organized and her mood is more stable. But her hallucinations and delusions are as strong as ever. I would have expected to see some decrease in these symptoms, but I'm not seeing much of that. It is a concern."

Sol leaned in. "Yeah, I agree, but it's not unusual for hallucinations and delusions to linger even with high doses of antipsychotics. Two months is not *that* long, but I hear you when you say something doesn't feel right."

Nicola spoke up. "Is there something more that's making you suspicious?"

"Yes. I know it can take a while for acute psychotic symptoms to resolve, but Raevyn has said some other things that give me pause." Idina lowered her voice. "You see, she's convinced her twin brother Finch is talking to her through the wall between their bedrooms—something they apparently did when they were kids. She also said she heard his voice when she was in jail but admitted that she was, to use her words, 'Off my fucking rocker and hearing things.' In effect, she acknowledged her auditory hallucinations before she was hospitalized. But now she's convinced about daily communication with Finch at night as the two whisper things back and forth through a vent in their wall."

"Interesting, Idina. She acknowledges she *was* hallucinating in jail but *is* actually hearing him speak to her now," said Sol. "Well, hmm . . . I still see this as symptomatic of an elaborate delusional system she's not ready to let go of, despite all the medication she's taking. A delusion may become less distressing with meds, but the conviction about its truth may remain high for quite a while longer."

"You're the expert, and you may be right, Sol. That's what I believed until recently when she told me that Finch is actually living in their house. You've heard of this thing called phrogging, where someone lives undetected in a house? They apparently have an enormous old house in Bethesda, and Raevyn swears that Finch is living there and comes out from his hiding places at night to communicate with her through the wall. Delusional, right? She said she's left food for him, which is gone in the morning."

Kitts shook her head. "Yeah, that phrogging shit gives me goosebumps, but all this is coming from someone who, as she put it, was pretty much off her rocker."

"Agreed. It sounded preposterous at first, but then she began telling me her brother knew things about several crime scenes in other states that I don't think have been released to the public. He even told her about mathematical plans he mapped out for the murders. I don't know if any of this is true. I don't think any of this has been in the news. The worst thing he supposedly told her was that the victim list might grow. This poor woman was not just conflicted about sharing this, but she became terrified that she had said too much."

The hair on the back of Kitts's neck stood on end. "That's some wild-sounding shit. What did she say when you told her you'd talk to Sol?"

"She totally freaked out and swore she'd never come back. I got her settled and asked what she was most afraid of. She told me she's afraid that Finch would find out and might try to hurt her and the people she told."

For the first time, Sol shed his cool, clinical demeanor and looked unnerved. "Did she say Finch would know if she was talking about this?"

"Yeah, Raevyn said he's a genius who always knew what she was thinking. She said he would make her tell him."

Nicola pushed back from the table. "This is crazy because Finch is supposed to be dead, right? Besides, he doesn't have the initials b and c."

Idina and Sol looked confused.

"Initials?" asked Sol.

"Yeah, the math guy we brought in to figure out the formulas at each crime scene said that the letters b and c in each equation, might be initials for the killer—some kind of sick signature. But there was no letter f for Finch or n for Nevenmoore, so that doesn't fit."

Now it was Idina who pushed her chair back. "You said, b and c? That's funny, because Raevyn refers to Finch as Birdie, and she says he called her Cobie—b and c . . . Oh my God!"

26

CLASS VALEDICTORIAN

October 25, 2013

She couldn't recall the moment she first felt afraid of her brother. It might have been their sophomore year at Walt Whitman High School when she saw him jab a knife through the tires of their neighbor's car. Earlier that week, Mr. Graves scolded Finch for cutting across his lawn. Two days later, the Graves family dog went missing.

For years, Raevyn had watched kids ignore, mock, and taunt her twin. They knocked books out of his arms, tripped him, and pulled down his pants. Sometimes he cried, but he mostly accepted the abuse while quietly looking for his sister to rescue him. When he found her eyes, Raevyn would usually look away. She was too frozen by her popularity and shame to claim Finch as her brother, let alone her twin. Later, when they'd talk, she'd try to console him, promising she wouldn't let these things happen again. But the taunts continued, and she did nothing.

During eighth grade, their parents complained about Finch's withdrawal and social isolation and decided to send him to a specialized treatment program. He had been seeing an important psychiatrist who included him in research studies at NIMH. Raevyn knew little about this because her life was governed by self-interest and a desire to please her mother and avoid her wrath.

The complex contradictions in their relationship always confused

Raevyn whose feelings ranged from *schadenfreude*—better him than me—to guilt that it was *always* him. She knew of his deep sadness, even though he rarely shared. But when he returned from the specialized treatment program, something had changed. With the torments of middle school behind him, Finch emerged from the darkness of his cocoon, not as a butterfly, but as a wasp. In their first year of high school, Raevyn became aware of Finch's dangerously cunning mind and hidden stinger. While she spent time socializing, perfecting gymnastics, and flaunting her popularity, he was reading every book he could touch, navigating the portals of the dark web, and perfecting his hacking skills. By habit, she continued to whisper through the wall, sharing her secret fears and insecurities, only to learn later that Finch was listening and quietly taking notes.

To the outside world, Raevyn still wore the halo of star student and all-conference gymnast, but it became increasingly difficult to keep up with her advanced classes. When she received her first C, she begged Finch to help with her homework, papers, lab reports, and examinations. From her perch high above his low branch, she became aware of a new feeling that further complicated their fraught relationship. Dependency. On a nightly basis, he completed her homework assignments after breezing through his own. Unlike Raevyn, Finch flew under the radar academically. Content with his image as an underachiever, Finch aced his easy classes and spent most of his time reading books and articles on the dark web.

"Birdieeee, I really need your help. Gymnastics ran late and I've got this stupid paper due tomorrow. Pleeease."

"Of course," and then sneeringly, "I'll just add it you your bill, Sister."

Bailing Raevyn out with term papers became the norm. Each time, he'd tell her not to worry, that he'd put it on her tab. Though she felt guilty about using him in this way and uneasy about her growing need for him, Raevyn said nothing when he snuck her black-market copies of her AP exams. In return, she promised to introduce him to her A-lister friends, but by that time, issues of social caste and inclusion no longer concerned him. Whenever she asked him what she could do in return, he always said the same thing: "There will be a price, Cobie. You'll know when I come to collect."

Apart from helping her look more academically gifted than she was, Raevyn turned to Finch to help stabilize her erratic moods. She experienced her first depressive episode in the fall of her senior year. She hid her symptoms under the guise of exhaustion from the demands of her AP classes, gymnastics, student council, and college applications. Her parents were too busy to notice, having already concluded that she was an immensely gifted and talented girl, and attributed any shifts in mood and energy to adolescence, her busy schedule, demanding courseload, and long hours at the gym. But Finch read her like a book and recognized that Raevyn was not her usual bubbly self. He gave her Adderall XR and later cocaine, which he said would drive away her depression. When she later began spiraling upward and staying up all night, he gave her Xanax to bring her down.

The golden crown above her head made it difficult for anyone— parents, older sister, teachers, coaches, or friends—to see Raevyn for who she was. A straight-A student taking five AP classes, she had honed her skills at fooling others and masking her symptoms. The only person who knew her brittleness was Finch, on whom she grew increasingly dependent for maintaining her grades, athletic standing, and general aura of perfection. To those around her, she was a beautiful young woman, a gifted student, and a star athlete. But she knew that Finch saw her as the fake she was, nothing more than a walking Potemkin village.

In the late fall of her senior year, Raevyn received early admission to Tufts. Her mother was thrilled, and even her emotionally vacuous father seemed pleased. Meanwhile, Finch informed them that he would take a year off. At best, they seemed indifferent about his vague plans.

He told them he'd be taking math courses at the community college and traveling. They didn't inquire where.

In the spring, Raevyn received word that she was selected as class valedictorian. She would be honored at graduation and expected to deliver the valedictory address. As graduation drew near, she spent most of her time preparing for the state gymnastics championships. Raevyn procrastinated working on her speech, just like she had with her term papers. At the last minute, she pleaded for Finch's help. Never one to collaborate, he wrote the entire address. When she implored him to tell her what he wanted in return, he told her to bring him their father's passport and some of the rare South African Krugerrands from the safe in his office. When she protested, Finch grinned ominously and said, "Oh, Cobie, I don't think you understand. This isn't a request, it's a payment notice. I've put you on an installment plan. I'll let you know when your next bill comes due."

27

FEATHER PICKING

"Sorry, I don't know why this is continuing and can't explain his lack of improvement." The bearded veterinarian's words did little to quell Nicola's worst fears. "Pterotillimania, or feather-damaging behavior, is seen in a lot of large birds—African greys, cockatoos, and unfortunately big guys like Langston. It looks like the spray we gave you didn't do much."

Seeking reassurance, Nicola implored, "Dr. Vernon, last time you said there were other things we could try to get him to stop doing this to himself."

"Sure, but as I told you before, this is *usually* a behavioral disorder caused by diet changes, stress, loneliness, or boredom. You told me about your recent move and job change."

"Yeah, guilty as charged. Work's been insane, and we've had our share of moves in the last couple of years, but he's never done *anything* like this before. I'm worried it could be something more serious."

Vernon stroked his beard. "There is always a possibility of allergies, ecto- and endoparasites. I think we should probably do more testing to rule out bacterial or fungal infections. There are other possibilities, but let's have you bring Langston in next week. We can keep him for a few days to do a more thorough workup and see if anything shows up. It's doubtful, but I think it's worth doing. Isn't that right, Langston?"

The bird fluffed out his neck feathers and began preening his long tail feathers as Nicola picked him up and placed him in his carrying cage. "Okay, thanks. I'll talk to your receptionist about a time to bring him in." She forced a smile but was distracted by the ping on her phone.

"Sorry, it's been like this, you know. Government work, right?" She glanced down and saw the message from Sidd about another urgent meeting that afternoon."

She hurried home to feed Langston and get him settled, but her life had been anything but settled, with unexpected meetings and late-night rendezvous. She could still smell Sol on her skin. She barely had time to shower and pull on some clean clothes before racing to Quantico.

The team was assembled when she walked in five minutes late. She avoided eye contact with everyone, especially Bernice De Vere, who'd scolded her the last time she was late.

"Nice you could join us, Agent Kitts. So glad you could wedge us into your calendar, dear."

Irked by De Vere's persistent picking, Kitts gave a sideways glance and caught a sparkle in Sol's eye.

Before Sidd continued, Nicola said that at some point, she wanted to brief everyone about their meeting with Raevyn's therapist. "I don't know if Sol mentioned this, but Ms. Madrigal shared some things that may be relevant to our investigat—"

Before she could finish, De Vere cut in. "If you had arrived five minutes earlier, dear, you'd have heard the good doctor inform us of this meeting. However, I seriously doubt that Idina Madrigal's news, shall we say, is as important as the lead we've just become aware of. Punctuality is not just a social courtesy but a necessity when weighing critical bits of information. I'm afraid you're losing sight of the Marine Corps ethos, you know, *First to fight*. Do I make myself clear about being on time?"

Fuck this shit, De Vere. Kitts swallowed her anger and took a breath to smooth her ruffled feathers. She was about to respond when Sidd stood.

"I'm sure Agent Kitts doesn't need more lecturing and will be here on time in the future. We do have a new piece of information. Shall we continue with what Agent Potter was saying? Go ahead Toby."

Nicola watched as Toby straightened his shoulders and shot her a scornful smile. "As I was saying, we've been looking at all the people connected with the Ann Arbor study, specifically for anyone with the initials *bc* or *cb*. Some of the files are restricted, like those involving kids in the program. We've tried to subpoena those records, but there are a lot of hoops to jump through. But we did get the personnel files of research associates involved in the study. And that's when we found the name, Cosmo Burroughs." With a clicker in hand, Toby projected an image of a sour-looking man with thin hair, thick glasses, and dark eyes.

Saks stood and took the clicker from Potter's hand. "Good work, Tobias. I'll take it from here. Dr. Cosmo Burroughs was the lead statistician at the university responsible for collecting and analyzing all the data from the Ann Arbor, Baltimore, Philadelphia, and Georgetown research sites. He had been a respected figure in applied mathematics and statistics. However, it was rumored he had an appetite for young coeds."

Sidd uncharacteristically intervened. "Dr. Burroughs was removed from the project after one of his graduate students discovered an extensive library of child pornography on his computer. Please continue Toby?"

"Yes, Sir. We've partnered with the field office in Green Bay, which sent us all the case files on Burroughs. It seems that after he was found out, his lawyer and the university's legal department were angling for a quiet dismissal from the project on the condition he accepted an early retirement. They all wanted this to go away. So, the head honchos apparently signed off on this, but then they did an about-face and decided to hang Burroughs out to dry. Tamerlane and the other guys ended up signing a letter condemning Burroughs, stating that his behavior hurt the reputation of their universities and screwed with their investigation. So, they dumped him. They recommended he be booted from the study and then fired from the university and charged by the prosecutor's office."

The room was silent, all eyes fixed on the photograph of the man glaring at them from the screen. Sidd nodded for Toby to continue.

"His life kind of collapsed like a house of cards." Toby glanced at Saks to see if his chief tormentor approved of his simile. "The guy pretty much lost the farm—his job, university pension, and ultimately his home and marriage—not to mention the legal charges he was facing. He was convicted of possession of kiddie porn and somehow got a suspended sentence. He had to register as a sex offender. His case even made the national news."

Saks said, "But that's not the end of the story, is it, Tobias? Seems like our man Burroughs crashed a faculty meeting and in front of a room full of witnesses threatened to kill Arthur Tamerlane. He claimed to know where the bodies were buried and said he could bring the vaunted ARES Project to its knees with what he knew. Fortunately for Dr. Tamerlane, the university police subdued him. Unfortunately for the community, a careless police officer left him unattended in his cruiser. Burroughs did a Harry Houdini and hasn't been seen since. And upon his disappearance, he took with him all the information he threatened to expose about ARES. So, we have no idea whether he knew something about the study or was simply blustering and posturing. Most likely the latter. Spurious counteraccusations are a common refuge for the desperate who find themselves boxed in by their own criminal activity."

Kitts spoke up, "So, there's obviously a motive for the killing of Tamerlane and maybe the others too. I mean, he told a room full of people that he wanted to commit murder."

"True," said Sidd. "Whatever else he was threatening to expose remains unknown. But there is more, isn't there?"

"That's right," said Toby. "Burroughs was off the radar for about a year until someone spotted him on the campus of Bay de Noc

Community College in Escanaba, Michigan, on the coast about 100 miles northeast of Green Bay. He had been teaching a stat class there, going by the name of Carl Burnley, keeping the *cb* initials. Then, about four months ago, boom! He went missing again. Just stopped showing up for work. One of his students thought they recognized him from all the news hype after he went missing a year earlier."

Saks stopped his cup doodling. "So, boys and girls, Cosmo Burroughs, AKA Carl Burnley, is a person of keenest interest. Tobias, I assume you are coordinating with the field office and local authorities in Escanaba to find him."

"Yes, Sir."

"Good," responded Sidd. "I'd like for Agent Kitts to accompany you on this, Toby. The two of you can coordinate with the field office in Green Bay to set up a task force in Escanaba to find Burroughs and bring him in for questioning. You ready for this one, Nicola?"

"I am. Yes, absolutely, Sir."

"Toby, coordinate your travel plans with Pat and the local field office. Let's make this happen. Before we end here, Agent Kitts, would you and Dr. Mendelson like to tell us more about your meeting with Ms. Nevenmoore's therapist?"

Kitts began, "Yes, Sir. Mrs. Madrigal wanted to share with Dr. Mendelson some of the concerns she had about her patient Raevyn. He brought me along because there were things that might have bearing on our investigation. Sol can talk about the psych angle better than me."

Sol shifted in his seat. "Right. I've known Idina Madrigal for years. She has a reputation as one of the best therapists for complex cases like this. In fact, most in the field have considered her the go-to person for patients who have multiple psychiatric disorders like Raevyn. Idina is not an alarmist, so I was quite interested to hear about her concerns."

Saks interrupted. "Please dispense with the hagiography, Sol. Not everyone shares your views about Idina Madrigal. Whatever concerns she may have about the Nevenmoore woman are best addressed in the consulting room."

Sidd held up his hand. "Please, continue with what you were saying."

"Well, she's not convinced that Raevyn's claim of hearing her brother Finch's voice is, in fact, an auditory hallucination—"

Saks interrupted again. "Please. I can assure you that—"

Sidd held up his hand, this time more forcefully. "I'm sure Dr. Saks will appreciate the importance of having a complete picture of all elements of our investigation. Isn't that correct, Gideon?"

Saks was about to speak when Sidd turned again to Sol. "Continue, please."

"Idina feels that Raevyn should be responding to her whopping dose of antipsychotic medication by now but is continuing to claim that she is speaking with her brother. Nicola, do you want to add to this?"

"Yes, thanks. She said that Raevyn talks to him through the wall separating their bedrooms, like they did when they were younger. But she also said that he is actually living in the house, unbeknownst to their older sister who works late and travels frequently. I know this sounds crazy but—"

"Indeed," said Saks dismissively. "I would not use the term 'crazy' as you put it, but this sounds like the workings of a deluded mind. The brother went missing, ended his own life, and was declared legally dead. Tell me, Sol, has Ms. Madrigal entertained a diagnosis of dissociative identity disorder for her patient? Antipsychotic medication may be less effective in addressing pseudo perceptions that are part of a dissociative personality."

"I honestly don't know, Gideon. But regardless of what's going on psychopathologically with Ms. Nevenmoore, Idina said that, according to her patient, Finch knew accurate details about the crime scenes—details that have *not* been made public. That raised the hackles on my neck."

Kitts jumped in. "The stuff with this Burroughs guy is at the top of the list. I get that. But I was pretty creeped out at the thought of brother Finch hiding out in the house and knowing all this stuff about the murders."

"Interesting, Nicola," said De Vere. "But we will need much more information about what this disturbed woman has told her therapist. Might I add that feeling creeped out, as you put it, is not grounds for action when we have limited resources. Same with your ruffled neck feathers, Sol. Let us keep to the objective data and hold our subjectivity in check. And dare I say, Finch Nevenmoore has been declared dead."

Sidd agreed. "True, but I think we can walk and chew gum simultaneously. If we need to bring in additional resources, so be it. I'd like Agent Patterson and Dr. Mendelson to follow up on this by arranging an interview with the older sister. Find out more about the brother's death and what he supposedly told his sister about the crime scenes."

Lenore spoke for the first time. "I did touch base with Yeardley Nevenmoore after Raevyn was sent to the hospital. Pat, could you see if you can schedule an interview for tomorrow. Does that work for you too, Dr. Mendelson?"

28

HAGONE

Her bag sat on the couch next to the pile of clothes. She sorted through them while listening to the bluesy voice of Sippie Wallace singing "Bedroom Blues." Sol hadn't returned her last three calls. She worried about what this meant, focusing on worst-case scenarios. Nicola shook off her paranoia and focused on her trip to Escanaba instead. She felt a surge of adrenalin preparing for the mission but was concerned about working with Potter. Since they'd first met, the tension between them was palpable. She wasn't sure how things would go, especially since he was the lead agent responsible for finding and interrogating Cosmo Burroughs.

Langston sat on his perch, surveying the mess in the living room. His small bag of toys was packed for his week with the vet, where he would get a complete diagnostic workup. Nicola tried to bury her worries, but the grave was too shallow. Thoughts about Langston and Sol had breached her perimeter. She continued sorting her clothes, not noticing that Langston was vigorously picking the pinfeathers on his chest again.

Langston suddenly looked up. He heard the soft tapping before she did. "Graaawk?"

"What is it, Langs? I'm gonna miss you standing guard duty, boy." Then she heard the knocking and went to the door.

It was Carmine. He wore a colorful dashiki incongruously paired with a black pork pie hat sporting a long feather from its band. She noticed an airline ticket sticking out of his pocket.

"Books! What a surprise, man. What are *you* doing here? Hey, come on in. I'm packing up for Michigan. We got a person of interest we need to locate and question."

Carmine entered cautiously and noticed Langston, who held his foot up and tilted his head. "Hey. Hi, L-Langston. I came to say goodbye. My work here is done. I finished my r-report and told Dr. Ramachandran, uh, S-Sidd, I wanted to see you one more time. I d-don't leave until tonight, so I thought I'd drop by. That's all."

"Wow, well hell. Sorry we didn't get to visit more, Books. You can't stay around any longer? What you gonna do back in Colorado?"

Carmine shrugged. "Don't know . . . m-maybe learn to play the mandolin. Paint some. Write poems, I guess. Noni wants to t-take care of some animals. That's it."

"Dude, man, I wish you could just see yourself and how much you've changed."

"Yeah, same. I wish you could see that about yourself, too."

"Huh?" Kitts tilted her head and picked a thread on her sweater. "What's that supposed to mean, Books?"

"How much you've changed." Carmine brought up how they met 10 years ago when she was the deputy who drove him to the Colorado State Hospital, where he had been committed for assaulting a woman at work. "You were kind to me. I th-thought I'd lost everything. P-people thought I was crazy and might hurt someone else. I-I wasn't right then. But you saw something others d-didn't."

"How could I forget Books? You sitting in the back seat all quiet like that, and me thinking you were asleep. But there you were, listening to me pour out my shit. Yeah, dude, you were pretty messed up back then."

"I was. But I noticed something about you too. I have this thing in my brain where I can feel things in p-people's faces. I felt things when I saw your eyes in the mirror."

"Yeah, I remember. That was pretty wild, Books. I told you something like how folks at the hospital would help you feel better, and you asked who was gonna help *me*. Something like that. That was some pretty intense shit."

He paused. "I see that again . . . your eyes are like they were that day. S-something's not right. It's not my business, but you're my f-friend, Nicola. That's all."

"Damn, Carmine. What do you want me to say, dude? You can kinda see I'm knee-deep in trying to find this psycho killer. You know, working for the F goddam BI doesn't leave a lot of time for navel-gazing, Books."

Carmine walked over to Langston who held a large nut in his talon. "What about him?"

"What about him?"

Shifting uncomfortably, Carmine said, "He d-doesn't look well either. Do they know what's wrong?"

"Nah. I gotta take him to the vet for more tests while I'm gone so they can figure out why he keeps picking at himself. They call it feather-damaging syndrome or something like that. It's like he can't stop doing this to himself."

"Hmm. Do they know what causes it?"

"Still trying to figure it out. Vet said it could be diet, parasites, or stress with all the moving and whatnot. Maybe loneliness. He's just a bird, so he can't tell me."

Carmine lightly stroked the bird's wing. "G-guess he can't say what he doesn't see."

"Yeah, he just keeps showing me something's not right."

"Yep. I see that too."

"But I ain't got a lot of time to speculate about this right now with all these folks getting carved up by some serial killer. Books, you know I gotta finish packing and get him to the vet before getting my ass to the airport. When you leaving?"

"T-tonight. I'll just sit at the airport and wait."

Nicola's face softened. "Look, Carmine, I really appreciate you coming by. And I *do* plan on paying you back for my tuition money. I just—"

"Why? I never expected you to. I d-don't need the money. You did. I don't. I wanted you to have it. That's it."

"But Books, come on. How can I pay you back? What can I do for you?"

Carmine didn't answer for several seconds. "Maybe just stop, look inside, and see what you're d-doing to yourself. I never believed that stuff my sister said in her book about how people should put bad feelings into c-compartments. I think she n-needed to do that for herself. So, that's it."

The softness around Nicola's eyes hardened once more. She crossed her arms and pinched at her skin. "Yeah, well, maybe someday, but I can't do that now. I just can't. This shit don't mean nuthin.'"

Carmine's eyes shifted to the tattoo on his arm. "Neither d-did $e^{i\pi} + 1 = 0$. That stuff you hold onto, thinking it will k-keep you safe. It doesn't. It just puts you to sleep. That's it. *Hagone.*"

"The fuck. What's that mean?"

"It's Navajo for goodbye. I hope you can f-find yourself." He reached up to his hat and pulled out the feather. "T-take this. It's an eagle feather. It might help you see better." With that, he turned and walked out the door.

With a tear in her eye and a feather in her hand, she watched through the window as he disappeared around the corner, uncertain if she would ever see him again.

29

A Frog in the House

They sat in the living room, waiting for Yeardley to pour the coffee. Lenore took the lead and explained the reasons for their visit.

Sidd had instructed Lenore and Sol to wait before mentioning Raevyn's story about Finch being alive and hiding in the house. Their strategy was to find out more about her siblings and parents first, then ask about Raevyn's bizarre allegation.

"Like I said, Ms. Nevenmoore, we want to understand more about your family. Dr. Mendelson has some specific questions about both Raevyn and Finch's mental health history and especially anything you can tell us about Finch's disappearance and suicide."

"First, please call me Yeardley. Ms. Nevenmoore sounds too formal, like 'Spake the Raven Nevermore.' Honestly, I've had a lifetime of that, as you might imagine. I'd rather keep this low-keyed if we could. So, where would you like me to start? I could write a book about my family, and the picture wouldn't be all that pretty." Her eyes welled up. "We began as five, and now we are two. I'll do anything now to protect Raevyn. She's all I have left. Poor dear has been through so much."

Lenore sipped her coffee and leaned forward. "We're aware of the tragedies in your family, with losing your parents four years ago and Finch's suspected suicide a year later. Can you tell us more about Finch?"

"First, it was not a *suspected* suicide, Agent. Just to be clear, my brother killed himself. He was legally declared dead. That's a fact. Where to start? I'm sure you know that our parents were brutally murdered—shot, both of them. How does one describe what this does to a family? They went to our vacation home in Calvert Cliffs for a weekend and never returned. The police couldn't identify any suspects. Can you *imagine* what this is like? They said this was a home invasion and burglary gone wrong. It infuriates me that they're now classifying this as a cold case. God, I hate that term—cold case. There is *nothing* cold about this." She wiped her eyes with a tissue and blew her nose.

Lenore replied, "I'm *so* sorry for what you've gone through and the fact that we're bringing all this up again, but we think it's important. Can you tell us how long after the murders Finch disappeared?"

"I'm not sure. He was away when they died. He came back for the service and disappeared shortly after that. He was in and out of our lives. We always knew where Raevyn was and what she was up to, but Finch was an ongoing mystery. He was a revolving door, returning and leaving at odd times. He'd just disappear for months, sometimes longer, and then suddenly turn up out of the blue. So, let's see, Raev started medical school in August, and they were killed in October. October 13th—how do you ever forget the worst day of your life? So, it must have been sometime in February or March after our parents were killed when he came back. But I can't be certain. He was around for several months before his . . . you know."

Sol asked, "What was it like for the family, having him just disappear for months at a time?"

Yeardley paused as she teared up again. "Truly, I think Finch was gone long before he decided to jump off that bridge. He was our lost brother. My heart still aches for him. I sensed his quiet brilliance even though Raevyn was always the one with a Midas touch. She was gifted at everything and was also the favorite in the family, at least for our mother. She was the shining star while Finch was pretty much ignored—the family stain, if you will. I was a bit like that too; not an embarrassment, mind you, but more taken for granted—part nanny, chauffeur, and tutor until I made my escape. Would you like more coffee, Agents?"

Sol responded, "No thank you, Yeardley. And, by the way, I'm not an agent. Now, can you tell us more about how your parents treated the twins differently?"

"Let's just say that our mother, truth be told, was a self-absorbed bitch. That's an awful thing for a daughter to say about her own mother, but it's true. She was a well-known thoracic surgeon at a time when you could count on one hand the number of women in that field. She was brilliant and loved reminding everyone that she was the smartest person in the room. Father was a pathologist who worked for the county. Bless his heart. He shared a lot with the patients in the morgue, except that he was still breathing, and they were not. They worked ungodly hours and would tell us they needed to spend all their time at the hospital caring for their patients, living and dead. But honestly, I think they couldn't stand each other, and it was obvious they weren't too keen on being parents."

Lenore inquired, "How do you mean?"

"You know, too much messiness, so they pretty much out-sourced parenting to nannies, au pairs, and *moi*. Since I was eight years older, I became the in-house babysitter. The only time I'd see our parents' eyes light up was when Raevyn walked into the room. At least, this was the case for Mother. Father, well, not much ever brightened his eyes. He was missing in action even when he was home. I always thought it strange that our parents spent their entire professional lives cutting up bodies, slicing through other people's tissue, muscle, and bone while hardly ever touching us. The only difference was mother cut into people who were alive, people she could talk to before and after she'd slice into their chests, while our father did this to people he'd never have to talk to."

"Can you tell us more about Finch's comings and goings?"

"Don't get me wrong; I loved Finch, but I never understood him.

He was a puzzle with missing pieces. My heart aches for all the abuse he suffered when he was a kid. Life was tough for him. But I think he was hard to connect with, too, for everyone except Raevyn."

"What do you mean, except for Raevyn?" asked Sol.

"Well, they were twins, you know. Twins are like that. They had these pet names for each other; Cobie was Raevyn's little nickname, and Birdie was Finch's. I guess that pretty much describes how the whole world saw them. I think our grandmother gave them those names. She was Cobie, which stands for Corvidae, the family of crows and ravens. It was supposed to be 'Corbie,' but Finch couldn't say his "R's." The crows and ravens are bigger, smarter, more aggressive birds. The name Birdie for Finch pretty much speaks for itself. Honestly, I hated those names. It was so unfair. But aside from all of that, they were extremely close. Even though Raevyn had everything going for her and didn't always stick up for Finch, she loved her little brother. See, I'm doing it too—referring to Finch as her *little* brother. That's so sad." She looked wistful and began to cry.

Sol passed her a box of tissues. "Do you need to take a break?"

"No . . . I'm alright. They were such cute little kids. Mother would dress them in these precious little outfits. From a very young age, they'd get into trouble for talking to each other late at night. I think Raevyn was always the instigator. That girl just couldn't sleep. Looking back, I think this is likely when her bipolar problems began—maybe not in a clinical way but, you know, the early signs of the illness for sure. And all that energy! Oh my God, she was a force of nature, always cartwheeling and backflipping throughout the house.

"Tell us more about Finch," urged Lenore.

"He was certainly not social and athletic like his sister. Finch liked reading about math and playing his little computer games in his room. There I go again, using the word *little* to describe him. He kept to himself and unfortunately didn't have friendships with real people."

"Real people?"

"Well, like people he saw in the real world. There was some little friend, Ricky, maybe Robbie. I don't remember his name. They would message each other on the computer, but I don't think anyone ever came to our house to see Finch."

Sol said, "Raevyn told her therapist that she and Finch used to communicate with each other at night. What do you know about that?"

"Their bedrooms were next to each other. They moved their beds so they could whisper through the wall they shared." Yeardley stopped and began to weep. "I'm sorry. I promised myself I wouldn't do this, but Raevyn told me she started talking to Finch again. I don't think she's ever really processed his suicide. She imagines she can hear his voice. My friend, Dorine, who's a counselor, said it's a symptom of Raevyn's grief, and that people hear the voices of their lost loved ones."

Sol added, "Yes, that can be true." Pivoting back to Finch's suicide, he spoke gingerly. "About his death, the body was never recovered. You were certain he took his own life long before the police classified this as a suicide. With all due respect, how were you always so certain?"

Her voice betrayed a hint of anger. "Because I knew he was *deeply* depressed and had tried to take his life before. That's how I know! Why they refused to say this from the start galls me—calling it a *suspected* suicide when he had left a note. They found his jacket, for God's sake. And a body *was* recovered, a year later, north of the bay, *exactly* where tidal waters would have carried him."

Lenore gently probed. "But they weren't able to get a DNA sample because the body had been in the water so long. Isn't that right, Yeardley?"

"Yes, but why are you pushing this!? Forensic examiners did all sorts of other tests on the body and concluded it was Finch. I am at peace with this."

Seeing Yeardley so upset, Sol returned to the issue of the suicide note. "We've seen that note. It said he wanted to get away from it all—"

Yeardley interrupted, "and that there was *nothing* to live for. He sounded desperate when he told me to my face it was over for him. Finch was no stranger to suicide. He tried to end his life by taking an overdose when he was just 15 years old. Hopelessness was no stranger to Finch."

Sol wrinkled his brow. "We knew he was in the hospital at age 15, but the records didn't document this as a suicide attempt. I think he was diagnosed with anxiety and avoidant personality, but—"

"Yes, more socially palatable diagnoses. That was the handiwork of our dear mother. She knew all the doctors in town. They were her friends and colleagues and knowing her, she might have even slept with one or two, but that's a story for another day. The point is, Mother couldn't tolerate that a child of hers would try to take his own life. Why, what would people think? How might this reflect on her parenting? So, they kept anything about his overdose out of the records."

Sol asked, "Wasn't there another treatment program before that?"

"You're referring to the place he went to in Florida when he was around 13. Honestly, that was very hush-hush in the family. I had long been away from home for college, graduate school, and the like, so there was a lot going on I didn't know about. Mother was as silent about the Florida program as she was about his overdose. She always thought there was something wrong with Finch. I don't think she liked him much because he embarrassed her. I once heard her call him a "little queer." How sad is that? It was painful to see her put him into experimental studies at places like NIMH, where I think they treated him like a lab rat. Again, I lived away from the family, so I didn't see the day-to-day of it all."

Lenore spoke up, "The program in Florida . . . can you remember the name or anything about it?"

"No, sorry. All I know is, Mother said it was an Outward-Bound type program to build up his confidence. I was away at the time, but I do remember how he seemed different from then on."

"Different? How?" Asked Sol.

"When I came home that summer, he was even more reclusive than before, like a little dark cloud was following him around. He was pretty much a loner before that, but at least he'd speak to me. That place really did a number on him. He wouldn't say a word to anyone that summer, not even to me, and we used to be able to talk. Honestly, it was so frustrating trying to get information from anyone in this family. I don't know what Raevyn would say, but that's another story. She's the same way when you try to get *anything* from her about what went on in her treatment programs. She takes after Mother in some of these ways. Like after her hospitalization at Georgetown following her disaster at the Olympic trials—God, how that broke my heart to see her out there just going to pieces—they sent her to these other programs. Nothing seemed to help. She was so angry. She finally ended up at this Austen Riggs place in Western Massachusetts for about three months. But programs like that pretty much shut down during COVID, and most of the patients were sent back home. So, Raevyn came back here. Where else was she supposed to go? She was not well and refused to get help, but at least she had a safe place to live. Honestly, she can be so stubborn."

Sol shared, "We didn't know about Austen Riggs. We saw the records from Georgetown and Menninger, and we should get the records from Austen Riggs as well. But we would really like to learn more about the place in Florida. If you can remember the name, that would help."

"Honestly, no one ever talked about that, so I simply have no idea. I don't think I'd even recognize the name if you said it."

"Thanks," Lenore continued. "Back to Raevyn, how long had she been Linus Prokop's patient?"

"Linus pulled some strings to get her into all these programs. After she was sent back here from Austen Riggs, I pushed her to start seeing him. She went back for maybe a month, if that long, back in 2021 to 2022, but then refused to continue. It took an act of God to get her to see him again a month ago. She had stopped her lithium and was cycling. She was going to clubs at all hours and coming in when I was leaving for work. She wouldn't, maybe couldn't, stop or slow down. Then she'd crash and wouldn't get out of bed for days. She fought me when I suggested seeing Prokop again. I was careful not to push too hard because I didn't want to sound like our mother, always pressuring her to do more. If Raev objected, Mother would punish her with silence. Of course, she always ended up doing exactly what Mother wanted. The whole medical school thing was her idea, by the way. I don't think Raevyn ever wanted to be a doctor. Now I feel horrible about pushing her to see Prokop again a couple of months ago." Yeardley paused and pulled out a tissue.

Lenore recognized this as her cue to ask about Raevyn's belief that Finch was hiding in the house. "Sol, would you share what we learned from Mrs. Madrigal?"

"Of course. Idina Madrigal, who you know has been treating Raevyn, asked to meet with me because she is concerned about Raevyn's ongoing communications with Finch. Mrs. Madrigal thinks Raevyn should be showing a lessening of her psychotic symptoms by now, and I agree. She's been in treatment for over two months and is on a lot of medication. Usually, within the first month of antipsychotic medication, we expect to see some lessening of hallucinations. But Raevyn is convinced that Finch is living in your house and talking to her nightly."

Lenore quickly added, "According to Raevyn, Finch was doing something called phrogging. It's when someone lives in a house without the residents knowing. I know this must sound—"

"Absurd? *Yeah*. I'd say crazy." Yeardley looked stunned. "You're saying like a *frog* in the house? How could he do that? What, he just comes back from the dead to hide in my attic? Do you know how outlandish this sounds? Are you forgetting my sister is mentally ill? Talking with her dead twin brother is nothing new. I told you she's started hearing his voice again. I'm not a doctor, but she hallucinates. End of story. I don't know how this is any different."

Lenore jumped in. "I know. It sounds wild, especially for someone with Raevyn's mental health history, but here's what really got our attention. She told her therapist that Finch described specific details of the crime scenes that happen to be true. The problem is that *none* of those details has been released to the public. So how would Raevyn know any of this? It doesn't seem like it could be a product of her grief or delusional thinking."

Sol treaded cautiously. "Raevyn also told her therapist that she was afraid of what Finch might do to her if she shared this information. Mrs. Madrigal said Raevyn became terrified and refused to say more."

Yeardley gasped and shook her head. "I-I...."

Lenore said they'd like a team of officers and forensic specialists to search the house for any indications that what Raevyn was saying might be true, that Finch could actually be hiding in their home. "I'm sure nothing will come of this, but we just need to put this to rest as part of our investigation."

Yeardley sat motionless, pale, as a look of fright and disbelief washed over her face.

"I-I just don't . . . can't—." Her voice trailed off.

Sol moved closer. "I know, this is a lot to take in. We can get some officers to watch your house, just in case. But I have one last question before we leave. Did you ever know Finch to be violent?"

PART THREE

RETURNS THE WHISPERER

Statistics abound and confound leading to a shell game
and sleight of hand
That will cull the hunters, like lambs, from the herd,
And be led to their deserved slaughter.
But alas,
Returns the Whisperer,
Responding to the trafficking in new secrets and
The betrayal of promises sworn to be kept in a sacred crypt,
Only to be announced loudly for all to behold.
Now, to thee come whispers of death to silence their tongues forever.

30

CARL BURNLEY

The flight to Green Bay and drive to the FBI field office reminded Kitts of the awkward silence riding with Jerry. There had been no small talk with her MAGA hat-wearing partner from the Arapahoe County Sheriff's Department. Back then, they responded to calls, period. No idle conversation, no mindless chatter. But Jerry was a racist asshole. Toby Potter was not Jerry, but his silent contempt for her felt the same. She and Toby exchanged a few words about logistics: rent a car, drive to the field office, and coordinate with the local agents and police. Escanaba was about two hours north along the bay. Sidd had spoken to the regional director about setting up a task force to locate and bring in Burroughs, AKA Carl Burnley.

When Kitts and Toby arrived at the field office, local agents Pfaall and Ricketts said they needed to call EAD Baldazzar ASAP. Potter placed the call. Boz told him to put it on speaker so Kitts could hear.

"BAU received another Whisperer message and equation. They're trying to make sense of it, but it looks like the UNSUB has more work to do. I'm faxing you what we've got."

They waited for one of the agents to bring in the fax. It looked the same as the others.

$$\frac{1}{3138-t\sqrt{2\pi^c}} \; -\tfrac{1}{2}(bc-XR)^2 X[x]$$

Boz continued, "According to the bookkeeper's cipher, he's planning to kill an *SM* on Tuesday the 13th. This one doesn't give a zip code like the others, so he's upping the ante and making us work. Oh, and check out how he ended it with an *x* in the bracket. They're telling me this indicates an unknown quantity. So, take that for what it is. Saks is a blowhard, but he was right on this one. The killer has no intention to stop his rampage. All we know is that he's targeting some *SM* vic on a specific date with no location. But I don't trust what the UNSUB is telling us. Something seems to have shifted for him. He's deviating from his pattern. This much seems clear: He's determined to keep on killing."

Potter appeared confused. "So *XR* stands for the initials *SM*?"

"Good boy, Agent. You were paying attention to the bookkeeper in class. Right now, we're trying to figure out who this *SM* could be, but whoever it is, he intends to kill them on Tuesday, August 13th. You gotta get to Cosmo Burroughs before then. We're looking at personnel files of anyone who worked on the Ann Arbor project who might have the initials *SM* or *MS*. When you locate Burroughs, see what he can tell you about anyone with those initials."

Kitts, jotting notes, stopped abruptly. "Sir, we don't know that he's only targeting people from the research team, right? His note seems to refer to new secrets and a betrayal of promises that were supposed to be kept in 'a sacred crypt' that someone then whispered. Sir, Raevyn's therapist shared information about her brother Finch with Sol and me. *SM* could stand for Sol Mendelson. The killer may be targeting another mental health professional for trafficking in secrets, you know, like breaking a patient's confidentiality."

There was a long silence. Boz said, "Or *Sancha* Madrigal. She's the one who crossed the line by calling Sol in the first place. I take it you didn't know that's her first name. She goes by Idina, but her legal name is Sancha. Smart lady. I wouldn't want to be called Sancha any more than I would Bozzio. So, we have two possible *SM* targets in our fold.

Today's the 10th. You've got three days to find Burroughs, and we'll see about anyone with the initials *SM* who worked on the research that Burroughs could have a vendetta against. In the meantime, we'll get some police protection for Mendelson and Madrigal. I still think we're looking at someone connected with the project that Burroughs feels betrayed him. He's taken out the doctors, but there were a lot of others who worked on that research. Let Sidd or me know what you've got. We're on a short clock, so fuck off kids."

While they were getting ready to leave, Toby looked at Nicola and said, "You can't let this Raevyn shit go, can you. That's bullshit, Kitts, and you know it. This whole thing with the brother living in the attic is bonkers. You just had to open Pandora's box."

Kitts bit her tongue, took a breath, and exhaled. "Maybe, Toby. But I was always taught to stay alert, keep an open mind, and look into all the buildings. Things aren't always what they seem to be. That's all I'm saying. Thought you knew all that now that you're walking point."

"Look, I don't know what you're talking about. You're not the only one who was in the military, Kitts. Let's keep our focus. We're here to do a job—find and detain Cosmo Burroughs. Oh, and by the by, the note he left mentioned statistics, right? Have you forgotten this guy taught statistics? It was his job, Kitts."

She chose to let it go for now. Ricketts and Pfaall took them to a conference room, where they briefed the director about Burroughs. When contacted, the local PD in Escanaba agreed to assist in finding and detaining Burroughs.

Kitts was preoccupied during the drive along the bay. Toby was becoming an asshole, but having Ricketts and Pfaall in the car broke the tension she felt riding solo with him.

Kitts, Potter, and the two Green Bay agents met with Sheriff Goodfellow of the Delta County Sheriff's Office. Goodfellow had a wide girth and folksy manner reminiscent of Oliver Burwinkle. The agents crowded into his office.

The first thing Kitts noticed was a large gray cat sitting on his desk. She looked into the yellow eyes which stared back at her. In a world made up of those who loved cats and those who didn't, she stood among the latter. It wasn't simply that she was a bird person. The truth, which no one knew, was that Kitts had an unnatural fear of cats—a direct consequence of being terrorized as a kid by her Aunt Rhea's nasty tomcat, aptly named Claude.

Goodfellow saw her staring at the feline. "Don't mind him, Agent, he's a good ol' boy, aren't you Sniper. Wouldn't hurt a flea."

Sniper maintained his unearthly stare, arched his back, and hissed. Kitts blinked, then turned away. *Fucking cats.*

The sheriff cleared his throat in true Burwinkle fashion. "You folks traveled a long way to find this fella. I'll brief you about what we know. Made some inquiries to the folks at the college where Burnley'd been teaching. Thing is, he's been MIA for the last three or four months. Just stopped showing up for his classes. No explanation whatsoever. His department head filed a missing person's report, but nothin' much came of that. It seems that no one knew much about him. Got his address, which we've checked out a couple of times. Didn't find much. We were expecting to find a stash of porn, but maybe he took all that with him. But I figure you all will want to see it for yourself. I'll get Deputy Hicks here to take you there."

Kitts asked, "Sheriff, what did they have to say about Burnley before he went missing?"

"Not much, Agent, except his department head said something kind of seemed off about him."

"Like what, Sheriff?"

"She said she caught him staring at some of the students in a way that made her skin crawl. She was gonna talk to him about this, but about four months back, he up and vanished."

Not wanting to be upstaged by his female partner, Toby inserted himself. "Figures. Fits his profile. Seems his going AWOL corresponds to the period of the murders. We'll go check out his address and see what we can dig up. Meanwhile, we need to talk to people at the college."

Agent Ricketts responded, "Will do. I can see to that. I'll talk to the department head, find other teachers and former students who knew him, and see if we can follow up on any leads."

"Just so ya know," the sheriff added, "we did talk to those folks when he went missing, but figure you need to do all this again. I'll assign you a couple of armed deputies to help you check out his apartment," volunteered the sheriff. "Who knows, maybe he came back and is lying low. Probably won't look the same. Folks like him have a way of changing their appearance. Pictures of him at the college don't look much like he did when he was in Ann Arbor, 'cept for them thick glasses. You know, the kind that make your eyes real big."

Kitts had grown quiet. Everything about Sheriff Goodfellow summoned intrusive memories of Burwinkle and his ultimate betrayal. She was also distracted by thoughts of Sol. "Okay, thanks, Sheriff. We'll let you know if we find anything."

Sniper had not taken his eyes off Kitts.

Goodfellow said, "There's one more thing, Agents. I haven't heard nothing about his being a violent type but figured you wouldn't be here if he wasn't."

31

GOING ROGUE

Burnley's cramped apartment had been untouched since the deputies searched it four months before. Deputy Hicks led the way. "It was pretty clean—well, not *clean*. Place was a pigsty when we first searched it. We didn't find much except a pile of worthless papers and dirty dishes but no whips or chains, ha! Whatever else is true about this guy, he wasn't much of a housekeeper or porn freak."

The tiny kitchen showcased a sink full of foul-smelling dishes, left untouched since the original search. Kitts held her nose as she walked to his desk, while Potter followed Hicks into the bedroom. She looked through a stack of mail opened during previous searches. "Doesn't look like there's much here. I guess you guys already processed all this, but how come you left all this stuff here and didn't take it back to your station?"

Hicks answered from the bedroom. "Honestly, Agent Kitts, there was nothing here worth hauling back to our evidence closet. We have so much crapola in there already. Since this was a cold scene, we didn't bother collecting all his stuff."

She shook her head, opened the drawers, and looked through the papers, finding nothing of interest—mostly bills and memos from the community college. She tugged at the bottom drawer, which appeared to be stuck. "Did you guys check out all the drawers?"

"Yeah, we must have done that."

"But this one was stuck and doesn't look like it's been opened." She tried to yank it open, peeked inside, and slipped her hand through the crack.

The deputy walked back into the living room. "Oh, yeah, that one. We didn't get it open all the way but just felt around. There was nothing there, just more papers and bills. Nothing seemed out of the ordinary. Honestly, we found bubkes."

Kitts felt that the back side of the drawer was wobbly. She wiggled it loose and pulled it out. Then she reached her hand back in and felt another compartment hidden below. "There's something in here. You got a flashlight, Deputy?"

Hicks handed her his flashlight, which she angled into the opening. "Looks like a box. Seems to be stuck."

Toby walked back in. "What you got, Kitts?"

"It's a metal box." She pulled it out and could see it was locked.

Both of their pagers suddenly sounded. Toby looked at his, then toward Kitts. "It's from Pat. There's been another goddamn killing in Ann Arbor! I gotta call in."

Kitts pulled out her pocketknife and tried to pry open the box, while Toby got through to Pat.

The lid gave way. "Hold on. There are more papers inside." She shuffled through them and pulled out a list of about 10 names. Among them were Tamerlane, Fortunato, Prokop, and Pough. One name jumped out at her. "Hey, Toby, you got a name on the last vic?"

"Yeah, Pat says it's someone named Morella . . . Sophie Morella."

Kitts froze as she read the name. "Damn, looks like he got his *SM*. But wait, this isn't the 13th, right? That's two days from now. Didn't the last equation say the hit would be then? He's ahead of schedule. Looks like Saks's right again. He's going rogue."

32

Unbalanced Beam

"I understand you're still angry with me, but I'm really glad you came back."

Raevyn turned her head away. It had been weeks since she'd seen Madrigal, but Yeardley wouldn't let up. She was determined not to say anything. When she finally spoke, she said she was torn between feeling betrayed and relieved that someone might finally do something to help free her from the confusion and fear.

Madrigal asked her to say more.

"So much for being a secret keeper. Look, I'm not stupid. I get why you did it. It's not like you went behind my back, but damn, did you ever think it wouldn't be cool for me when he finds out I've been leaking this information?"

"How would he know, Raevyn? Who would tell him?"

"I would, of course! What do you think? I have to tell him everything."

"And did you?"

"*Yeah.* I don't think you're getting this. I just told you. I had to."

"See, that's what I don't understand. This obligation you feel toward your brother, whom you also seem to fear. Can we talk about that?"

Raevyn's eyes welled up. "Because like I told you before, I treated him like shit when we were kids. I betrayed him, my own twin brother.

In public I always pretended he wasn't related to me but was just some weird little kid following me around. Then when we got older, I used him. He wrote my papers and got me answers to exams. He even wrote my fucking valedictory speech." Tears ran down her cheeks. "Then, he got me speed and coke, so he . . . became my supplier. You get it now? I . . . *needed . . . him*."

"Wow Raevyn, there's a lot to unpack about this relationship. I'm guessing you've never talked to anyone about this, not even Dr. Prokop or your treaters at Menninger or Austen Riggs."

"Are you serious? I didn't trust any of them. Anyway, I always knew he'd find out. I couldn't get his voice out of my head. I was *always* hearing him. Then, he came back."

"When? You said he came back a lot. I thought he committed suicide after your parents were killed. So, you're saying he *didn't* kill himself?"

"Yes. No, before all that . . . a couple months before the trials, he showed up at the house again. Yeard and I didn't know where he had been, but's that's pretty much how Finch rolled. I had started medical school in the summer, a few months before my folks were killed, and knew instantly I was in over my head with all this bullshit—a school I didn't want *and* the trials. But hey, I was Raevyn the Maven, so I couldn't tell anyone what was going on with me. I realized the fucking medical school thing was a joke. I didn't belong there. Then my parents got murdered. I was just so numb and wasn't dealing with reality. I couldn't sleep. What I needed was something to knock me out at night and Adderall to get me through the day before the trials, but I couldn't have that on my medical record."

"Because?"

"Duh, the whole USOC thing! You know, the Olympic committee. They have rules about what you can and can't take, and they do drug testing."

"Weren't you in medical school then?"

"No, I ended up taking a semester off from school in February and went back to Bethesda to train nonstop for the trials. Then fucking Finch shows up from God knows where, and all this shit got real again. I felt desperate and needed his help again. I had three months before the trials and begged him to get me the drugs he used to give me in high school. He said he still knew some people he could contact, but there would be another payment due."

"Another payment, Raevyn?"

"Yeah, he always told me he would keep coming back to collect on what I owed him. I didn't know what he was capable of; only that I owed him big time. He knew all my secrets about being a cheater and druggie. He has held all of that over my head."

"Blackmail? And what do you mean that you didn't know what he was capable of?"

"I don't know. I mean, I never saw him actually do anything, but there was always some kind of threat. He wouldn't say it, but it was *always* there."

"Did he ever threaten to hurt you?"

"No, that's not like him, but he hints at things. There was this time when we were kids, I think maybe four years old. Our grandmother gave us kittens for our birthday and told us to never let them outside. I remember Finch's kitten bit him. He freaked out, and the next day, the cats were floating in our swimming pool. I think my mother was glad to see them go. Hell, maybe she drowned them. But this happened the night after Finch got bit. Then, there was the neighbor's dog that went missing. No one ever accused my brother of any of this, but...."

"So, what happened when he returned to your house and you asked him to help you? You must have felt the dependency starting all over again."

"Yeah, but I didn't know who else to turn to. Now it was me who was drowning. But when he showed up, he looked like a piece of shit. God, he'd lost all this weight. He looked so pathetic, and the darkness in him was worse than ever. He said he couldn't go on, and that he'd get me the pills I needed if I helped him . . . kill himself. He said it had to be me who helped him, and he started in again about everything I owed him. He got all dramatic and said this would be my final payment. No one needed to know. I couldn't believe this and tried to talk him out of it. He sounded crazy and kept telling me that he hated the world and especially our parents because they wrecked his life. I knew he always had a lot of problems with them, with how our father would take him into the basement, and Mother would criticize him for everything. She'd scream, 'Why can't you be more like your sister?.'"

"I can't imagine how this was for you. Your own twin brother."

"I got good at ignoring it. I was always too busy with my own life to pay much attention. I was just glad she was going after him and not me."

"And what did Finch say about you owing him?"

"He kept accusing me of not backing him up and not wanting to hear anything about what people had done to him. Know what? He was right. I was even worse than our parents 'cause I never wanted to hear about any of that shit. I had my suspicions about his being gay, but we could never talk about anything like that in my house. I think my mother would have imploded and maybe even blamed me. I think there was something really wrong with her."

"My God, Raevyn, I hear your pain, and all your regret and guilt. But you're saying Finch held this over you?"

"Totally. He kept saying I owed him for everything he did for me, and now I could pay him back." Raevyn put her head down and began to cry softly.

Passing her the tissue box, Madrigal asked, "It almost sounds like he wanted to punish you by making you responsible for his suicide. That's rage. What were you supposed to do?"

"Just drive him to the Bay Bridge and drop him off. When I told him this was nuts, he grabbed my arm and said, 'You *have* to do this.

You *know* what I can do.'" She grabbed another Kleenex. "There was
no one I could talk to. Yeardley and I weren't on speaking terms. She
was trying to act like my mother, and I wanted nothing to do with her.
If I had told her, she'd have tried to stop him, and Finch would know."

"You have someone now to talk to, Raevyn, and I'm listening."

Raevyn reached for water from the pitcher. After taking another
moment, she continued, "So, I drove the fucker to the bridge, thinking
I could talk him out of it. I was afraid if I said anything, he would ruin
everything by telling people the truth about me. But I knew if he ended
up killing himself it would be all my fault. I pleaded with him not to
do this, but he kept saying I owed him and this would settle my debt.
When we got to the bridge, he ordered me to stop the car and started
to get out. I reached for him and begged, but he shoved me and bolted
from the car. I got out and screamed his name. I ran after him, but he
was gone. I panicked and called 911. I kept looking for him and was
so scared he'd already jumped. When the police arrived, they started
looking for him. I told them he wanted to kill himself. Then, one of the
cops gives me this weird disapproving look and says, 'But you said you
drove him here, didn't you?' They asked why I hadn't called for help
earlier. I said I couldn't control him and was afraid, but...."

"But? But what, Raevyn? You stopped your thoughts. I think
there's more."

Like the breaking of a dam, Raevyn began sobbing. "Part of me
felt so relieved that maybe I'd finally be free of him and his control and
all the shit he never let me forget. All the stuff about me *always* getting
more than him. He blamed me for *everything*. But he was right. I was
awful to him, but I needed him too. I needed his failure to make me
look good, then needed him to give me answers to tests and to get me
drugs. He said someday he'd tell *everyone* I was a junkie, a liar, and a
fake." She paused to pour more water.

"You 'needed his failure to make you look good.' What an interesting thing to say. I can take that two ways: You needed his failure in life

so you could look good. But I also wonder if Finch failed at making you look good because he knew the truth about what you were hiding. In other words, were you a failure in his eyes? Did you need him to view you this way, as a failure? Perhaps both are true. Either way, you don't have to pretend anymore. You can be real in here and tell your whole story about this horrible dilemma—needing him and hating him for it, not wanting him to take his life but hoping he would."

Raevyn stared at the floor and picked at the frayed holes in her jeans. "He started scaring me, and I wanted that to stop. But he was my brother. When we were little, he was like a little bird you find on the sidewalk. You know, like the ones that get thrown out of their nests? I should have protected him, but I didn't. Then he changed."

"It's a complicated story, Raevyn. You loved your brother but were ashamed of him. Then you found ways to punish yourself for these feelings. When you got older, you needed him but also resented and feared him. There was such a battle between guilt, fear, hatred, and sadness, and you never felt there was anyone you could turn to. Your brother's ultimate revenge, your final payment, was making you responsible for his suicide. Take your time, Raevyn. I'm listening."

"Three months later, I fell apart in St Louis. I could feel myself slipping. I was having withdrawal symptoms from going cold turkey off the drugs. I struggled everywhere. I couldn't admit I was a fraud and knew I'd eventually get kicked out of medical school. My training sucked. I wasn't sleeping. All this shit about my parents and secretly feeling glad to be free of Finch started closing in. But I was numb and good at blocking it all out like I did my whole fucking life. All I could think about was making the team and showing everyone, mostly me, that I was okay. At the time, I thought I could, but part of me knew this was my illness talking, and I was losing it. I just couldn't stand all those mopey-eyed people coming up to me saying, 'Oh, poor Raevyn. She lost her parents and then her brother, boo hoo. Poor little Raevyn, how does she do it all?' I knew I'd lost my edge but had one last chance on the balance beam to make everything right. If I could nail my routine, everything would be perfect again. But I felt really hyper and had a hard time focusing."

Speaking carefully, Idina said, "I've told you before, I watched the tape of that day. I'm so sorry, Raevyn."

"Yeah, Raevyn the Craven lost her shit and stripped for all the world to see. But what you don't know—what nobody ever knew—was that right before I was about to do the beam, I looked up and saw my dead brother sitting in the stands . . . *grinning* at me. He was there! Not dead, but alive, with that sadistic smirk, staring, smiling." She paused and continued in a halting monotone with a wide-eyed, hollow expression saying, "I'm totally freaking out. Have to get someone to see he is here. Sitting up there. The gym is so hot like someone turned the heat way up, and there's this loud ringing sound. I look up again, and . . . and he is still sitting there looking at me, mouthing something. They're cueing me to start my routine, but I can't get him out of my head. Then everything is spinning. I'm suffocating and...."

Idina leaned in. "Raevyn...Raevyn, stay with me in the room."

Raevyn rubbed her eyes and shook off the flashback. "Yeah, I'm here . . . but so is he."

33

SOPHIE MORELLA

The flight from Delta County Airport to Ann Arbor took a little over an hour. Few words passed between the agents as they studied the material Pat had faxed. The next stop was another sit-down at the Bureau field office before going to the crime scene.

They sat in a windowless office with Agent Camille Le Duc, who was apologizing for knocking over Toby's coffee cup and staining his suit jacket. Clearly irritated, he waved her off while muttering under his breath. "Let's get on with it, Le Duc. It's getting late, and we've still got the crime scene to get to. So, what do you know about this girl?"

Le Duc made eye contact with Kitts, who rolled her eyes. "Okay, so, Sophie Morella's the woman who blew the whistle on Burroughs after a grad student informed her she'd found kiddie porn on his computer. Apparently, Morella went to Dr. Tamerlane but asked to keep her name out of this."

Kitts asked, "Do we know why?"

"We don't. When the Burroughs thing broke, the spokesman just said that information had come to their attention from a reliable source. The focus shifted to Cosmo, and that took up all the oxygen until a week ago when Sophie began to talk."

"Hmm, why do you suppose, after all these years, she's willing to talk now?"

"Let's not waste time on the *why* here, Kitts, and just get to the what. So, *what* did this lady have to say?"

Le Duc was about to speak when Nicola said, "I think knowing *why* she chose to come out now *is* important, Agent Potter."

Ignoring her comment, he pushed forward. "So, *what* did she say?"

"She sat for an interview with *People Magazine* and provided new details about the whole Burroughs thing. After their recent book came out, reporting the results of the ARES Project, Tamerlane turns up dead, sparking a lot of interest. Of course, Burroughs' name surfaced again. People remembered he was dropped from the study in 2016 because of the whole computer porn thing. So, after this *Masculīnus* book came out and Tamerlane got killed, some investigative reporter tracked down Morella, who agreed to discuss the project. I don't know why she decided to finally speak, but she did. Here's the article in *People*." Le Duc pushed the file folder across the desk.

Toby picked it up and thumbed through the file. "She was one of the research assistants?"

"No, Morella was the project manager. She wasn't a scientist but the administrative backbone of the whole thing. In the interview that just dropped, she said a research assistant came to her about Burroughs, complete with graphic details about finding him masturbating in his office while looking at child porn. I guess the senior researchers wanted to keep the whole thing hush-hush what with Burroughs being the head statistical guy and their buddy to boot, but Morella said she pushed Arthur Tamerlane to kneecap Cosmo."

Le Duc picked up the magazine and read Sophie Morella's words. "'I had learned that a senior member of our research team, this man Burroughs, was engaging in immoral behavior, and that simply couldn't stand. We are a respectable university and have high standards to maintain. And let's just say that some of the senior investigators and university lawyers lacked the courage to take a principled stand. I could use a different word but won't. That's when I put my foot down to protect the university and integrity of the ARES Project.'"

Le Duc closed the magazine. "Morella thought quietly dismissing Burroughs from the project was bullshit, which is exactly what Tamerlane and his pals wanted to do. So, Morella goes after him and forces Tamerlane to get some balls and fire Burroughs. She said the university lawyers and Tamerlane had intended for Burroughs' dismissal to be done discretely, with few details released to the public. Morella disagreed on moral grounds and pushed for Burroughs to be burned at the stake. She insisted Tamerlane, Fortunato, Prokop, and the other doc write a letter condemning Burroughs, stating that his behavior not only sullied the reputation of the universities but seriously undermined the credibility of their investigation. So, she not only got him fired but made sure they took away his university pension and made him a public spectacle."

Kitts asked, "I'm still wondering why she waited all these years to come out publicly about Burroughs. Why *now*?"

"Again with the *whys*," snorted Toby.

Ignoring his protests, Le Duc explained, "Something about how she didn't want to draw any negative attention to ARES back in 2015. The project was still in full swing. There had been some glitches. They were still gathering a lot of data on their subjects. She feared that if they went public with too many details about Cosmo the pedo, it would stain their precious project. When the book was finally published and Tamerlane was murdered a few months later, maybe she felt freer to talk. I also think she felt obligated to speak out on behalf of the project and showcase it as a landmark study to promote the book. She bragged about the study's methodology and how they took special measures to ensure their sample was...." Le Duc stopped to read from the article, " . . . developmentally pure and free of deviant variants. Oh, and she probably got a nice paycheck for doing the interview."

Impatiently, Toby interjected, "Okay, I don't want the scene to get cold. I think we have all we need here. Let's get our asses in gear and take a look."

Both women continued as if mindlessly swatting an annoying gnat. Kitts mused, "To keep their sample pure and 'free of deviant *variants*,' ugh. That sounds, uh—"

"Like creepy Nazi stuff," shot Le Duc. "I am not sure what that meant, but she said each family was notified when their child was disqualified and dropped from the study. I think Morella wanted to remind everyone that Burroughs was the bad guy and to keep any bad press away from their all-important project."

Kitts asked, "Bad press? Wonder what they were afraid of."

Le Duc responded, "Beats me. But Sophie wanted to keep the focus on Burroughs. She even suggested that he might have been the one who killed Tamerlane. Remember, after he was fired, Cosmo crashed a staff meeting and threatened to kill Tamerlane." Le Duc reached for the *People* and read from the interview again. "Hear what Sophie said when asked about that meeting:

"'I was present during that faculty meeting when Mr. Burroughs burst through the doors. He appeared under the influence. He was wearing dirty clothes and looked as if he hadn't washed for days, probably longer. He ranted like a madman about betrayal and said he'd get his revenge because he knew where the bodies were buried. When he looked at Dr. Tamerlane, I could see such hatred in his eyes. We were all terrified about what he might do. I was afraid he had a gun and would just start shooting. Thankfully, the security guards arrived after they were alerted that a crazy person was threatening to kill Arthur Tamerlane.'"

Le Duc looked up. "I don't think Burroughs knew then that it was Sophie who pulled the trigger on him getting fired and losing his pension. But if he reads this, then look out."

Kitts thought of the last message from the Whisperer that said something about the *betrayal of promises sworn to be kept in a sacred vault*. Clearly, Burroughs had felt betrayed all over again. He may not have known then that Morella was responsible for ruining his life, but the *People Magazine* article must have made him feel that she was now trafficking in his secrets.

The three agents drove to the crime scene. Yellow tape surrounded Graeves Hall, where Sophie's body was found at her desk. White-suited forensic workers were hunched over her body, taking swabs, photographs, and dusting for prints. They stepped away when the agents approached. Kitts bent down to inspect the body. Although she was hardened to the gritty horror of crime scenes, she still had trouble keeping bloody images from her past secured in their mental boxes.

The cleaning crew found her at her desk. Spatters of blood stained the wall, leaving garish streaks of red on her artwork, certificates, and placards. Kitts stepped carefully over broken framed photographs, which were obviously the result of struggle. Photos of family, a picture of Sophie with her dog, and a group of colleagues celebrating at a bar lay scattered around the room. Books had been pulled from her shelf. Kitts spotted a hard copy of *Masculīnus* with a drop of blood on the cover.

Like the others, Sophie Morella lay face down in a pool of blood. Her throat was slit, but she also appeared to have been shot. Her hands showed cuts from trying to fight off her assailant. This woman who had years earlier taken a righteous stand against the indifferent researchers who had wanted to sweep an inconvenient truth about corruption and perversion under the rug now had paid the ultimate price. Whatever else Kitts was thinking about Raevyn and her bizarre story, she knew at that moment that Burroughs was a brutal monster who had to be hunted and put down.

34

ONE MAY BE TWO, OR TWO MAY BE ONE

With the Burnley trail having grown cold, Agents Potter and Kitts were summoned back to Quantico. Field offices throughout Michigan, Wisconsin, and Illinois remained on alert, and local law enforcement issued an APB for Carl Burnley or Cosmo Burroughs. Boz informed Toby and Nicola that once the locals found Burroughs and had him under surveillance, they'd be flown back to be on hand for his apprehension.

"Remember, this is a goddamn federal case. Don't let the local yokels try to ride shotgun. They're strictly backseaters for this. Now get your asses back here, pronto. You'll get your return tickets punched once they find this psycho."

Later that afternoon, the BAU squad gathered around the conference table. Kitts let her partner take the lead.

Toby showed photos of Burrough's apartment and crime scene images from Ann Arbor. "As you can see, the MO looked pretty much the same."

"Pretty much?" questioned Saks.

"Well, close enough . . . but maybe not identical."

"Just how do you mean, Tobias?" Pressed Saks with his trademark haughtiness.

"Sir, if you'll allow me," said Nicola as she waited for a nod from her partner.

Toby shrugged and murmured, "Knock yourself out."

Kitts looked at Saks. "The obvious difference began before the body was discovered."

"Meaning?"

"Meaning that the killing occurred on the 10th, three days before the date predicted on the latest equation. Also, there were no location codes."

Sidd asserted, "Yes, we're aware of those discontinuities, Agent. And what about differences at the crime scene?"

"Sir, this was a brutal crime scene. Worse than the others. Her office was trashed. Sophie Morella was shot and then stabbed or stabbed then shot. The forensic report hasn't come back yet. All the others were killed with a knife."

"It was an overkill. The woman didn't stand a chance," added Toby.

No one spoke as they studied the graphic photographs on the screen.

Lenore broke the silence, "We've already noted that this last equation targeting someone with the initials *SM* was incomplete compared to the others."

"And two days early," added Sidd. "And the x between the brackets seems to be the killer's way of further keeping us off balance. Perhaps he felt he'd given too much away and was making it too easy for us to track him. He may have changed his MO to avoid becoming predictable."

"Guess y'all saw Sophie's interview in *People*. Pretty much nailed Burroughs to the cross again. This time in public. Gave him a good reason to go after her."

Pat held up the magazine. "We've all read it."

Kitts asked, "So, if he is our killer, and it sure looks like he is, does this mean he got his *SM*?"

Saks took the question. "How we would like to believe this, Nicola, but as Siddharth has said, the bracketed x is a conundrum. X signifies an indeterminant number, meaning he is no longer telegraphing the number of victims he intends to execute. Does this mean the UNSUB plans to butcher an indeterminant number of psychiatrists or simply future victims with the initials *SM*? So, my darlings, which is it? Unfortunately, this proves my point that he is far from being done with his madness and mayhem."

De Vere added, "If that's the case, then Sancha Madrigal and Sol could still be in danger."

"I'm afraid that's correct," confirmed Sidd. "With this latest victim, the UNSUB might want us to assume that he has satisfied his plan to kill someone with those initials and that we will relax our vigilance and protection for Dr. Mendelson and Mrs. Madrigal. Because the threat remains high, both will continue having around-the-clock police protection."

Kitts glanced at Sol who was looking down at his hands and avoiding eye contact. He hadn't responded to her recent voicemails or texts, which set off an alarm bell she couldn't silence.

"I'd like to go back to the original point about the deviation in the pattern and suggest something else," offered Sidd.

"That's a fine idea," remarked De Vere. "As we've already noted, the shift in MO could reflect the UNSUB's feeling of insecurity, that they feel threatened at having relinquished their power by providing us with too many paint-by-numbers clues."

Sidd responded, "True, the deviation in patterning is important, but I think we also need to consider the possibility of an accomplice. I believe Agent Kitts wondered about this earlier. We've been assuming we are dealing with a single UNSUB, but perhaps one may be two. In other words, is someone else involved?

Toby jumped in. "But Burroughs is our number one guy."

Kitts studied the mug shot of Cosmo Burroughs on the screen. Mug shots show an ugly truth that other photographs hide. The face glowered at her, bloodshot eyes peering out through crooked wire-rimmed glasses. A face, not timid or contrite but defiant. Balding and bearded, he looked demented and dangerous. She was looking into the eyes of a killer.

"We got him dead to rights, and he's on the run," continued Toby. "He's got a motive and a history of violence. He felt betrayed by the ARES doctors, and now by this Morella woman for going public last week. He went after Tamerlane and the other guys because they got him fired, took away his pension, and trashed his life. That screams motive to me. And then he finds out that Morella was the one behind all this. Bam, he adds her to the list of victims."

Lenore shared, "I agree, Toby, about Burroughs, but Sidd or Nicola's idea is intriguing too. An accomplice. Yes, I can kind of see that. It would help explain the differences between crime scenes and MOs."

"At this point, we have nothing hard, and as Dr. De Vere has pointed out, there could be other explanations for his deviations. I'm simply suggesting that we need to keep all options open and consider something lurking outside the box." Sidd looked over at Kitts who had raised her finger. "You've got something to add, Nicola?"

"Yes, Sir. It's this thing with Raevyn Nevenmoore and her belief that her brother Finch is phrogging in their house and knows about the crime scenes. Don't get me wrong, I think Burroughs has blood on his hands, but this thing with the brother is like a stone in my shoe, especially now with you bringing up all this about a possible accomplice. Just thinking, Sir."

"Well as far as that goes, we interviewed the sister, Yeardley," said Lenore. "She thought Raevyn's claims were utter nonsense. She was adamant that Finch committed suicide in 2019, not long before Raevyn went to the Olympic trials."

Sidd probed, "Can you tell us more about your conversation, Lenore? Sol, I'm interested in what your thoughts are as well."

Lenore recounted the details of their interview. "Yeardley described how Finch had always been a lost soul and reportedly tried to commit suicide before. She said as kids, Raevyn and Finch called each other something like Bird and Covin—"

Sol cut in. "I think it was Birdie and Cobie, Lenore. These were their nicknames from the time they were small children. Raevyn walked on water, while poor Finch never learned to swim. She was the larger, more aggressive bird. You get the picture."

Lenore continued. "The murder of the parents in 2018 tore them apart, or so it seemed to Yeardley. But Finch had a habit of disappearing for long stretches of time with no one knowing his whereabouts. He would just come home, stay for a while, isolate himself in his room, and then disappear again."

Kitts thought of Finch, a pale-looking boy sitting in a darkened room with curtains drawn. She pictured him hunched over his computer, slender fingers rapidly executing keystrokes, eyes searching, a plate of half-eaten pop tarts by his side.

Lenore paused and added, "The sister also spoke at length about the parents—a father missing in action and the mother a severe narcissist who tormented Finch and kept Raevyn on a pedestal. It's like what Dr. De Vere was talking about, with the false self. The mother doling out praise and—"

Saks interrupted to finish her sentence, "Pushing her and feasting off her successes."

"Yeah, that's kind of what Yeardley said. But when Raevyn went off script, the mother would cut her off. Sounds pretty classic, huh? Oh, and she said going to medical school was the mother's idea too, that Raevyn wasn't keen on it."

Nicola asked if anything had been found in the search of the house.

"So far, the search teams and forensics haven't found a shred of evidence that he was ever there—no dishes or food crumbs in the attic or signs that his room has been lived in since he died. But they'll go back and do a final check of the house to—"

Saks interrupted again, "And they will not find *anything* because he was *never* there. Quite clearly, our dear Agent Kitts is now trafficking in fantasies that have been propagated by a severely disturbed woman."

"I totally agree," exclaimed Potter.

Kitts straightened her shoulders. "Yeah, I get it. Sounds creepy and crazy. But Finch's disappearance in 2019 was initially classified as a *suspected* suicide, not as a *completed* one. A year later, fishermen pulled a body out of the bay, but it had been in the water too long to get any DNA, so I'm just saying his body was technically never identified—"

"He's dead Kitts," corrected Saks. "Legally declared dead on May 23, 2022, three years after he jumped to his death from the Chesapeake Bay Bridge. He's dead, deceased, expired, departed, passed on to the pearly gates, and no longer amongst us. Is there something about the concept of death you have trouble with?"

"Plenty. I do have trouble with death, *Gideon*. Seen too much of it, but that's not the point here. And respectfully, phrogging is a real thing. Often strangers—"

Saks was not done with her. "And now I'm afraid you've succumbed to the popular media and fictionalized accounts, Agent. Maybe you've watched *Hider in My House*, too many times, hmm?"

Kitts pushed back, noting that she did a search on the central database and documented more than 20 cases of phrogging reported to the police over the last five years. "Look, I'm only going back to this 'cause you mentioned a possible accomplice, and Finch supposedly knew confidential things about the murders. And don't forget about his pattern of disappearing and—"

"And then . . . dying. Sadly, young Finch is dead. I, for one, do *not* believe he is lurking in the bowels of the house on Glenbrook Drive," pronounced De Vere. "In all due respect, I think you're reaching, Nicola. We don't need to impute such a chilling fantasy regarding the dead coming back to life. As far as knowledge about the crime scenes, let's employ our friend Occam's Razor, shall we? The simple explanation is the one that posits the fewest steps between observation and conclusion. I submit that our Raevyn only knew about these crimes because *she* was involved in them in the first place. I suggest we deploy our resources to find a nexus between Burroughs and Rav—"

Sidd uncharacteristically cut her off. "If you're going where I think you are, Bernice, we should widen the search for possible links between Burroughs and both Nevenmoore twins."

"Indeed, dear friend. When you've worked together as long as Sidd and I have, then like any old couple, you begin to finish each other's sentences and complete each other's thoughts. Yes, we must search for a nexus, as you suggest, but I'd like to raise you one. I think the sister may have identified herself *with* the brother. Given both her guilt and *schadenfreude* over poor Birdie's misfortunes, together with what is clearly her borderline level of character organization, I think our Ms. Nevenmoore may have taken on his identity. Wouldn't you agree, Gid?"

Looking confused, Toby interjected, "Wait, you mean like a split personality?"

Saks declared, "Indeed, and the precise term is dissociative identity disorder or DID, Tobias. Furthermore, remember Lenore told us that Raevyn and Finch were Birdie and Corvie. Ahem, *b and c.* Let's suppose that one became two or two are in fact one—"

Sol stood up. "With respect, I find this slightly offensive." He looked at Saks and De Vere. "I think you're both stepping off the razor by bringing in DID here. And frankly, you're the ones playing into Hollywood's worst stereotypes about violent DID sufferers. I'm surprised you would be willing to take us down that slippery slope."

De Vere paused to compose herself, as the rosy hue on her cheeks began to subside. She cleared her throat and said, "We're waiting for an alternative hypothesis from you, Dr. Mendelson. And by the way, Sol, I'm glad you've finally chosen to join the soiree this afternoon."

Lenore asserted, "All this sounds pretty incredible, but looking for a connection between the Nevenmoores and Burroughs makes sense. Maybe there isn't one, but I think we need to put this thing with Raevyn to rest."

Sidd stood, signaling their time was up. "Agreed. Let's search for a connection, even if it's a thread. Let's start with Raevyn. Agent Kitts, I'd like you to schedule another interview with her."

35

WHAT MATTERS MOST

She replayed his voicemail. "Hey Niki, we need to talk. Things have really been nuts. Can we meet tonight at that place near your apartment? I'll grab a table around 7:00."

We need to talk. Shit, Sol. Really? Part of her always knew the Sol thing was a distraction and interlude—a fling with another unavailable man scripted to leave her. But then, her loving feelings crashed the party.

She thought about the tender words he'd spoken: "Niki, can I call you that?" "I'm planning to leave Gin." "My feelings for you are like nothing I've ever known." "I can't get you out of my mind." "God, you're beautiful." But with this voicemail, his sweet words turned instantly to bitter bile.

Nicola glanced at Langston's empty cage, noticing a few feathers still resting at the bottom. He'd been at the vet for five days now. All they said was they were still running tests. *Shit, Langston. Not you too, boy.* Reflexively, she searched her mind for a distraction. She needed to refocus on the investigation and her interview with Raevyn tomorrow. *Yeah, girl, you got this.*

The case offered endless rabbit holes of distractions, but sometimes, the sought-after detours bled into intrusive reminders. Thinking about Raevyn led her back to Michigan and the brutalized body of Sophie Morella lying in her blood. Sophie's vacant eyes summoned the other dead: Wilson, Peters, Gonlin, and Garcia, all staring up from their bloody graves in Musa Qala. Then, she flashed back to the hollow look in the eyes of the man shot point blank in her living room by Burwinkle. Of course, these thoughts *always* led back to her little brother, whose bloody body she held in her arms when they were just kids. This case had pierced her armor. The killings haunted her. Her dam had sprung a leak, and she couldn't stop thinking about Raevyn. She wondered how long she could do this work when the distractions became the reminders. Now, her greatest distraction was about to end.

Kitts arrived at *No Goodbyes* on Euclid St. *Why choose this place? Are you trying to be clever and cute?* He was sitting at the same table as their first dinner date, which had launched the fires of a fleeting romance, now the ashes of a funeral pyre.

Sol stood and gave her a brotherly hug. "I hope this is okay. It's close to your place, so I thought it would be convenient."

"Yeah, it's fine. So, what's up with you? Pretty crazy times with all this *SM* shit, huh? Man, I was thinking what it must be like for you . . . and your family."

"Yeah, it's really been tough. Gin and the boys have been pretty freaked out by all this. The kids thought it was cool having police parked in front of the house, but I think it's really wearing on everyone with no end in sight. Work's been awful too, with the case plus my teaching and consultation schedule. Hey, I feel like a real putz. I'm sorry I haven't reached out more, you know, with all that's been going on."

She thought about her unanswered texts. "Sure, I get it. And you're not a putz, Sol. It's okay. You've had a lot on your plate."

"And sorry about not getting back to you when you texted. I've just had—"

"A lot going on. It's okay, really. All good."

Sol ordered a glass of white wine and Kitts a Jack Daniels on the rocks. They sipped silently, awkwardly. Then it came.

"This whole thing has made me think about my life differently, Niki. Not that I haven't been through tough times before, mind you.

But the thought that I, my family for God's sake, might be targeted .
. . well, that just feels like too much. What I'm trying to say, not very
clearly, is that this thing has gotten me thinking about what matters
most in life. Family is what it all comes down to. As I told you, Gin and
I have had our problems, and the distance between us has only grown.
But when you're suddenly faced with a life-and-death situation, that
kind of changes your calculus in life."

Nicola listened with a sympathetic look while she twirled her glass
with one hand and dug her fingernails into the palm of the other. Then
she drained her drink and thought of ordering another.

"So, this thing got us talking again. We talked all night and into the
morning. I had to tell her about you. I'm so sorry, Niki. I just had to
if Gin and I are going to have a chance of making this work. And the
boys, God, to think what their lives would be like if anything happened
to me, and I wasn't there for them, for any reason. Look, I think you're
fantastic, and I envy the guy who will have all the luck in the world
to end up with you, but it can't be me. You probably think I'm the
world's biggest putz, Niki. I know that." His hands shook as he sipped
his Chardonnay.

*My name is Nicola, you fucking putz! Suddenly, she shot up from the
table, kicked back her chair, slapped the wine from his hand, drew back,
punched him squarely in the nose, and watched him fall like an oak.*

She shook that fantasy from her mind and replied, "It's okay, Sol.
It was fun. I think we both knew what this was, right? It meant nothing more than it was. Family comes first, and we have this case. You
know, good guys need to catch bad guys. Tomorrow, I'm gonna talk
to Raevyn again, and we're on standby to fly back to Michigan when
they find Burroughs. Really, I get it. It's fine." She downed her drink
and stood up. "I should go over my notes on Raevyn. Got the report to
write up from the trip to Escanaba and Ann Arbor, too. Someone's not
done with their killing."

Sol remained seated and looked up at her intently. "Yeah, about the case . . . I'll need to step away for a bit. I've talked to Sidd about my schedule and recommended my colleague, Gail Masters. She's experienced and has been thoroughly briefed about the killings and the Nevenmoore family. She's great and will fit right in. I think you'll like her. Okay. You take good care, Niki." He stood up and reached to give her a hug.

Kitts held out her hand instead and gave him a cool look. "Let's keep it professional, Dr. Mendelson. And to set the record straight, my name is *not* Niki. It never was. You can call me Nicola. But actually, I prefer you address me as Special Agent Kitts." She shook her head and added, "Oh, and just so you know, I lied. You are a putz."

With that, Special Agent Nicola Kitts turned and walked away.

36

THE DARK SPIDER

Nicola's foul mood, amplified by several late-night shots of Jameson's, became the enemy of sleep. She thrashed about, haunted by dreams of those who had left her and fears of who would. She awakened at 5 a.m. with a hollow feeling in her gut and a pounding in her head, enraged but unable to decide who she was angrier at, Sol or herself. She settled on the latter. *How could you be so stupid? What did you think you were to him anyway?* She searched her unpacked boxes for an old book by Carmine's sister, the wildly obnoxious Professor Anne Schivalone, who'd preached how it was better to find a deep mental compartment to drop your shit into so you could sleep. She thumbed through the pages, searching for anything to help repair her leaky compartments, but all she found was useless drivel.

In true Kittsian fashion, she began to pull herself together, cramming her demons and any hint of vulnerability back into their band-aid tethered boxes. She softly chanted her father's mantra, *Don't mean nuthin', don't mean nuthin.'* After a shower and a quick bite, she dressed and got ready for her interview with Raevyn at 10:00. She reflexively looked in the fridge for Langston's fruit container, only to find nothing. *Shit, ain't got time for this now. Go away, bird. Can't be worrying about you too.*

Before leaving, she spent time reviewing her notes. On the drive, she thought about their first encounter and how rattled she was by

Raevyn's unhinged behavior. But surely there was more to this woman than her madness. There had to be a story behind this woman with Medusa-like hair. Suddenly, Kitts became curious about the *who* and *why*.

The housekeeper answered the door. Kitts stood in the foyer, while the woman called upstairs for Raevyn. After several minutes, she sauntered down the stairs. This was a very different person than Nicola had remembered. Then, she had a frightful countenance, threatening and unhinged. Today, she looked totally together in her flared jeans and an Armani sweatshirt, radiating normalcy and calm. Her hair was pulled back, highlighting her dark eyes, which no longer looked menacing but now warm and calm. Kitts was struck by a beauty that had been masked by her outrageous behavior in the jail.

Raevyn smiled and extended her hand. "Oh, hi. My sister said you'd be coming to talk today. I've spoken with the police before but don't think we've talked . . . have we?"

"Well, actually, Ms. Nevenmoore—"

"Call me Raevyn, okay?"

Bracing for what might come next, Kitts said, "Sure, Raevyn. Actually, we *did* meet several months ago when you were in the DC Jail. But that was quite a while back."

The agent saw a spark of recognition and a hint of a smile. "*Oh, yeah.* Nicola from Mineola, right?"

Glad that her blush was not easily detected, Kitts responded, "Yeah, it was something like that."

Raevyn gave an impish smile. "I must have freaked you out that day."

"Did it show?"

"Kind of, I guess, but that time is pretty much a blur."

"Yeah, I get it. You were, uh...."

"Fuckin' nuts, right?"

"Well, that's not how I'd put it, but—"

"Cuckoo, batshit crazy. How's that? It's how my sister describes it when she's annoyed. She tries hard not to show it, but you can always tell with some people when they're mad or scared of you. So, yeah, I do remember. Hey, do you mind if we talk outside? There's a lovely park nearby. It's nice out, and I'm tired of being cooped up inside."

Kitts did a quick mental scan of the situation. Raevyn was no longer a suspect—at most a person of interest. She had no known history of violence and seemed entirely in control of herself this morning. Nicola dismissed a twinge of doubt about protocol and agreed to walk to the park.

They walked for roughly twenty minutes, chatting about the break in the summer heat. When they reached the park, a few blocks from the Crescent Trail, they found a bench and sat.

"I was one of the folks who spoke with your therapist recently. She was concerned about some things you'd been talking about and felt compelled to let us know." Nicola took a breath and tried to flush Sol from her mind.

"I was really pissed at Encanto about that whole thing. That's what I like to call Madrigal. You know, from the movie? Anyway, I guess she had to break confidentiality. Still, it pretty much sucked, but I guess I'm over it. She's alright, as long as she doesn't die on me."

Kitts thought she must be referring to Madrigal's cancer, which Sol—*the fucking putz*—had said was in remission. "I understand how you must have felt when she came to talk with us. But Ms. Neven, uh Raevyn, it was important."

"You were going to call me Ms. Neven. That's cute." Raevyn nodded, as two little girls came running by. "What was it you wanted to talk about?"

"For starters, what can you tell me about Finch living in your house now? How does that work?"

Raevyn paused and looked off toward the nearby playground. "Oh snap, here we go again. Okay. We'd always whispered through the wall ever since we were kids. I couldn't sleep; he'd tell me stories. That's pretty much it."

"What kind of stories?"

"All kinds, but mostly about dragons and princesses—shit like that. He was really into the whole Harry Potter thing. I wasn't, but I liked his stories. We did this pretty much until we started high school. But then Finch changed."

"How so?"

"Man, I've already talked about this. He never had any real friends, just some kid he used to text with but no real friends. Know what I mean? He kind of checked out of the world and spent most of his time in his room. Then, we kind of stopped talking."

"What do you think caused the change back then?" Kitts was making mental notes. She didn't want to spoil the conversational flow by taking out her notebook, thus turning this into a formal interrogation.

"Okay, when he was 12 or 13, they sent him to some camp for reasons no one would talk about. He didn't say much, except...."

"Except what Raevyn? What did he tell you?"

She fidgeted and said, "He was trying to tell me . . . he thought he was gay. I told him he was crazy and shouldn't think that way. I really fucked up with that, you know. He was trying to reach out, and I wasn't there for him." A tear ran down her cheek.

"Yeah, it can be rough with brothers. You don't know where he went for this camp, do you?"

"No. No one talked about any of that. Maybe somewhere in Florida. To tell the truth, and I hate to say this 'cause it shows what a bona fide piece of shit I am, but I was glad he was gone. I was totally embarrassed by him, you know. If that makes me a terrible, selfish person, well busted. It's all true." Another tear fell down her cheek.

"If you do remember anything about that camp, I'll give you my card so you can call, okay? And wasn't there another hospitalization at Georgetown a few years later?"

"I'm not sure. Like I said, I was pretty caught up in teenage bull-shit. But by that time, we weren't talking much. A couple of times, I tried calling out to him at night, and he stopped whispering back. Can't say that I blame him."

Kitts refocused. "You said he used to talk with someone online. You wouldn't happen to know if Finch knew anyone named Cosmo Burroughs? Or, he may have gone by the name of Carl Burnley?"

"Nope. Not that I know of."

"And that name's not familiar to you? He would have been an older man. Can you think of anyone he was talking to?"

Raevyn shook her head. "No. Next question."

"Okay. This is awkward, but I have to ask. You said that Finch thought he was gay. Is it possible that he may have been talking to some-one online about this?"

Raevyn yawned. "Really, I don't know. Ya know, I'm not liking you so much right now. This is beginning to sound like an interrogation."

"Sorry, I'm only asking because there are so many online predators trying to groom vulnerable and lonely kids like your brother. Is there any chance that Finch may have had contact with someone older like this?"

"Geez, will you stop! How should I know? Like I said, we weren't talking much. When he was a kid, he wanted to tell me things, but when we got older, he kept his life in a vault."

Raevyn asked if they could walk around.

"This is a nice area, Raevyn."

"Yeah. When we were kids, we'd come here all the time."

They strolled in silence, watching children on the swings. Kitts couldn't help herself. "So, you told your doctor about conversations you and Finch were having through the wall between your rooms and—"

"First of all, Encanto is not a doctor. She's a social worker. Second, you're probably thinking this was just me being psychotic like I was in the jail. I may be crazy but I'm not out of touch with reality."

"Hey, I'm not here to judge. Can you tell me when this started up again? When he returned and you started talking at night again?"

"Maybe a couple months ago. Like I keep telling everyone, he always disappears and then just shows up. He did this too when he faked his suicide."

"Faked?"

"Yeah, f-a-k-e-d. You know the word? He showed up at the house a few months before I went to the trials. I assume you know all about that. I really hate it when you people play dumb to get me to repeat stuff you already know. Okay . . . he made me drive him to the Bay Bridge; he said he wanted to kill himself; I went along. I was thinking I could talk him out of it. You know, like humoring him. When we got there, I begged him not to do it. He started to open the door, and I grabbed his arm, but he got loose and ran from the car." Raevyn's voice broke. She suppressed a sob and looked toward her lap.

"You need a break?"

She shook her head. "I called 911, but we couldn't find him. I told them I thought I could stop him. I was always stronger. I thought I could stop him."

Kitts thought that a sister driving her suicidal brother to the bridge he wanted to jump off was like a parent giving their suicidal child a gun, hoping they could talk him out of it. She dismissed this thought and studied Raevyn's face, curiously noting the absence of tears.

"Two months later, Finch just shows up again in St. Louis. I was already a basket case. Seeing him in the stands, laughing at me, put me over the top."

"When did you see him next?"

Totally annoyed, she blurted, "You already asked me that! Go back to interviewing school, Mineola. I don't know. Maybe two or three months ago."

"Are you still in contact with him?"

"No."

"No, because?"

"God! Because he's gone again, *okay?* I tried to talk with him and even looked around the house, in the attic and cellar, but he was gone. Whoosh."

"Gone?"

"Why are you just repeating my words!? Yes, gone. He's here, and then he disappears into the wind. But I already said that. I don't think you are listening very well. You should take a refresher course in listening."

Kitts brushed off her snipes and asked about Finch knowing details of the other crime scenes, not just Prokop's.

Raevyn shook her head. "That again? Snap, I guess Madrigal didn't hold much back from you guys. Not very helpful for a girl with trust issues."

"Well, did he . . . know things? Did he tell you details about other crime scenes besides the one with Prokop?"

Raevyn hesitated. "Kind of. I guess . . . but I'm not really sure. That part is fuzzy. I guess he told me where I could find those things online. I think he said he knew about others who were killed like Prokop, and told me where I could find out about those killings on the dark spider. That's what he called it, you know, the dark web."

Kitts was stunned. "Wait, he *didn't* tell you about the details himself?"

"I'm not sure. Maybe he did, maybe he didn't. He could've just told me where to look. Birdie could hack into anything. I figured he'd hacked into the police records and must've told me about that. I just can't remember."

"Whoa, let me get this right. You're saying he didn't *actually* share these details himself? *You* looked them up yourself?"

"Whoa, have your hearing checked. I just said I don't know. Why are you making a deal of this? You're upsetting the patient. I think he might have told me, but maybe he just told me where I could look them up. I really can't remember. This sucks. It's a big blur, and I'm done, okay? The mentally deranged have memory issues, you know."

37

DIFFERENT KINDS OF MONSTERS

The relentless buzzing wouldn't stop. Nicola awakened, groped for her phone, and cursed after knocking over a near-empty bottle of Irish whiskey.

"What! You better have a damn good reason for calling at 3:15."

"Oh, I do, Kitts," cackled Boz. "Wakey, wakey. They've found Burroughs up in Masonville, Michigan working at a 7-Eleven. Someone recognized him. Now, he is calling himself Barney Pike. Got you and Potter on a 7 a.m. flight. Locals got him under surveillance and are waiting for you two to be on hand when they collar him."

She sat up in bed. "Yes, Sir. I'm on the road in 20."

"Make it 10."

After a two-minute shower, she threw on clothes, took Tylenol, and inhaled a container of yogurt. On her way out, she eyed an unopened envelope from Potomac Animal Hospital. Fearing what she'd find inside, she just left it on top of the pile. *Best put that aside for now, boy.*

In a flash, she was speeding on I-95 toward Quantico, just 15-minutes after Boz's rude wake-up call. The darkness and rush of cold air settled her queasy stomach.

Toby Potter was sitting in Boz's outer office when she arrived. He nodded and gave her a slight smile, which left her wondering what he wanted. "It's show time. Hey, Kittsy, you don't look so—"

"She looks fine, Potter," interjected Boz, who had suddenly appeared at his office door. "How about you worry about yourself, okay?"

They followed him inside and took seats at his conference table where Siddharth sat in sphinxlike stillness.

He nodded and handed each a large envelope while Boz gave instructions. "Here are your tickets and the surveillance report. Burroughs was last seen going into his motel room last night and hasn't come out. We have people posted around the 7-Eleven and a tactical team at the Days Inn outside of Masonville. So, coordinate with the locals. Agent Le Duc will pick you up and drive you to the motel about 15 miles from the airport. You'll find the latest intel in your packets. Keep us dialed in. Any questions?"

They shook their heads and answered, "No, Sir."

Sidd cautioned, "We're assuming he's armed, so consider him dangerous. Watch out for each other."

Kitts nodded at Toby and replied, "Will do, Sidd. Got each other's backs."

They spent the first part of their flight silently scanning the surveillance reports. Then Nicola reclined her seat to get some sleep.

Potter broke the silence, spoiling both her nap and the nascent truce between them. "Remember, Kitts, I'm lead on this."

Without opening her eyes, she shot him a flippant salute and then dozed off.

LeDuc was waiting at the gate. "How was the flight, guys?"

"Peachy," smiled Nicola. "Any change in the target's whereabouts or movements?"

"No, considering it's still early, he's probably in bed. The TAC unit is on site. We've got armed officers and plain clothes there as well. You guys ready?"

The Days Inn looked like all low-budget motels. LeDuc pointed out the grounds crew and housekeeping staff working undercover. "We've got personnel on all sides, in and outside. This is your rodeo, so our instructions are to follow your lead."

"Roger that," barked Potter. "Locked and loaded. Let's go knock on the fucker's door, set the hook, and see what size catfish we pull up."

Kitts felt a wave of nausea at his cowboy lingo. "Hey Toby, we should try to talk to him before going all commando."

"Not your call, Kitts."

They put on Kevlar vests and FBI jackets. Officers were positioned in both stairwells. The two agents, Le Duc, and three armored officers climbed the stairs to the third floor and crept to room 322. They positioned themselves silently in front of the door. Kitts held a radio with a channel to Boz's office. Toby pulled his revolver from its holster, gave a hand signal, and the officers rammed the door.

"FBI! Cosmo Burroughs, you're under arrest!"

Clearly surprised, a disheveled man struggled to sit up in the bed.

"Put your fucking hands where we can see them! You can run, but you can't hide, asshole," shouted the lead agent. "Looks like you've been a busy boy, Burroughs. You did a number on the Morella woman and thought you'd get away scot-free, but surprise, surprise, here we are! Let's get him cuffed and bring him in for questioning."

Potter lowered his gun, turned, and shot Kitts a smirk, just as Burroughs lunged from the bed and grabbed the agent from behind, quickly yanking the weapon from his hand. He dragged Toby by the neck to the corner of the room, while pointing the revolver at the agent's temple.

The officers quickly aimed their guns at Burroughs.

"You've got the wrong person, Officers. I'm just an innocent man responding in self-defense to armed intruders breaking into my room. Besides, I don't know this Burroughs fellow. My name is Pike, Barney Pike."

"No, I'm afraid it's not Pike or Burnley for that matter, Dr. Burroughs." Kitts was quick to recognize the need to de-escalate. She spoke in a calm and measured tone. "And it's not Officer. I'm Agent Kitts, from the good ol' F bleeping BI. You can call me Nicola, if that makes this any easier, Doctor." She inched forward and slowly raised her hands. She could see shame and terror in Toby's eyes. Motioning for Le Duc and the officers to take a step back, she continued, "Let's all take a breath, okay? Hey, Dr. Burroughs, you're right about the intrusion. We just want to ask some questions. Sometimes my partner likes to act like a cowboy, if you know what I mean. He gets a bit rambunctious, but let's just slow this down before someone gets hurt."

Burroughs listened and tightened his grip around Toby's neck. He stared at her. She also saw fear in his eyes—the same fear she'd seen in the eyes of the village women they questioned in Afghanistan. Hollow eyes, no longer the menacing glare in his mug shot. He looked frightened, small, and gaunt. Vulnerable. She thought that he had once been a boy, someone's son. But like any cornered animal, his terror could quickly turn violent.

Agent Kitts continued, slowing her words and cadence. "I hear you . . . I do. Chattin's a good thing, right Doctor? Let's do that, okay? But first, you gotta put that gun down 'cause you're scaring the shit out of my partner."

Burroughs pressed the gun more firmly into the side of Toby's head. "Well, don't you think it's a little late for a friendly palaver? You're aware, of course, that Michigan has a stand-your-ground law. I'd feel more secure if we chat while your partner and I remain in this lovely embrace."

"Fair enough, Doctor. That's cool. Just don't shoot him, okay? So, let's talk then. I got some questions maybe you can answer to clear all this up. To begin with, why did you up and disappear from the community college? That got people suspicious and wondering."

After a pause, Burroughs answered, "Because people can't seem to forget or unsee. It doesn't matter if it's not true." Feigning a country accent, he drawled, "Y'all must know I'm a cause célèbre in these here parts. My picture has been in the newspaper more than Big Gretch, but not for the same reasons. Wherever I go, there I am, to quote John

Kabat Zinn. Meditate on that, thank you very much. It's not long before people stare, and then it clicks. 'Hey, he looks a lot like that perv from Ann Arbor. Same nose and deranged look.' They stare, and I stare back. Then, it's time to move on."

"I get it. That's gotta be tough. The way the stigma keeps following you. I'm sorry for that, but I also want to ask about the recent murder of a woman named Sophie Morella. I believe you might know her."

Burroughs didn't respond but held tight to Toby's neck.

"We know you both worked on the Ann Arbor research project with a lot of other folks, and that you were dismissed from that project. We're not here to judge, okay? We're just doing our jobs, trying to get our facts straight. We were hoping you could tell us what you know about Sophie Morella."

Almost 30 seconds passed before he spoke again. "Okay, Nicola . . . you asked and shall receive. About Sophie Morella, yes, I knew her, but I didn't kill her. I've committed sins, but killing is not in my repertoire. Can't say I'll send roses to her funeral though."

"Gotcha. Yeah, that's good. But Doctor, we found a box hidden in a desk drawer at your apartment in Escanaba with her name, along with those of the other dead doctors you worked with on the research, so...."

"Ah, the ARES Project as it was called. Yes, I knew them all quite well. ARES was an elegant study until it wasn't. It's a shame about their demise."

Toby began to wiggle around.

"Please tell your colleague to cease and desist, or I will shoot him in the head, Nicola."

"Hey Toby, chill dude. It's gonna be okay, isn't that right, Dr. Burroughs?"

After a beat, Cosmo continued. "I saw that dear Sophie recently decided to talk about ARES, perhaps to promote the book. But she took it upon herself to tell more stories about me than the project."

"Stories, huh? Yeah, I read the article in *People*. Pretty harsh. That must have been hard to have all that stuff about you brought up again."

"Oh, Nicola, if you're trying to curry my favor and be my buddy, I'm afraid it's a little late for that. Yes, I've been pilloried and thoroughly buggered. A monster—the community's boogeyman and village pederast. As I said, I'm a sinner with a weakness for pretty coeds, not children. I pled guilty but *not* to their lies about me. You must know there are different kinds of monsters."

"I hear you, believe me, I do . . . but I am curious why you kept those names in a locked box."

"Just my feeble attempt to cleanse my soul, Nicola. You see, I *hated* those people, Sophie included. I suppose I was a monster in my own way, but I was punished and lost everything for something I did *not* do. I doubt I'll ever see my children again. They'll deny they ever had a father. I could have sought retribution against them all or ended my own life. But, alas, I'm afraid I was a coward for both. Locking their names in a box was my foolish effort to eradicate them from my consciousness. I'm afraid it didn't work very well."

"Yeah, it never does. Believe me, I get that one. Tell me, what did you mean when you said the ARES was elegant until it was not?"

"I'm suggesting you're looking in the wrong place. Not everything is how it seems. What they were doing made the moral lapses of the Milgram experiment look like a peccadillo. Let's say I was something of a stalking horse for the ARES Project."

"Meaning what?"

"They ignored one abomination to invent something so horrendous they could make everyone look the other way. They feared I would blow the whistle on what they were doing, so they needed something to discredit me. Accusing someone of being a pedo and a wanker gets everyone to stop looking elsewhere. It's the beginning and end of the story."

Kitts was confused and didn't know how long she could keep him talking. She saw that his hand holding the gun began to tremble.

"You said different kinds of monsters. I'm not sure what you mean by that."

"What they did to those poor boys was the original sin. It was criminal. If you want to understand what is behind all of this, I suggest you look more closely at ARES. And don't expect to find any saints or the truth in their book."

Sweat poured down Burrough's face, and his hand shook. "It's been too long now. I'm afraid our chat has ended. I'm weary of the accusations, name-calling, tarring, feathering, and running from it all. No one ever believes a man when there are whispers about pedophilia. I was no saint when I raised concerns about what they were doing, and they took everything from me, and now I'm being accused of these murders. It's never going to stop when the equation of crime and punishment remains unbalanced. I'm afraid it's done."

At that, Cosmo loosened his grip around Toby's neck and pushed him forward. "My story ends here, Nicola." Before anyone could react, he put the revolver in his mouth and pulled the trigger.

38

Banished Boys

July 15, 2008
Oak Harbor Boys Camp
Pahokee, Florida

A quiet boy sat on his bunk, clutching his backpack. Beside him stood a large suitcase, home to all things he would need for the next eight weeks. The temperature was in the mid 80s. The camp brochure cautioned parents about the midsummer heat. Condensation began to form on the lenses of his thick glasses.

Quiet Boy had arrived by himself earlier that day. He waited with six other silent and awkward boys for the bus to Oak Harbor. When they arrived, he was escorted to Cabin 6, where the sign on the door read, ***Beware! Wolves Live Here.*** The quiet boy was told he would be sharing this cabin with three other boys and their counselor. Two boys were already inside unpacking clothes from their duffle bags. A thin, wispy-haired boy wore tight-fitting jeans and a blue dress shirt. The other boy, short and pudgy, had begun to change into his camp tee shirt and shorts.

The wispy-haired boy welcomed him. "Hi, I'm Kieran from Cherry Hill, New Jersey, and this is Jordie. I heard they have some snacks for us at the canteen. Wanna come?"

"No thanks," answered Quiet Boy with a tight smile.

The other boy, Jordie, spoke in a high-pitched voice. "They said that supper would be at 5:30 sharp, so maybe we can all go together."

The quiet boy shook his head, knowing he would not be hungry.

Jordie and Kieran filed out of the cabin, donning their black Wolf Pack tee shirts. As soon as they left, Quiet Boy began digging through his backpack searching for the comfort of his Gameboy. The cabin door swung open, and a tall boy with a suitcase and shoulder bag entered. He wore his long hair in a ponytail. He was neatly dressed in khakis and a tee shirt that read, "No, I Don't Think So."

He scanned the room before seeing the quiet boy sitting motionlessly on the lower bunk. Their eyes locked.

"Uh, dude you're on my bed."

Quiet Boy froze and then quickly moved without questioning the newcomer. He was scurrying to the top bunk when the tall boy spoke again.

"Damn, you didn't even ask me why. Do you always do as you're told? We'll need to work on that." After a beat, he smiled, held out his hand, and introduced himself. "I think we're going to be friends."

They exchanged names and shared their nicknames.

"Hey, dude. Our nicknames even sound alike," said Tall Boy.

Jordie and Kieran returned munching on beef jerky and Fritos. They introduced themselves to the tall boy. Chattery exchanges about their hometowns, schools, and favorite video games were suddenly interrupted when a large man entered the cabin. He wore a black and gray camp tee shirt and looked to be in his mid-30s. His name tag said, "Chase Bransby, Alpha Wolf."

He called out the camper's names from the pages on his clipboard and began to review the daily schedule and camp rules.

Counselor Chase fit the stereotype of the worst kind of bully, who wore his tee shirts two sizes too small and had a love affair with his own biceps. "Here's the deal, men. I'm gonna be your big brother, role model, drill sergeant, and coach. You've come here as whip socks and sissy boys, but I guarantee you'll be leaving here as men. We have a lot of smart people here who are gonna set you right. No more being prey. We want *you* to become the predators. That's right! You're gonna learn and grow. We're here to toughen you up. Your muscles are gonna be tired because I'm gonna be on your sorry asses in the weight room. But you'll learn to be tough. We have a full schedule for you boys. There are required activities and meetings throughout the week. You'll each be assigned an individual therapist who'll meet with you three times a week, more if they think it's necessary, to get your head screwed on right and get rid of your bad habits. We'll feed you three squares a day. You won't be hungry here. Have dogs, burgers, and pizza on the menu every day and barbecue on weekends. Plenty of good whole milk and ice cream for those who get with the program and—"

Tall Boy interrupted. "Excuse me Counselor Chase, but I'm vegetarian and lactose intolerant. I don't eat those things."

Chase seemed unprepared for such an interruption by a boy wearing a ponytail. He glared at the tall boy and sneered, "Is that right? What's your name, Ponytail?"

Tall Boy stated his name.

"See, I don't think you understand, Pretty Boy. This isn't Camp Minnehaha or the Fairy Village. You princesses didn't come here so we could cater to your likes and dislikes. Nope. Your parents sent you here because they weren't too happy with where you boys were headed. They sent your fat asses here to learn to conform, which means *we* dictate the terms so that *you boys* can get on a path of growth that'll lead you back to your natural God-given state as young men. So, no, we don't do vegetarian here. By the way, you'll need to lose that ponytail. There's plenty of healthy food here. So, when you get good and hungry, you'll eat." He looked at Jordie. "And you, Roly-poly, look like you could slim down. Turn some baby fat into muscle, Russell. Get you on a high-protein diet, son."

Counselor Chase read through the rest of the orientation materials and handed the boys their schedules, which included 6 a.m. wake-up, morning PT, and a hearty breakfast of eggs, bacon, sausage, and toast with pitchers of fresh homogenized milk. After breakfast, there was a Christian religious service, weight training, soccer or football, then classes. In the afternoon, the programming included individual and group therapy sessions.

After reviewing the camp schedule, Counselor Chase re-emphasized that each camper had been sent there because they had drifted and strayed from their natural course. "Fellas, it's our job, my job, to get each and every one of you boys back on that path to become the kind of young men that the Lord intended you to be."

And that's how the midsummer session of Oak Harbor Boys Camp began.

‚ ‚ ‚

Morning chapel services were led by Chaplain Dave. With fire and brimstone, he read biblical passages from Genesis 19 about Sodom and Gomorrah. He lectured about Leviticus 18:22, which taught that "You shall not lie with a male as with a woman; it is an abomination." He preached about the immorality and sinfulness of homosexuality based on I Corinthians 6:9-10, and Romans 1:26-28.

"Take heed, young sinners. Our Lord did not create the Garden of Eden for Adam and Steve. Do not forget this."

The chaplain recited this during every session lest the boys forget. He ended his sermons promptly and did not encourage discussion. This was strictly a one-man show.

Once, Tall Boy raised his hand and asked about biblical passages that spoke about agape, tolerance, and unconditional love.

"Aren't there Bible verses that don't condemn homosexuality, like I Peter 3:15-16, Ephesians 4:32, and Galatians 3:28? And some religions like Hinduism and the United Church of Christ welcome all people. So, I guess not everyone agrees with you, Chaplain Dave."

The chaplain glowered at him and called him a Jezebel who needed to listen and not question the word of the Lord.

After every chapel service, the boys marched off to their counseling sessions and group therapy. Quiet Boy and Tall Boy spent much of their time together. During downtime, they talked about their lives and families. Slowly, the quiet boy came out of his shell. They sat together during mealtime, while the tall boy picked at his food. They took walks together during breaks. One afternoon, they spotted a coral and black colored snake slithering across the path. They shared their interests in Dungeons and Dragons and Warcraft. They talked about their love for math and poetry. They confided in each other about hating their schools and how their parents were ashamed of them.

Both saw Dr. Sondra for individual reparative and aversion therapy as well as gender exploratory group therapy. She was a tall woman with a pointy chin and bony elbows. Sondra's dyed red hair fell carelessly to her shoulders, and her black-rimmed glasses encircled smudged lenses that refused to refract the sunlight. She referred to her techniques as "your treatments." Additional behavioral techniques were utilized with the goal of extinguishing non-traditional male interests and arousal patterns while attempting to shape what were deemed natural masculine interests and identities. Not one to question authority, Quiet Boy complied with his therapist's methods and techniques, but his quiet obedience ended when she began administering electric shocks.

One afternoon, Tall Boy saw bruising on his friend's wrists. "What is this?"

The quiet boy hung his head. After a minute, he wiped away a tear and said, "She didn't like my answers to her test, so she tied my arms to the chair and started giving me shocks when I said I still liked pictures of boys better than girls. When I cried, she got mad and started calling me a little wart. She said I wasn't ready to change my disgusting habits because I was a prissy little wart. She told me that her treatments were just like getting a shot from your doctor when you're sick, that they would sting a little now but would cure my unfortunate disease."

"These are evil people," responded Tall Boy. "They can't tell us who we are and who we should love. These are not good people. Dr. Sondra is a witch."

Unlike the quiet boy, accustomed to enduring hectoring and humiliation, Tall Boy never stopped challenging authority. One evening, when Quiet Boy returned to the cabin, he found his bunkmate missing. He walked outside and followed the sound of angry, drunk voices. He peered through the bushes and saw Counselor Chase and three others standing around the tall boy. They had stripped him naked and tied him to a tree.

A tall, skinny counselor with a menacing tone whacked him on the back with a stick. He slurred the words, "You're a fucking troublemaker, Alice, and we're here to help you learn respect and how to take your medicine like a man."

Counselor Chase barked, "See the problem with you, Ponytail, is you always think you're the smartest goddamn person in the room. You just can't listen and keep your mouth shut. You always gotta question everything and talk back. Well, I've had about as much of your crap as I can stand. The way I figure it, you can either get with the program and show us what you're learning here or face another three weeks of misery. It's your choice, Ponytail, but if I were you, I'd wise up and start showing us that you're getting what we're teaching here. I'm just asking you to cut the crap and stop whispering your bullshit to the other campers. So, what do you say?"

Tall Boy tried to speak.

"I can't hear you, ponytail. A little louder this time."

"I said, FUCK YOU."

The skinny counselor hit him again.

"That's unfortunate, ponytail. You can stay here all night for all I care." He turned to the skinny counselor and said, "You guys do what you want with him. Just make sure he's back in his cabin before dawn. And cut the shit with the stick, Darin, I don't want there to be a lot of marks on him like with the Geflin kid."

Quiet Boy watched as Counselor Chase and another senior alpha walked away, leaving Tall Boy with the two other counselors. When the others were out of sight, they began laughing and taunting, "Hey pussy, we know what you *really* want." Then, the quiet boy watched in horror . . . he opened his mouth and tried to scream, but paralyzed by fear and gasping for words that would not come, he backed away and retreated to the cabin.

The tall boy never spoke about what had happened that night by the tree, and the quiet boy never had the courage to ask. Over the next several weeks, Tall Boy continued to be subjected to late night taunting, name calling, and hostile treatment at the hands of the counselors. He lost weight because he refused to eat the food. He was made to do extra PT and not allowed to attend evening movies. He was given drugs that made him sick when he continued to react more strongly to photos of males than females. One night after movie time, Quiet Boy entered the cabin and saw the tall boy holding something in his pillowcase. It wiggled and writhed.

"W-what's in there?"

"Coral snake. They're all over this place if you get close to the lake. Time for payback, dude."

"B-but. You'll really get in trouble. Someone might get hurt."

Tall Boy looked at him intently. "And *you* haven't already been hurt with their name-calling, bullying, and electric shocks? You like being called a little wart? You realize they're all calling you that now. I'm sick of this freak show and everyone in it, you being the exception. These are bad people, and they must pay. Remember, they told us they wanted us to become the predators and stop being the prey. You ever heard the term apex predators? Time to show them we learned our lessons. I'm gonna start with our own alpha male and work up the food chain. With me?"

Quiet Boy began to shake, and his mouth was dry. He thought of his nickname. Then he flashed on what they had done to his friend. After a pause, he nodded and answered, "Yes!"

After lights out, the stillness of the night was punctured by shrieks coming from their counselor's bed. Somehow a poisonous snake had found its way into their cabin, crawled in between his sheets, and bitten him on the penis.

Counselor Chase was medevaced to Everglades Memorial Hospital. But with only two weeks remaining in the camp, the director and staff agreed the snake incident posed too significant a liability. The midsummer session at Oak Harbor was brought to an abrupt end. Parents were called, and their young men were sent home.

The boys in Cabin 6 packed their bags. By that time, Kieran's wispy locks had been shaved, and he was sporting a buzz cut. He now went by the name K-Man and had stopped talking to the others. As for Jordie, he had not developed the muscles their counselor promised but had gained 10 pounds from a daily diet of pizza and ice cream. There was a rumor circulating that Dr. Sondra and Chaplain Dave had developed severe infections after someone placed poison ivy in their beds. This story remained shrouded in secrecy because the camp director didn't want anyone to know that the two senior staff members were fornicating and committing adultery in the chaplain's quarters.

No one had been aware of this, not even the other counselors and professional staff. No one knew, except for a quiet boy and a tall boy, who were determined they would no longer be anyone's prey.

39

ARES

"What I'm trying to say is, if it hadn't been for her, I wouldn't be here. There, I said it, okay." Toby fidgeted and spoke haltingly in response to Sidd's question about his partner's actions during the Masonville incident. The others listened and thumbed through his report.

Kitts was feeling the heat of their collective eyes when Lenore began to applaud. The others, except for Saks, joined in to acknowledge her heroic action.

De Vere hailed, "Your quick reflexes in assessing the risks to protect Agent Potter reflect well on your military and law enforcement experience. Well done, Nicola."

Kitts smiled faintly and fought against the numbness she'd felt since Cosmo blew his brains out just five feet from where she was standing. She had been through this before. While others shared their praise and admiration, all she could think of was her frenzied efforts that night to scrub the blood and brain tissue from her skin and hair. She sat in the shower with a bottle of bourbon until the hot water turned cold. Still, she scoured ferociously until her skin felt raw.

Saks put down his cup and pen and said dryly, "Yes, kudos Agent Kitts. Tobias is now obliged to name his firstborn after you. But alas, you didn't find out if Burroughs knew anything about the Nevenmoores. I understand that in the heat of the moment, with the Sword of Damocles dangling over our young colleague's head, you had to act decisively. Bravo, indeed; however, I hasten to add that we do not rush to assume that Burroughs was telling us the truth about his innocence. To quote myself, nothing is ever as it seems, my darlings. He may have been involved but wanted to further excoriate the ARES team for, shall we say, throwing him to the wolves. Vengeance does not only exist for the living, hmm?"

After a pause, Sol's replacement spoke up. "Hello, Agent Kitts. I'm Dr. Gail Masters. Well done. It's clear why Dr. Mendelson had such great things to say about you."

I'll bet he did. Nicola gave a weak smile of acknowledgment.

Masters continued, "Bernice and I, with Pat's help, did a deep dive into the ARES Project, and I must say it wasn't easy. They have placed their internal files under lock and key, and it literally took a letter from Congressman Stiles of the Judiciary Committee to subpoena their records. I hear what Gideon is saying questioning Burrough's veracity and motives, but we found plenty of fire beneath all the smoke he was blowing."

De Vere looked at Pat as she spoke. "Thanks to Pat for her dogged persistence with the congressman. And Gideon, you are right when you say nothing is as it seems. This was most certainly the case with the ARES Project, especially the principal investigators. Tamerlane and Prokop, maybe the others too, had a political agenda masked by their landmark study." She reached for the remote and showed pictures of Arthur Tamerlane and Linus Prokop. "It's clear that the study's two lead investigators shared a secret from our ignominious past, which they quietly carried forward into the ARES Project."

Saks looked up. "Pray tell this secret, Bernie. We wait with bated breath."

"These so-called distinguished psychiatrists subscribed to a long-discredited offshoot of the American Psychiatric Association's gender studies interest group, which they called Gender Identity Modification Theory or GIMT. You may recall that though the Kinsey Report in the late 40s argued that homosexuality was a normal variation along a developmental continuum, ardent members of the GIMT group held fast to the categorical separation of homosexuality from normalcy. Their position was that it was a psychopathological divergence from normality, which should be identified as such and treated as any other form of mental illness or disease. We know that the American Psychiatric, Psychological, and Psychoanalytic Associations all renounced these beliefs and delisted homosexuality as a disorder over 50 years ago. But sadly, not everyone agreed. Gail has more on this."

"That's right. As recently as 2001, a handful of preeminent psychiatrists and psychoanalysts, like Robert Spitzer and Robert Stoller, were interested in psychological treatments that could change sexual orientation and identity. These were largely discredited, and Spitzer himself later repudiated this research, but unfortunately, these theories never disappeared completely. Powerful conservative religious and political groups poured millions into creating therapies and treatment centers to alter what they argued were deviant sexual developmental patterns, collectively referred to as DSDP."

De Vere shook her head in disgust. "The ARES internal documents show us that they used a systematic method to identify these DSDP subjects whom they concluded were showing signs of deviant sexual orientation or gender nonconformity."

Lenore said, "'Subjects' is such a cold term, isn't it, when we're talking about human beings? And these were just boys."

Kitts felt her numbness begin to thaw as she focused on Tamerlane and Prokop's faces on the screen. She recalled Sophie Morella's words about ensuring their sample was developmentally pure and free of deviant variants, and she suddenly grasped what Burroughs was saying about there being different kinds of monsters.

Pat spoke for the first time. "If I may add something here. I don't know if you will get to this, Dr. D, but the researchers sanctioned the admin team headed by Ms. Morella to notify parents about the boys they identified as developmentally unfit for the study."

"It gets worse," interjected Masters. "Tamerlane, but mostly Prokop, we think, recommended sexual orientation or gender-changing treatment programs when they debriefed the parents and explained why their sons had been dropped from ARES."

Sidd asked, "Did Congressman Stiles gain access to the names of these boys, by chance?"

Pat stood up and distributed two pages with the names of subjects who had been dropped from the study. "These are all the boys who were terminated between 2005 when they started the study, and 2020, when it ended. Their records show that they began with a total of 200 boys or subjects between the ages of 10 and 13 and disqualified 40 for various reasons. They coded 17 boys who were terminated as DSDP."

Saks asked, "Did they ever make clear their method for making such determinations, or should I say, *discriminations?*"

De Vere answered, "They employed screening scales and interviews to make these decisions. It appears that Tamerlane and Prokop conducted most of the interviews. But just to be clear, the crime was not simply labeling developmental differences as psychopathological or using psychometrically unsound methods to conclude which adolescent subjects exhibited these so-called deviant patterns. It was their outing these young subjects to their parents without involving the boys in *any* of it. Effectively, they went behind their backs and, in several cases, actually arranged for them to be sent to these questionable programs in the dead of night, in an attempt to change their sexual orientation and identification."

The room fell silent as the team members turned to read the names on the first page.

"Oh my God," blurted Kitts. "*Finch Nevenmoore* was in that study!"

Lenore said, "I know. It took my breath away when I saw his name. Of the 17 boys, three, including young Finch, ended up committing suicide. It's—"

Saks interrupted, "It looks like one or two more on this page have the initials *bc* or *cb* somewhere in their names."

The room was filled with sounds of shuffling paper as the team members turned to the second page. The room fell silent. One name leaped off the page—Roderick B. Cummings, the mathematics professor from Lawrence University, who was on sabbatical and unable to consult with the team.

"Why, *Hello*, Roddy. It's our old friend. Be still my beating heart," chimed Saks, who looked at others around the room. "To quote my dearly departed Aunt Maeve, 'Faith, bejaysus, and begorrah,' or in your parlance Tobias, "this is a *big fucking deal!*"

Sidd spoke up, "So, it seems that we should try to locate our friend who's been on sabbatical. It may be a coincidence—"

Saks tried to interrupt, but Sidd raised his hand to silence him. "Of course, Drs. Saks and De Vere will remind us that there is no such thing in this business."

Pat told the group that when they'd reached out to the dean's office at Lawrence University, she was informed that Cummings was unavailable because he was supposedly traveling abroad.

Sidd continued, "We must get on that, but in the meantime, we should arrange another conversation with the Nevenmoores about the ARES and Florida programs."

"Yeardley wasn't much help with the camp," added Lenore. "She said their mother was secretive and only divulged that Finch was at a Florida wilderness program to boost his self-confidence and social skills."

Kitts jumped in. "Ditto with Raevyn and the camp thing. She wasn't tuned in but said that Finch had tried to tell her he was gay. All she remembered was that he became a shut-in when he got back."

Sidd nodded. "Let's make this a joint interview to see what they can remember about ARES and Florida when they're sitting in the same room. I'm especially curious to know if Finch had ever been in contact with someone like Roderick Cummings from either program."

"Yeardley did say something about Finch talking to someone online, a Robbie or Ricky. She wasn't sure. I'll have to check my notes, but could she have meant *Roddy*?"

"Yeah, Raevyn said there was someone he would email," added Kitts, "but again, she was clueless and got pretty defensive when I asked about any of this. Truth is, I don't think she ever wanted to know."

Sidd replied, "All the same, let's go at them again and see what we can shake loose. I'd like you two to conduct the joint interview. Pat, can you arrange this?"

"Yes, Sir. I'll get on that today."

"In the meantime," suggested De Vere, "we should check all the residential programs and camps in Florida that provided some form of conversion therapy to adolescents during that period. We want to know if any of those programs treated boys like Finch Nevenmoore, who had been dropped from the ARES program."

Saks inserted, "And let's not forget the name of the eminent mathematics professor from Lawrence."

"My preliminary survey showed a lot of programs, more than you'd have expected," shared Pat. "Again, we might need to call on the congressman's office again to grease the skids for names of the boys who attended their programs. I'll let the boss know and get right on it."

Sidd brought the meeting to a close. As the others filed out, he walked over to Kitts. "You did a fine job, Nicola. I wonder, though, if you need a few days off? I can ask Lenore and Dr. Masters to meet with the Nevenmoores."

She flashed to the moment Burroughs' head exploded and drew in a breath. "No, Sir. I'm okay." Her thoughts then turned to the unopened envelope from Potomac Veterinary Hospital. She realized she hadn't been home for several days. "I'm good. Really. . .I'm fine."

40

ONE PATH FORWARD

That afternoon, Kitts joined Pat to work on canvasing the 15 programs in Florida that had offered conversion therapy between 2005 and 2015. She knew Pat Smith only from her quiet presence sitting on the periphery of the conference table. Pat always spoke deferentially and provided definitive answers, but never unfounded speculation.

Pat broke the silence as they started reviewing the list of programs. "Just so you know, Agent Kitts, I've always thought that true bravery and verbosity don't line up. The correlation is not high. I thought what you did in Michigan was impressive. Thank you for your service."

Kitts blushed. "I appreciate that. But I think the ones who do the most, say the least. Kinda like you, Pat."

"Well, with all that fanfare, let's see what we can find out about these programs. I phoned the Boz's office. He said he'd talk to the director about making calls to the congressman's staff if we need backup."

They worked for the next three hours calling the offices of program and personnel directors. For some, simply announcing that they were with the FBI was enough to cut through red tape. Nearly half of the programs sent rosters of adolescents they had treated in the last twenty years. The numbers were staggering.

"Well, this is interesting," muttered Pat. "Several of these programs apparently received hefty donations from One Path Forward. It was endowed by someone named Dr. Javier Weisman, a billionaire from

Cuba who lives in Miami. He's been an outspoken critic of LGBTQ rights for the last 25 years, way before it became politically popular among conservative groups. I'm curious if he had any links to ARES. They funded their research with institutional and private grants. Let's see if One Path Forward provided one of them."

After a series of deftly executed keystrokes, she chimed, "Voila. This shit—'scuse my French—is amazing. Like all studies that have used public funds, ARES was obligated to list all their funding sources. There it is, hidden in plain sight. OPF, One Path Forward, donated 2.5 million to the project in 2007, just as they were gearing up to admit their subjects."

Over the next two hours, Kitts and Pat burrowed through the records. Of the nearly three hundred boys who were treated by these programs, they identified 10 who had been dropped from the ARES Project.

Pat observed, "So, more than half the boys classified with deviant sexual developmental patterns from ARES were sent to these programs. Oh no! Here are the names of two of those boys who ended up killing themselves."

Kitts looked at the names. Still nothing about Finch or Cummings. "I guess it's possible that Finch went to some other kind of camp, and we don't know if Cummings ever did. Shit, if we widen our search to all the programs in Florida that *didn't* do conversion therapy, we're probably about—"

"Yeah, way too many."

Nicola's shoulders ached and her eyes grew bleary. "It looks like a few of these kids had been to another place that didn't appear on our original list, probably because it's no longer in business. It was a center called Oak Harbor in Pahokee, Florida, a tiny town along Lake Okeechobee."

"That's interesting," remarked Pat as her keyboard sprang to life. "Let me see what I can find out. It looks like . . . yeah, here's an old webpage from 10 years ago. Oh my, Prokop was on the board. He was a busy man who seemed involved in just about everything. Hold on a minute . . . *Holy cow*! It looks like the camp burned down in 2015. There was an electrical fire, but they never ruled out arson. Several of the boys who had been there were transferred to other programs. Yikes, it looks like some staff members died in that fire."

"Can we get some names of the boys who had been there?"

"No can do. All their records were lost in the fire. They didn't store anything on the cloud either, so everything went up in smoke. If Finch was at that place, there wouldn't be any records."

Nicola added, "All the more reason to check in again with the Nevenmoores. Maybe we can squeeze a few more drops from their memories."

Pat got up. "We've been at this for too many hours. I've got to get home and see what kind of monstrosity my husband has concocted for dinner. You should get some rest, too. But before I go, let me call Yeardley to set something up for tomorrow." She stepped out of the room.

Alone, Nicola thought about Sol. She pictured her empty apartment, where only a half-empty bottle of Jameson's and a dreaded letter from the vet awaited her. She glanced at her phone and saw five missed messages from the animal hospital. Kitts gritted her teeth and rubbed her temples, trying to narrow her thoughts about meeting with the sisters tomorrow. She had the ability to silence her humanity and adapt to the needs of the mission. It had always been her way. Lessons learned from the old Marines who raised her.

Pat suddenly burst through the door. "Um, Houston, we have a problem. It looks like Raevyn's gone missing!"

41

The Angels of Madness

A tall woman opened the door. "Hi, I'm Yeardley's friend, Dorine. She's back there with the police. Poor dear is just beside herself."

Kitts and Lenore followed her back to the sitting room. In a large, upholstered chair across from Yeardley slumped the hygienically challenged Lt. Edgar Bilch. Kitts immediately smelled the stale odor of tobacco. Behind Bilch stood a female detective taking notes.

He looked at the two agents and dismissively said, "This is a matter for the police. You must not have gotten the memo about jurisdictional priorities."

Fed up with this man's fuckery, Kitts snapped, "Oh, I'm sorry, this *is* an active federal investigation. You must've missed that part of your detective's exam, and maybe you should just—"

Lenore lightly touched Kitts's elbow and interrupted. "We understand, Lieutenant. Raevyn Nevenmoore has been a person of some interest in our ongoing investigation of Dr. Prokop's murder and the deaths of others we feel are related." Looking toward Yeardley, she said, "She is not a suspect, but we think she might have vital information that could aid in our investigation, Lieutenant."

They locked eyes until Bilch blinked. "Fine." He turned toward Yeardley. "We have what we need. If you think of anything, let us know. But from what you've said, your sister might be away on a bender and will show up like before. In the meantime, we'll get her picture out there and see what turns up. He stood up, put a Camel between his lips, motioned to the other detective, and asserted, "We're done here... for now, that is."

Dorine stepped forward to show them out. Kitts avoided looking at him but reflexively held her breath as he passed. She muttered, "Such a dick." The female detective heard and gave a faint smile as she walked out.

Yeardley waved her hand in front of her nose and coughed. "I'm sorry, he is not a very nice man. The woman was pleasant enough, but the lieutenant, he was here before and well."

Lenore sat on the couch next to Yeardley. "I'm sorry you're having to go through this. You must be—"

"Completely frazzled, at wit's end, and destroyed. Yes, I'm *very* worried."

Dorine took a seat on the other side of Yeardley. "She's been a wreck."

"Of course. We understand and will do anything we can to help. This is Special Agent Kitts, by the way. I'm not sure you've met, but she's talked with Raevyn a couple of times."

Yeardley looked up. "Yes, you were here the other day. Raevyn told me you took a nice walk together." Her voice broke, "I just can't believe this is happening."

Kitts took the chair across from them. "Did Raevyn say anything before disappearing? Was she acting differently?"

"No. We haven't spoken much. Since Dr. Prokop . . . well, sadly before that too. What with my work and travel and her moods, our communication hasn't been good."

"When exactly did you notice her missing?" Kitts pulled out her notepad.

"The day before yesterday, or was it the day before? I'm sorry. I'm not thinking straight." She looked toward Dorine.

"You told me it's been more like three days ago, hon," corrected

Dorine.

Kitts explained. "Gotcha. This is a whole lot to deal with, but if you can think of anything out of the ordinary that you noticed it could be really important."

Yeardley shook her head. "No . . . nothing. Everything has been—"

Dorine perked up. "The note that came in the mail the other day. Yeard, didn't you tell me that it didn't seem right or something?"

"The note? Oh, yes. I found it in the mailbox. I don't know how long it had been there. I thought it was from some religious group, like Jehovah's Witnesses, or something. I just threw it away because it seemed like nonsense, talking about angels and retribution. I think those groups can make people feel so uncomfortable."

Patterson and Kitts looked at each other. Lenore asked, "Do you still have it? Might it still be in the trash?"

"I don't know. I didn't think it meant anything. It was just annoying."

"Your trash doesn't get picked up until Friday, so maybe it's still in the bin in the garage. I can check if you think it might be important," offered Dorine.

"Yes Ma'am, that would be *very* helpful," Kitts enthusiastically replied.

Dorine was back in five minutes, holding the envelope in a tea towel. "I think this is it."

"Good thinking, using the towel. It might have prints other than Yeardley's," noted Lenore who took the towel from Dorine. She used her pen to open the envelope, gingerly pulled out the note, and read out loud.

The Angels of Madness are but masks for the righteous retribution that will follow,

Leading the betrayers to their final judgment.

Lenore spoke slowly, "Is it okay for us to keep this? It might be important." She shot Kitts a glance.

"Of course. Like I said, I thought it was just some nonsense that a fringe group was putting in all the mailboxes."

Kitts refocused. "Back to Raevyn's disappearance, I'm sure you already told the police, but has she ever disappeared for days at a time?"

"No, well yes. But that was something her brother would do. Raevyn was gone for a few weeks in the early spring. She went to visit a college friend in Boston, and she always told me about things like that so I wouldn't worry. But she wouldn't take her phone with her! It drove me crazy. She'd call me to check in, but I couldn't reach her. Can you imagine? When I'd object, Raevyn would say she wanted to disconnect her busy brain from all my chatter and worry. Sometimes, she stays out all night and maybe into the next day, but this is three or four days now." She began to cry.

Lenore placed her hand gently on Yeardley's shoulder. "Do you have the name of the friend she went to see in Boston? We can check with her too. Maybe your sister went back to see her."

"No, I'm frazzled, and my memory is fuzzy," Yeardley sniffled. "It might have been her friend Marney, but I'm not sure. I can probably find it."

Lenore noted it would be helpful to know names of all people Raevyn had been in contact with.

Dorine reached for Yeardley's hand. "It'll be okay, honey. They'll find her."

Kitts asked Dorine, "You can't think of any place she might have gone?"

"Like we told the detectives, her car is missing, so I guess that means she must have driven somewhere, right?"

Lenore clarified, "You must have told the police that her car was missing."

Composing herself, Yeardley responded, "Yes, no. I must have. I—"

"Actually, Yeard, you did, remember they said they'd run her plates."

Kitts asked again, "Can you think of where she might have gone?

Like, is there a friend she might have gone to visit?"

"I wish that was true, but Raevyn stopped having friends long ago. There is no place she would have gone, and she would have told me if she was going away for any length of time."

Dorine's eyes lit up. "What about the bay house, Yeard?"

"Oh my, no. I can't imagine that. Why would she go *there*? No one has been there for . . . I can't imagine it. I don't think she ever liked Calvert Cliffs all that much, even before."

Looking at the agents, Dorine sighed, "You're familiar, I assume, with how their parents were murdered seven years ago. Yeardley kept it—"

"Well, I *couldn't* let it go. I was *all* we had left."

Dorine explained, "They thought of putting it on the market, but that was too much to deal with. I helped her hire a management company to rent it, but there was very little interest. Truthfully, no one wanted to stay in a house with . . . you know, that kind of history."

"I think we should check that house." Lenore looked at Kitts. "What do you say?"

"You bet. A missing person is a police matter, but we need to find her first. Can you give us the address? Do you have a key?"

Yeardley nodded and slowly got up from the sofa. They followed her into an office. On the wall hung a portrait of a well-coifed woman, a grim-looking man, and three children—an older girl and two youngsters. The little girl had an ear-to ear-grin, while the bespectacled boy wore a dull and somber expression.

"It's a mess in here. I'm sorry, we don't use this anymore. Let's see . . . we keep it with some papers in Mother and Father's safe."

Yeardley leaned down to open the safe, cursing her memory as she tried to retrieve the combination. "No one has been in here. I don't think I've opened . . . there."

The door swung open. Three pairs of eyes peered into the small opening as Yeardley fished around inside the safe. She turned around.

The blood had drained from her cheeks. "The keys . . . they're not in here!" She began to frantically grope inside the safe. "They were on a key ring but...."

Kitts and Lenore moved in closely.

Yeardley dropped to her knees and cried, "Oh, please God, no! The gun is missing too!"

42

THE CLIFFS

The agents left Yeardley with Dorine, hurried to their car, and immediately called Quantico. Boz patched in Sidd. Lenore read the note.

Sidd responded, "We'll need to process that, but it sounds like the other notes."

"Yes, Sir. Sounds right out of Whisperer 1.0. We gotta find out who mailed it," volunteered Kitts.

Lenore added, "Or put it in the mailbox. It had no stamp. Boz, I don't think we can rule out Raevyn in all this. The note shows up, she disappears, and the keys to their house on the bay and gun go missing possibly at the same time. Plus, she was apparently away and incommunicado when the second murder took place."

Sidd continued, "The note speaks of hiding behind a mask of madness, possibly disguising murderous intent as insanity. We can't be sure, but I agree, she is certainly not looking any less suspicious."

Boz's voice boomed over the speaker. "Yeah, it may be starting to add up. Raevyn the bird just went from being a person of interest to a possible suspect. You two need to get your buns down to Calvert Cliffs pronto. We'll have state troopers in Maryland put out an APB on Nevenmoore. I don't know where she's gone, but right now, the Chesapeake Bay is our best bet. Ladies, she may not just be looney tunes, but a dangerous loon with a gun. That missing weapon changes the calculus."

Lenore agreed. "Right, Boss. The sister said no one has been to their vacation home for years. And as far as she knows, there was just this one set of keys. So, I'm thinking you want us to drive down there."

"Hell, no. I'll get a chopper to pick you up on the pad at Walter Reed. You'll be on the ground in Calvert County in about an hour. The state troopers and local PD will meet you at the Calvert Memorial Heliport." Boz paused before saying, "Put Kitts on."

"Hey, Boz. We're less than 15 minutes from Walter Reed. We can stand by for further instructions once we get aboard."

"Good. I'm sending Toby too. The boy needs to get back in the game. Just wanted you to know that he'll be meeting up with you at the hospital heliport near Calvert Cliffs. He knows that you and Patterson are calling the shots. Lenore's senior on this, but you two can work out the particulars."

"Will do. All good, Boz. Glad he'll be joining us."

"Ditto, Boss," said Lenore. "We're on our way. Will check back in when we get there."

They arrived at Walter Reed 10 minutes later and waited another 15 for the chopper. Once onboard, they radioed their ETA.

Boz cautioned, "Hey Kitts, she might not be alone. Remember, we're thinking there might be someone else involved. On the other hand, if that nutball Saks is right and she's got this split personality thing going on and thinks she's her dead brother, maybe that's who her partner is. God, I'm getting too old for this shit. Okay, now piss off."

"Gotcha. We'll be careful," assured Kitts. She got a grin out of Boz's thinly veiled disdain for Saks' psychobabble. *Oorah.* She also thought the DID thing was a bridge too far, but then again, she'd left all that mental health stuff back in Northampton.

They were met at the heliport by several state troopers. The local police chief had deployed a small tactical unit. Calvert Cliffs was a state park overlooking the Chesapeake Bay. Named after the massive cliffs that dominate the shoreline, Calvert Cliffs sat next to a small marine community. Although the quiet community was shaken by the Nevenmoore killings seven years earlier, it was unlikely the tactical team had seen any action since.

Ten minutes later, Toby Potter's chopper landed. "Hey. I've been briefed. We're locked and loaded on this side."

"Yeah, Toby, 'bout that—"

"I know, I know. Boz-man made it clear. You guys are in charge. I can play nice, be a team member, and all that. Really, it's cool, Kitts. I got your back this time."

The police chief arrived a few minutes later. He told them the Nevenmoore house was located in an area called The Cliffs, a handful of multimillion-dollar homes on a wooded bluff overlooking a rocky beach. Each had gargantuan windows with sweeping views of the steep cliffs and the bay below. The Chief called the area "Moneyville" and said that most of the homes were used only once or twice a year. He said that other than being the site of a double homicide, the Nevenmoore house had been badly neglected and would probably be torn down within the next year.

The property spanned more than an acre. Perched on a knoll, the house, large and white, enjoyed an expansive view of the rocky shoreline. A long driveway lined with black cherry trees led to its front. The lone car there was quickly identified as Raevyn's. The house was desolate and dark, a place time wanted to forget. The bushes, neglected and overgrown, surrounded an ornate front door, now home to a thriving colony of mold.

The agents and police officers gathered on the driveway. Kitts deferred to Patterson as the OIC. Lenore directed the small tach squad and four troopers to split into two groups to approach the house from both sides in the back. With earpieces and mics in place, the teams took position at the bottom of the hill in back of the house. Nicola and Toby accompanied one group while Lenore led the other.

Kitts's team positioned themselves behind a clump of spicebushes that provided a view of a large back deck. They could see a person in one of the Adirondack chairs.

Kitts focused her binoculars and radioed Lenore. "I have eyes on someone sitting on the deck. I can't tell if it's Raevyn. They're not moving. Gonna see if I can get closer." She signaled for Toby to stay put. Kitts drew her pistol and followed closely behind two tactical officers. As she got closer, she saw it was Raevyn, who appeared to be covered by a large blanket.

When they were within 30 yards, Kitts called out her name. There was no response. She signaled to the officers to let her approach on her own. Moving cautiously, she communicated her position to Lenore.

As she stepped cautiously onto the deck, she was stunned by Raevyn's appearance. Unresponsive, looking pale and gaunt, dark rings encircled Raevyn's eyes. Her lips were dry and cracked. She stared vacantly and did not react as Kitts moved closer.

"Hey, Raevyn. Whassup, girl? We've been—" Kitts stopped when she noticed Raevyn's right wrist chained to the arm of the chair. "Raevyn...Raevyn? Hey, it's me, Agent Kitts. You know, Nicola Mineola. Raevyn?"

Raevyn robotically lifted her left arm and pointed toward the bluff overlooking the beach. Nicola followed the unresponsive woman's finger, which she held frozen in place. Nicola squinted and shielded her eyes from the glaring sun on the water. Using her binoculars, she could see what looked like a lone figure walking along the rocky beach beneath the cliffs.

"Who is it? Who *is it*, Raevyn?" Nicola sharpened the focus and tightened her grip on the binoculars. Her eyes were drawn to the red-colored hat. The figure suddenly stopped, turned and looked up toward the house, then lifted the hat to wipe his brow. Sunlight reflected off his glasses. The same thick glasses she'd seen in the portrait. The same thick glasses she'd seen at the restaurant when a strange man delivered his cryptic message to Sol and her. She felt a chill. In a moment of clarity, she knew. She was looking at Finch Nevenmoore, very much alive and looking right at her with a grin on his face.

"Oh my God. Is it . . . it's your brother."

Raevyn remained mute.

Catching her breath, Kitts radioed Lenore and Toby. "There's a man on the beach. You're not going to believe this but, fuck, it looks like Finch Nevenmoore, come back from the dead! I've got Raevyn here, and she's in bad shape. We need to call an ambulance, but you guys get down to the rocky beach now and stop whoever that is."

"Right," shot Lenore, who quickly instructed her team to get to the beach ASAP. "There's a set of stairs down to the beach. We're on it!"

Kitts gently lowered Raevyn's wooden arm. "What did he . . . did he do this to you?"

Raevyn nodded slowly.

"I got you. It's gonna be alright. Help will be here soon." She sat with Raevyn, who kept her eyes closed. Kitts lowered the blanket to see the bruising around her chained wrist. She saw what looked like needle marks on her forearm. "I got you, Raevyn."

Fifteen minutes passed before the EMTs arrived. They brought a stretcher onto the deck and checked Raevyn's vitals.

The EMT said, "She's badly dehydrated and appears to be drugged. We'll get an IV started and get her to the ER."

At that moment, Lenore radioed that they were still searching for the figure on the beach. "We haven't found him yet. It's a bit of a labyrinth down here. Whoever it was must've gone back up into the trees or down into the caves here at the base of the cliffs. We've called for backup. We need more bodies to cover the area, but if he's down here, we'll get him."

43

Lament of the Loons

Kitts was still reeling when she phoned Boz about Raevyn and the figure on the beach. "She's getting checked out by the EMTs who'll take her to the hospital. Meanwhile, we got Lenore's team still searching the beach. Boz, you won't believe it, but I swear, I think it's Finch Nevenmoore. He's—"

"Dead, Kitts. Maybe you didn't get the memo. The whole damn family was full of loons, but unless they've done some voodoo to bring him back, you saw something else. We'll have to get your eyes checked when this thing's over. For now, we've got people searching for who or whatever you think you saw. In the meantime, you need to go with that girl to the hospital. She's still a suspect, you know. Keep us posted with what's going on down there. I'll let Sidd know where we're at. And Kitts, no more ghost talk, okay? Now fuck—"

"Yes, Sir, I will definitely do that. And no more ghost stories."

She radioed Lenore. "Hey, Raevyn's in bad shape. Boz wants me to ride in the ambulance and question her when she's more stable. He doesn't buy the Finch thing, but I think she could still be in danger."

Lenore was slow to respond. "If you *did* see someone, they're gone now."

"*If?*"

"Yeah, we've seen no sign of him or anyone on the beach. You sure it was a person down here?"

"Positive."

"Well, the sun against the water was pretty bright, and we were all looking up at the deck. So, I don't know . . . but we just got a new crew to help search the caves. We'll keep looking, Nicola."

Kitts tried to brush off her uneasiness at Lenore's words, "*If you did see someone.*" She climbed into the back of the ambulance. Raevyn was on an IV drip and still unconscious. At the hospital, they triaged her in the ER and admitted her an hour later. Nicola had spoken with the police chief and requested a deputy be posted outside her door.

The doctor found Kitts by the nursing station and provided an update on Raevyn's condition. They found fentanyl in her system and treated her with Naloxone. He said they expected a full recovery.

"We got ahold of her sister who told us about the patient's bipolar disorder. Her lithium levels are pretty low, so we'll restart her on that as soon as she is medically clear. She's coming out of her fog but is still in rough shape. On top of a near-fatal drug overdose, she was badly dehydrated. And what with the bruising around her arms and wrists, looks like she might have been beaten as well. You should be able to see her when the nurse comes out, but don't get her worked up."

Kitts nodded to the deputy seated outside her room. Raevyn was awake and immediately responded to seeing Kitts. She appeared surprisingly subdued.

"Mineola."

"As you live and breathe. How ya feeling?"

"Like a building collapsed on my head." She hesitated, then broke down. "I–I thought I was going to die. He said he was going to kill me. I'm so sorry. I—"

"Hey, shhh. What are you sorry about?"

Raevyn choked on her tears. "I should have told you he was dangerous, but I was afraid and didn't want to face it."

"Afraid of what, Raevyn? What couldn't you face?"

"That he killed people. Prokop, and I think our parents."

Kitts poured her a cup of water. "Here, take a sip. You know this for a fact, that your brother killed Prokop *and your parents*?"

"My parents. I . . . he never said this, but he always dropped hints. He used creepy words like a 'final retribution' and said that the wicked would be punished. But I never...."

"What about the others?"

"I don't know; I'm not sure. He was gone for a long time, then showed up again this spring."

"Weren't you gone around that time too, seeing a friend or someone?"

"Yes, but that was before. He came back before then. It's hard to focus."

"Raevyn, who was the friend you visited then? I'm just trying to clear this up."

"Yeah . . . Marney, I think. But that has nothing to do with this. Can we please talk about that later? I'm just...."

"Okay, sure. You've been through hell and back. I get it."

"When he showed up again, I had no idea where he'd been. He would never tell me. Everyone thought he died five years ago. So did I. But when I saw him in St. Louis, sitting there with his shit-eating grin, I lost it. Then, when he showed up again like some kind of ghost, he made me keep it secret. He said everyone would just think I was psychotic if I said anything."

Kitts struggled to keep track of Raevyn's stories about Finch's repeated disappearances from her life only to reappear from nowhere. "Man, that's a lot of comings and goings. So, no one else saw him sitting in the stands that day?"

"No! Of course not. Like I said, everyone thought I was crazy anyway, so I never said anything. When he came back, he told me I owed him, and that this was interest on the debt or some kind of Finch bullshit like that. He knew all the hiding places in the house. Birdie, uh, Finch made me tell him when Yeardley was away or working late so she wouldn't find out he was there."

"And Prokop?"

"He hated Linus and talked about killing him. He pressured me to help, but I said no way. That was too much. I may be a complete lunatic, but I'm not a killer. But I did tell him Yeardley was making me see Prokop again. Then, when I got to his office that night, he was dead. It was horrible and I—"

"So, you *were* there but weren't involved in his—?"

"No! Of course not! I just found him and panicked."

Kitts worried that her questions had become irritants. "It's okay. Hey, I get that." After a pause, she asked, "So, you walked in and found him like that. Wow, that must have been—"

Raevyn cut her off with a rapid flood of words. "Horrible. What do you think! I didn't know *what* to do, just had to get into his file cabinet, wasn't thinking straight but had to get my records and Finch's too, 'cause I knew they'd be looking into all his patients, especially me because I was the last one that day."

"Hey, hey Raevyn, just slow it down, girl. Take a breath. Now, you're saying you knew you were his last patient?"

"It was 6:00. I knew he didn't see anyone after that. Why are you asking me this? Are you listening? I didn't kill him!"

"I'm sorry, I'll let it rest. I know you've been through hell." Kitts realized her questions were making things worse. She decided to back off and let Raevyn talk freely.

Over the next hour, she detailed the whispered communications with her brother and how one night they just stopped. Raevyn hoped he'd disappeared, once and for all, so she could go on pretending he would finally leave her alone.

Then she slowed down. Her speech became halting. "Like that night I drove him to the bridge . . . I wished he would jump and be out of my life forever. But he *always* comes back, like in St. Louis . . . and now."

"And then you heard from him again?"

Raevyn's words came more slowly. "He called a week ago begging me for help just like he did before the bridge. He *always* twists my feelings and squeezes out more guilt. Every time I saw him, I felt like crap, and he knew it. I tried to get rid of these feelings, but like my brother, they *always* come back. To tell the truth, when I drove him to the bridge that night, I hoped he'd jump. I did. I wanted him dead. Wanna know the whole truth? I thought I should jump *with* him. Like we've always been joined in this sick bond and could never really get away from each other. If I jumped too, I'd never have to see him or feel like shit again. But I chickened out. No surprise, huh? When he called last week, he sounded desperate like before. I had to make it stop. So, I came up with a plan to end this sickness between us." Her words gave way to more tears.

Kitts poured water. "Here, Raevyn. Take another sip. Just breathe, okay? Man, it sounds like you've been carrying a ton of shit." She waited for Raevyn's tears to subside. "You were telling me what happened when you got to Calvert Cliffs."

"When he called this time, he begged me to come to the bay house. He wanted to be with me one last time. He was crying and said he was miserable, that he was done with his crap life, this time for real. He said he was *so* sorry for making me feel guilty and scared. He just needed me to be with him, 'cause he was tired and in so much pain, right? So, I went," she said, making air quotes, "*to help* him this one last time. He said I would never have to worry about him again. My debt would *finally* be paid, like he was giving me a break or something. But I knew he was manipulating me, like he always has. I wanted to make it stop. And what better place to end this horror show than the house on the cliffs? You know, return to the scene of the crime."

"You said you had a plan, and that's why you took the gun. You were going to stop your brother from—"

"Killing more people and even maybe me! Have you heard any of this? I didn't know what I was going to do. I just knew I had to stop him."

"Yeah, I'm listening. Sorry, I *am* hearing you . . . so, you were going to end things for both of you."

"Yes! No! I don't know! I just had to make it all stop—him, and me being tortured by these feelings."

Mindful of her fragile state, Kitts tried to balance the need for information with concerns that more questions could push Raevyn off a cliff and lead to a repeat of what happened in the DC Jail. "Okay. I get it, Raevyn. You wanted your pain to stop. You were starting to tell me what happened when you got there."

"He acted *so* happy to see me. 'Oh, Cobie, you came. You're the only one, Sister. We can be together one last time before we say our final goodbye. You were with me when I came into the world, and I want you with me when I leave it.'"

"That's some heavy shit, Raevyn. It sounds like what he was telling you on the drive to the bridge five years ago."

"Yeah, but he wasn't threatening like he was back then. He seemed calm. He had prepared this elaborate feast—appetizers, pasta alfredo, Caesar salad, a bottle of merlot. He called it 'a celebration of life'—typical Finch weasel bullshit. When we were eating, he said it was Birdie and Cobie's last supper. Can you believe that?"

Kitts sat motionless, transfixed by Raevyn's story. She realized there was no need for further questions. What she needed was to sit with her and let Raevyn get her story out. She had pulled back the curtain and was giving Kitts a front-row seat.

"Then, he whispered that he had one final story to tell me but that it would have to wait. We finished dinner, and he laid out his plan for the evening. We would sit together, sip our wine, and listen to music. When the time was right, I was supposed to administer the potassium chloride, the stuff he'd gotten for this special occasion. That's what he was calling it. I wanted to vomit. It was so pathetic. He told me he needed me to sit with him and hold his hand while he just drifted away from a world that had been so cruel to him. That's how he put it. But then his mood changed, and he got really quiet. He put on this old Carole King song, *It's Too Late,* and I thought, *What the fuck. Why this song? What are you trying to tell me Birdie?* He got this scary look and said it was time for his final story. It was a twisted version of the Grimm fairytale *The Juniper Tree,* about a wicked family that committed evil acts against a helpless little boy. He got this really crazy look in his eyes and started blaming me for his miserable life. That's when I felt dizzy and realized my fucking brother had put something in my wine. I passed out. When I came to, I was tied to the bed."

"Oh my God, Raevyn, you were tied to that bed for three days? I can't imagine what that must have been like."

"He was acting like someone I didn't know. He got really agitated, and I heard him screaming at someone on the phone. My own brother put a needle in my arm and said he wanted to watch me waste away. No food, no water. 'Now, *you* will be the vanishing twin and *you* will see what it's like to have *everything* taken from you. *You* did this to me my whole life. Now, it's your turn to waste away, *Cobie.*' He said our parents had to pay and now it was time for my final payment." Raevyn's words stopped, and she began to sob like a child alone in the world.

Kitts noticed that no tears accompanied her mournful cries, but she told herself that people cry in different ways. Still, she couldn't shake her confusion as her empathy wrestled with her doubts. When she first met Raevyn at the jail, Kitts was unbalanced and unnerved by this woman's chilling, Medusa-like stare. Now, she felt unbalanced and confused by what she was hearing. She struggled to find her edge as a sharp-minded investigator but found herself wanting to believe Raevyn. She felt sympathy for her pain, which seemed raw and visceral. When Kitts went to speak, there were no further questions, no false words of comfort. In the void, she reached to hold Raevyn's hand. "I'm so sorry."

Raevyn composed herself. "My whole family was insane. My

mother and father were sick fucks but knew how to hide it from the world. I did that for a long time too, until I couldn't. An almost perfect fucking family—doctors as parents, a famous mother, money, a big house, and me, Raevyn the champion on a box of Wheaties. Only Finch wore his emotional scars for everyone to see. But no one knew I was just as fucked up. Probably even more. I feel I've lost everything, but I'm not sure what I ever really had. So much of it was fake. Only Finch knew the truth. I was *always* broken; now, I'm just hollowed out and empty. I should have died in that house."

Over the next hour, Kitts listened to Raevyn's account of what had happened while she lay drugged and chained to the bed. She told of Finch's rants about their parents' abuse—their mother's disgust and demeaning names for him, and their father's physical punishments that turned into sexual torment.

Later, Raevyn's lament turned fearful. "Did you find him!? He was on the beach. Did they get him!?"

"They have a bunch of people looking. They'll find him. I promise." Kitts winced, knowing she'd made a promise she might not be able to keep. "In the meantime, I'll make sure we post another deputy outside your door."

A nurse came in and said it was time to bring the visit to a close. The patient needed to rest.

Kitts was on emotional overload. Sickened by what she'd heard, she was also saddened that Raevyn had turned a blind eye to her brother's torment as a child. But regardless of how much Finch had suffered, Raevyn had been badly damaged too. Cobie and Birdie. Fledglings hatched from the same egg and left in the nest. One fell out. She felt sorry for Raevyn and afraid for what lay ahead—recovery from severe trauma, a chronic mental illness, and being a suspect in an ongoing FBI investigation, and if what she was saying was true, a target for her brother's revenge. She wondered if it was too late for her, if Raevyn was beyond help. And how much of her outrageous story was even true?

Nicola decided to schedule an appointment with Idina Madrigal in hopes of getting answers to those questions before finalizing her report on the events at Calvert Cliffs.

Still, there was another feeling she couldn't shake. Fear. From their first contact to the last, there was something about Raevyn that frightened her.

Nicola radioed Lenore. There had been no sighting of the man on the beach. Two more deputies arrived at the hospital. One offered to drive her back to the Cliffs to continue the search.

The sun beat down, and the traffic thickened on the way back. The air inside the police car felts heavy. Kitts rolled down the window and saw cars parked alongside the road. People were lined up and carrying signs. Some read, "Stop Killing the Birds NOW." She heard others chanting, "Save the loons!"

She asked, "What's with all this?"

"Got a big protest goin' on 'bout all our birds dying around here," replied the deputy. "They say it's the pollutants in the water. Mercury and lead poisoning from the fishing lures and whatnot is making the birds sick. Some are just wasting away. It's so damned sad what's happening to the loons."

PART FIVE

EVERMORE THE WHISPERER

Their selfishness knows no bounds as they've destroyed others
Whom they've abused and thrown away.
But the sword of retribution will never rest and will ris—

44

THE TALL MAN

Armed officers were stationed at each entry to Briggs Hall. The Lawrence University campus police accompanied the officers and SWAT Team. Agents Kitts and Potter entered the front door and found the administrative suite. Toby read the directory and found his office on the third floor. Kitts and three officers entered the admin space. One was carrying a tactical entry tool. A worried-looking woman got up from her desk and approached them.

"Uh . . . hello. I'm Ms. Cassidy. May I help you?"

Kitts introduced herself and told her who they needed to see.

"I'm afraid that's not possible, right now. The professor has been away and is unavailable right now. He's blocked off his afternoon schedule to prepare for his convocation address. But I can make an appointment. He'll have time in his schedule sometime after 1:00 tomorrow."

Nicola flashed her badge. "Thank you, Ms. Cassidy, but we'll see him now."

Toby called out, "Third floor!"

The two agents and officers walked up three flights of stairs as Trudy Cassidy chattered nervously at their heels.

"Honestly, if I can just tell him what this is about, I can—"

"Not going to happen, lady. We've got this," snapped Toby.

Things had come together quickly since leaving Calvert Cliffs.

Search teams were still looking for the man on the beach, who so far had eluded detection. Pat and her team had tracked the professor's movements in the last four months and found his credit cards had been used in the cities where each victim had been killed. Analysts also found a multitude of encrypted messages on a laptop in the bay house, sent to an email in Appleton, Wisconsin. They traced the IP address to an apartment near the university.

They reached the third floor and followed the signs to the Mathematics Department. The hall was dimly lit and lined with yellowed photographs of dour-looking faculty from the last 100 years. The agents and officers reached his office and read the name beside his door. "Rodrick Bertram Cummings, Ph.D., Assistant Chair, Mathematics Department."

Trudy pleaded, "*Please*, let me tell him you're here. I'm not sure he's even in there." She suddenly called out, "Professor! Professor? Bertie? Are you in there? I have some people here who insist on seeing you."

After a long pause, the professor responded dismissively, "I asked not to be disturbed until after the ceremony, Trudy. Please have them make an appointment."

Trudy shrugged and looked helpless. "Well, they really are quite insistent and have some officers with them and—"

At that, Kitts nodded to the officer with the entry tool, who burst through the door.

A tall man with a graying ponytail pushed back from his computer. "WHAT THE HELL! Trudy, call the campus police now!"

With fear in her voice, the confused secretary responded, "I'm sorry, Professor, but they're already here."

"What do you think you're doing!? I'm a tenured professor and have an important event this afternoon. This is completely outrageous! Trudy, call Dean Ellison."

"Already been notified," answered Kitts. "Back away from your desk and keep your hands where we can see them." She drew her gun and directed the officers to confiscate his computer.

The tall man turned and barked at her, "Just *who* do you think you are!?"

"Tweet, tweet, *Bertie*. We're the F motherfuckin' BI, and your ass is under arrest!"

45

The Truth is Out There

The BAU team greeted her warmly, praising her field operations that led to the arrest of Bertie Cummings while he was in the act of writing another twisted poem. Since his apprehension, there had been no further killings, and with Raevyn back under surveillance, police protection had been discontinued for Sol Mendelson and Idina Madrigal.

When Nicola asked about Finch, there was an uncomfortable silence and shifting in chairs.

Sidd spoke after a pause. "About that. It has been over a week, and we haven't had any leads. Professor Cummings has been implicated in the killings, and we have locked him down. As to the question of an accomplice—"

"Excuse me," interrupted Saks, "Siddharth, if I may, as they say, cut to the bone. We simply do not have any real evidence to suggest the presumptively deceased Finch Nevenmoore was involved in her abduction, if there ever was one, or in any of these murders. However, the sister, who is very much alive, is not in the clear."

"Thank you for that Gideon, but I think we need to give serious consideration to what Agent Kitts is telling us in light of what she found and reported observing on the beach at Calvert Cliffs." He turned to Nicola and continued, "The sun was high overhead and reflecting off the ocean when you attempted to shield your eyes from the glare as you raised your binoculars toward the east. Isn't this what you reported?"

"Yes, but I was still able to see."

An uncomfortable silence settled over the room.

Sidd turned to Pat who projected two large photographs of the beach on the screen. "Nicola, please look at these photographs that were taken from your exact position on the deck at the same time of day you found Raevyn. Please direct your attention to the area where you saw a figure you believed to be Finch Nevenmoore."

Kitts and the others studied the photographs with arrows pointing to a rock formation on the left side of the beach. "Take your time, Nicola. Now, is this the area of the beach you were looking at through your binoculars?"

Nicola examined the pictures. "I . . . believe it was generally, Sir, but—"

Pointing to the area beneath the arrows, he asked, "Can you tell me what this looks like?"

"I don't know. It's a pile of rocks. But—"

"It is a rock formation, but what else does it look like?"

"A person? It looks like it could be a person." Her stomach dropped. Nicola suddenly felt she was on trial, but more disorienting was the abrupt assault to her senses and her confusion about what she had seen. She tried to recompose herself. "But this is *not* what I saw."

Gail Masters was quick with a comment. "Perception and memory can be easily distorted and molded to fit our belief systems. I'm sure you've heard of the Rorschach Test," lectured Masters with a patronizing tone.

The room was silent again. Despite her misgivings, Nicola wanted to believe Raevyn, but even more than that, she wanted to believe her own eyes. Her survival as a Marine and deputy had always depended on her clarity of perception and ability to survey and accurately interpret the environment. Staying alive depended on the acuity of her senses and judgment. She had replayed the events of that day—what she'd witnessed on the deck and the beach—a thousand times. Now, uncertainty and confusion began to rock her confidence.

Lenore came to her defense. "But what Nicola saw on the beach was not the only thing she found that day."

Kitts's words tumbled out. "That's right. Look, I hear what you're saying about the beach and sun and all that, but again, what I saw *wasn't* a pile of rocks. And are y'all forgetting we found *his* computer with messages from Cummings? They *were* communicating. Plus, we have Raevyn's account that he drugged her, not to mention my finding her chained to a chair like an animal and dying of thirst. We have evidence from the hospital of fentanyl in her system and signs of physical trauma. We have her as a witness. She said he was gonna kill her. And I didn't see some rock. I saw *him* on the beach. And remember, they never could prove with complete certainty that the body they pulled out of the ocean was Finch. No DNA? Doesn't that make you wonder? I sure do."

De Vere looked up. "That's all true, Nicola, and that fact has bothered me. They never found *his* body, but they did recover the remains of *a* male body. They conducted detailed anthropometric analyses on the remains. It wasn't DNA, but the examiners used these other means and concluded it was most likely Finch Nevenmoore. With regard to your other points, *yes*, we can all agree that you saw something. And *yes*, you found *a* computer, and *yes*, Raevyn was certainly in bad condition. All true. But what we're saying is that we haven't established that Finch Nevenmoore, or anyone else for that matter, was ever there."

"But I *saw* him. He looked right at me."

Lenore looked at her, a trace of sadness in her voice. "But, but we didn't. I'm sorry Nicola."

Surely, Raevyn's report of how her brother had drugged, beaten, and starved her would make others realize what she was saying was true. But no one did. They had all made up their minds.

Gideon Saks aggressively pushed his theory that Raevyn suffered from severe DID with multiple alters and had colluded with Cummings while she acted as her dead brother. "Our favorite Poe character, Miss Raevyn N, has *always* remained at the center of the storm. Her psychopathology *is* the driving factor. You'll recall that I believed her to have a dissociative identity disorder, and I think my theory has been borne out. As I've described thoroughly in my many publications, Miss Nevenmoore suffered multiple traumata—growing up in a narcissistically neglectful household, then suffering the brutal murder of her parents, the suicide of her brother, and humiliation on the world stage. We know that she loathed her brother, felt guilty about her mistreatment of him, resented her dependency on him, and, in the end, wanted him dead." Looking toward Toby, he added, "And as one of our colleagues might say, 'Slam, bam, and thank you, Ma'am.' Against the backdrop of her trauma, she was unable to contain, much less integrate and accept, the multitudinous contradictions and highly charged affectivity. Thus, our dear Raevyn formed internal splits, creating a central alter personality of her dead brother. By assuming his identity, she simultaneously saw to it that she enacted his revenge in partnership with a cohort—another boy Finch had told her about, i.e. our dead friend Roddy Cummings, who had also been ejected and abused by the ARES Project. You see, by taking on the identity of her dead Birdie, she was able to make good on her debt to him and join forces with another Bertie to assuage her guilt and atone for how badly she treated him."

Kitts was stunned. "Sure, I get it. Their relationship was messed up, and she was mixed up, but she was also really scared of him."

"Precisely, Agent Kitts. She was so scared that she wanted him dead. We hate that which scares us the most. Isn't this what she told you? That she'd gone to the beach house with a gun to kill him, just as she had driven him to the bridge so he could kill himself five years earlier?"

Kitts tried to parry. "But I think she was desperate and afraid of what he might try to do to her. She knew he was involved in the murders and felt threatened."

"I'm afraid you're overlooking the fact that she drove her suicidal brother to the Bay Bridge five years ago. Who does that? Let me remind you that this event took place long before any of these people were killed or her declaration that she was frightened of him. She simply despised her twin brother and wanted him dead."

Masters cleared her throat, leaned forward, and folded her hands on the table. "I agree with my colleague that Raevyn has deep-seated issues that are relevant here. But, with all due respect, Gid, I think your elegant construction of DID as an explanation is a bridge too far, a top-heavy and theory-laden formulation, when a simpler explanation for her behavior will suffice. Despite the marvelous work that you've done in the field, Gideon, let's put aside the whole DID thing and view Raven as a narcissistically disturbed young woman. Yes, there is trauma and severe bipolarity involved, but what you're not seeing is the degree of psychopathy. Gideon asks who would drive a suicidal brother to the bridge he was intending to jump off? A psychopath would."

Toby nodded forcefully at the word "psychopath" and quietly muttered, "I knew it."

As if speaking to a jury, Masters continued to argue her theory of the case. "Raevyn knew she was a suspect, so what better way to remove suspicions than to make herself look like another victim. I don't think there is a better explanation than to view her as a clever, malignant narcissist who's been playing us all along. I believe she facilitated the death of her brother, then pretended, *not dissociated*, to be him, and established contact with someone, i.e., Cummings, whom she knew from her brother lusted for revenge and would go on a killing spree. Let's not forget that Raevyn had plenty of reasons to hate those in the psychiatric field. In Cummings, she found a fellow psychopath—another twin, if you will—who shared her thirst for blood."

Sidd interrupted, "I'm sure you realize that dual serial killers are quite rare and more often the stuff of fiction."

Lenore mused, "Weren't there two serial killers in that James Patterson book, *Kiss the Girls*?"

Masters responded, "Sure, it is quite rare, but this isn't an Alex Cross novel. I submit that like the documented case of Leonard Lake and Charles Ng in the 1980s, Raevyn and Cummings formed a killing bond. Finally, I also believe that she may have used her bipolar illness to throw us off the trail. First, she played up her insanity. Then, when she continued to be viewed as a suspect, she played the victim card, all the while concealing her clever deception with an air of helplessness and manic confusion. The fact that she has a bipolar disorder and has previously been psychotic does not define her. She has a personality too, which is driven by dark traits and fueled by revenge. Just because one suffers from a major mental illness does not mean that his or her symptoms cannot be employed in the service of other aims. Oh, and after murdering Prokop, she tried to get into his file cabinet and remove any previous records that might have documented her murderous fantasies."

Sidd listened as the dueling specialists espoused their competing theories. "Thank you, Gideon and Gail. My learned colleagues raise interesting points for us to consider. Now allow me to offer my own analysis of Ms. Nevenmoore, whose psychopathology has been central to our discussions."

Saks looked up while the others fixed their eyes on Sidd as he uncharacteristically began to walk around the room like a trial attorney in his closing argument to the jury.

"Complex cases such as this rarely are reduced to single diagnostic formulation. Her mania, characterological patterns, trauma, and history of neglectful and malignant parenting cannot be disputed. Gid's hypothesis about dissociation is interesting in light of the violent deaths of three family members in less than a year, followed by another traumatic event in 2019. Surely, that's more than any of us could metabolize. And Dr. Masters posits the dark triad of narcissism, psychopathy, and Machiavellianism, putting forth a fascinating theory that Raevyn formed a dual killing bond with another malignant narcissist, Roddy

Cummings, as the two sought revenge against psychiatrists whom they felt had harmed them. Earlier, our colleagues Dr. Mendelson and Mrs. Madrigal wondered whether her auditory hallucinations could actually have been the voice of her brother, who had feigned his death and was hiding in the house. All interesting formulations."

Kitts assumed that Sidd was merely summing up the theories of the others and preparing to offer a grand synthesis of opposing points of view. She was surprised by what followed.

"But I offer something different. I question whether a fundamental illness may have been missed all along. Twenty-five to thirty-three percent of individuals suffering from schizophrenia have treatment-resistant hallucinations and delusions that continue despite multiple trials of antipsychotic medication. I believe Ms. Nevenmoore is one of those individuals who may be suffering from an undiagnosed schizophrenia spectrum or schizoaffective disorder and that her auditory hallucinations and delusional thinking have never disappeared. Of course, as I said, a single diagnosis does not obviate the others. We know that trauma is found in the backgrounds of many suffering from psychotic illnesses. But I suggest that schizophrenia, not bipolarity, DID, or psychopathy lies at the heart of Ms. Nevenmoore's condition."

Kitts's eyes glazed over listening to the psychological gymnastics espoused by leading experts who danced on the head of a pin as they sought to find explanations for the killings, the events at the Cliffs, and Raevyn's deep-seated psychological problems. She was about to push back against their theoretical constructions when Sidd continued.

"Diagnostic clarification is necessary in understanding a potential UNSUB but in no way removes Ms. Nevenmoore as a suspect in this investigation. In fact, we have additional information that further entangles her in these killings. Pat, would you please share what we've recently learned?"

"Sure. Let me begin by saying that before he left the team, Dr. Mendelson emailed information about Raevyn's treatment at Austen

Riggs. Unfortunately, he did not respond to requests for clarification. We only recently followed up on this and sent for her records. I'm sorry it's taken this long. Anyway, it gets complicated but interesting."

Kitts was waiting for another shoe to drop when Sidd suggested they take a 15-minute break. Sitting alone in the coffee nook while the others chit-chatted about their gardens and dogs, she struggled to process what she was hearing about Raevyn's illness and the tension between perception and illusion, and to anticipate what new evidence Pat was about to share.

When they returned to their seats, Pat had passed out a summary of Raevyn's three-month residential treatment at Austen Riggs. Kitts was familiar with the celebrated institution that had treated celebrities like Judy Garland, Sinclair Lewis, and James Taylor.

Pat began, "We recently learned that Raevyn had a connection with another of the dead ARES doctors, Julius Fortunato. It just so happens that Fortunato was her psychiatrist at Austen Riggs. He left Penn after the project was completed and was hired as a senior psychiatrist at Riggs in 2020. He ended up being Raevyn's doctor during her treatment there until patients were sent home due to COVID."

Sidd added, "If you read between the lines of his clinical notes, it sounds like Dr. Fortunato struggled with Raevyn during her residential treatment there. In other words, as our analytic colleagues would say, his negative countertransference toward her is suggested by the pejorative language he used to describe his patient in his chart entries, progress—or dare I say lack of progress—notes, and final treatment summary. The language he used reveals his thinly veiled contempt for his patient. Raevyn surely read his summaries after she was discharged. There is documentation that her records were released to her in 2023."

Lenore stated, "And it looks like Fortunato was killed during the time Raevyn was away, supposedly visiting someone in Boston. We've looked into this. Seems like she did actually visit a friend named Marney Peters during that time. But Marney said that Raevyn came and went as she pleased during her stay. Fortunato still had an office in Philly, where he was killed. Raevyn could have easily taken the train down from Boston."

De Vere, who had been silent, spoke up. "So, it seems that Ms. Nevenmoore had a troubled history with Dr. Fortunato. And let's not forget who sent her to Austen Riggs in the first place—Linus Prokop. In essence, it was Prokop who sent both Nevenmoore twins into treatment programs against their will."

"And their bitterness festered like a boil," added Saks, "giving both grounds for hating his guts."

"And a motive," said Lenore.

Masters conjectured, "I also think she's lied to her therapist. Idina is a marvelous clinician, but we've all been fooled before. But some would say we can't be helpful if we don't believe our patients."

Kitts couldn't ignore what she was hearing, but she was sure of what she had seen when she found Raevyn. She tried to explain again. "I hear what you're all saying.Not everything fits into neat little boxes here, but man, she was in sorry shape when I found her. I just can't see her doing that to herself."

De Vere commiserated. "That's another thing that's bothered me, dear. It's hard to imagine the miseries people can inflict on themselves in pursuit of an aim or cause. History is replete with examples of those who have done great violence to themselves, including the hunger strikes during the Troubles by Irish Republican prisoners in Northern Ireland. They went for weeks without eating or taking liquid. Can you imagine their gaunt faces and desiccated lips?"

Masters added, "And Raevyn trained for years as a gymnast. Surely, she learned to tolerate excruciating pain in pursuit of a goal, as Bernie just said."

Nicola could no longer dismiss what she was hearing. She had been trying to silence her doubts about how defensive and evasive Raevyn had been about her trip to Boston and her admission that she wanted

Finch dead. And why had she lied to the police? It was true that she had links with two of the dead shrinks, which spoke to motive. They were right; she would remain at the center of all this. Maybe Saks was right all along about Raevyn playing a long game. As for what she had seen on the beach that day, no one else saw it except for a woman with a documented history of psychosis, now possibly psychopathy, *and* a motive to kill. Nicola was beginning to doubt what she had seen. The sun *had* been bright, and the glare *had* obscured a crisp image of who or whatever she thought she saw on the rocky beach that afternoon. She knew Masters was right. The eyes can create what the mind wants to see.

Sidd signaled the meeting was over. "We are assembling the pieces. There are more gaps, but what we've heard today deserves serious consideration while we gather and synthesize more data before reaching our final conclusions. But there are indisputable facts. First, we can make a strong case against Professor Cummings, who seems eager to take credit for the murders, and second, Ms. Nevenmoore suffers from a mental illness, which I believe is an undiagnosed schizophrenia. Regarding her involvement in these murders, she will remain a suspect. As more evidence is collected, we will likely charge her as well. And finally, as for her brother, until we have evidence to the contrary, we'll assume the record is correct. The official police report was that Finch Nevenmoore took his own life on that bridge on May 23, 2019."

As the others were preparing to leave, Bernice De Vere stood and looked, first at Sidd and then to Kitts, whose arm she reached out to touch. "I would just like to say that it is indeed a privilege to be a part of this group that functions as a sentient brain, weighing the facts and engaging in the dialectical process of searching for the best formulation of the case. However, with great respect," she added, turning to Sidd, "I think we've overlooked something important. The eminent group therapist turned novelist, Irving Yalom, wrote one of my favorite books called, *When Nietzsche Wept*. It tells of an imaginary clinical encounter between Josef Breuer and Friedrich Nietzsche. In it, Yalom imagines a conversation about differential diagnosis between Breuer and his disciple Sigmund Freud, in which the elder physician says to the younger Freud, that some dogs have ticks, and some dogs have fleas, and that some have ticks *and* fleas.*"

"And your point is *what* exactly, Bernice?" queried a bored-looking Saks.

"My point is that I fear we're falling victim to an all-too-common cognitive distortion—absolutist or binary thinking—wrestling over the either versus the or, when in fact both may be true. That Raevyn suffers treatment-resistant hallucinations and delusions does not mean that she wasn't actually hearing her brother communicating with her. Isn't it possible for both to be true? She could be quite ill and have hallucinated his voice at one moment, while at other times heard his actual whispers from the room next door. Like the hackneyed saying, 'just because you are paranoid doesn't mean there aren't people out to get you,' both illness and actuality may coexist in a complex way for Raevyn. And as I've said before, I *am* troubled by the lack of DNA evidence supporting his suicide. I, for one, am not ready to dismiss the possibility that Finch Nevenmoore *is* still out there."

Kitts shrugged and gave a half-smile. "Thanks. I never said that Raevyn didn't have major issues, but this other stuff about Finch . . . I just don't know."

De Vere looked at her. "You're right. Despite everything said here today, we simply don't know what we don't know. Of course, Raevyn suffers from a severe mental illness—a bipolar disorder, maybe schizoaffective psychosis—and at the same time may have heard her brother's actual words. She may have even formed some kind of twisted bond with Cummings and collaborated in the killing of five people. Maybe there are more to come. But sometimes we can be so sure of things that we have trouble looking beyond our certainty, however wrong it ends up being. So, all I'm saying is that we don't really know, do we?

To quote from my favorite 90s program, *The X Files*, 'The truth is out there somewhere.' It may take us a while to find it, but 'The truth will out,' as Hamlet put it. Regardless of how this story ends, *Semper Fidelis*, Nicola. You've done admirable work. Now, take a much-earned rest."

46

Goodbye Blue

Three Weeks Later . . .

Steam rose from Nicola's hot coffee into the cool morning air. She enjoyed her tiny lanai, watching the sunrise and listening to Billie Holiday sing "Good Morning Heartache." She felt guilty about taking a three-week leave, but she was exhausted. The last several months had taken all she had. The brief relationship with Sol had affected her more than she could admit. She felt raw. Her steely exterior had cracked, laying open the tenderness she'd long kept hidden. Feeling vulnerable didn't suit her. She continued to be haunted by Raevyn's story but even more troubled by her own self-doubt. She was having trouble putting a lid on either.

Just before her leave, she sat in on the interrogation of Roderick Cummings. Even without his cooperation, they had irrefutable evidence from his computer, but like many serial killers with monumental egos, Bertie Cummings couldn't stand it that others might not recognize his brilliance. He wanted everyone to know how clever he was. He proudly laid claim to the killings of the four psychiatrists and Sophie Morella for their "breathtaking breach of ethics and soul-crushing cruelty." He declared they deserved to die and had planned the same fate for others. But when it came to the Nevenmoores, Bertie denied knowing either, despite the volume of messages found not only on the laptop at the bay house, but on the cell phone and computer in his apartment.

He claimed his phone and computer had been stolen and denied any knowledge of the emails or calls.

The kudos from Boz and the BAU team were nice but felt a bit hollow. Still, she tried reminding herself that this was what she had wanted. They had a small ceremony at which several members of the team spoke. Lenore repeatedly thanked Nicola for her service, and Pat baked a cake. Sidd kept his remarks brief, while De Vere spoke about Kitt's heroic, lifelong service as a Marine, a deputy, and now as an FBI agent. Toby came by for cake and orange juice, and Gideon Saks never showed up.

After presenting her with a commendation, Boz had to "piss off" to another meeting. On his way out, he pulled Kitts aside and whispered something about wanting to set up a meeting to discuss the "fast-tracking of her career." In the past, such words were intoxicating, no matter the cost. But now, they only warned of a hangover.

*, *, *

Nicola finished her coffee and went inside to change the music when she caught sight of the empty cage. *Oh, Langston.* Her heart sank. The hardest part of returning home from Wisconsin was having to read the letter from Potomac Valley and listen to the unanswered voicemails. Though they had initially thought his feather picking was related to stress and boredom, they discovered a fibrosarcoma on his breast. He may have been lonely, but he was suffering from a large tumor that had become ulcerated from his picking. They had wanted her permission to begin experimental treatment, though they cautioned that the prognosis was grim. The last voicemail was to inform her that Langston hadn't made it. He was gone.

How she sobbed at this news, sitting for hours, rocking and wailing at the loss of her blue companion. She was drowning in guilt for leaving him alone in her apartment while she chased her career, thinking only of herself. Sorrow over Langston led to a hidden reservoir of grief for her brother Blue. Somehow thoughts of her lost brother made her think of Finch Nevenmoore, another boy who'd been lost long ago. Nicola sat for the rest of the day, crying like she had never cried before. She wept as she remembered her little brother's peaceful innocence as he squeezed her hand one last time. She cried when she remembered the silly song that Privates Gonlin and Garcia used to sing in the barracks. When her tears and bourbon ran dry, she cried some more.

Feeling lost and alone, she reached for her phone and called the one person she knew she could trust—Carmine. When he answered, she spoke words unfamiliar to her: "I need you."

Carmine flew out the next day and stayed for a week. He straightened out her apartment, did loads of laundry, shopped, and cooked for her. Mostly, he sat with her in silence, a state they both knew so well. He listened when she blamed herself for leaving Langston alone, just as she blamed herself for leaving her brother behind before he was shot. At one point, Carmine reached out to hold her hand and began to cry with her.

Toward the end of the week, Nicola felt somewhat purged of the grief and self-loathing and began to bargain. During breakfast, before driving Carmine to the airport, she asked if he thought she should get another bird. "I know I can do better this time. I mean, I won't leave him like I did Langs."

Carmine smiled and muttered, "You could, Nicola. But maybe it's t-time to be done with cages. B-birds need to fly free. People need that t-too. That's all."

With Carmine gone, Nicola decided to take down his cage. She found a long blue tail feather at the bottom and tied it to the eagle feather Carmine had given her. She hung them on her bedroom ceiling, knowing she had been blind for too long.

It was time to go back to work. The case of the dead shrinks hadn't been completely closed, but it felt like the center of gravity had shifted. Raevyn would remain under investigation, but with Cummings in custody, the killings had stopped. Lenore and Toby were assigned another case. Dr. Gilbert returned to her practice. BAU-4 had caught their UNSUB who'd confessed to the killings. They would await more proof of an accomplice. But Kitts was plagued by unanswered questions about Raevyn and what she'd seen on the cliffs. Still, one question loomed above the others—could she trust herself?

47

Reawakening

Her leave felt cleansing, yet it left her sad and empty. Langston was gone and Carmine had left. Her tiny apartment rang with the silence of too many echoes. Ruminations about Raevyn and Calvert Cliffs continued to inhabit her mind. She wanted to move on but needed one last meeting with Idina Madrigal to get the updated information for her final report. She hoped their meeting would put all of this to rest. Kitts thought again about the twisting of facts and lofty theories spewed by the insufferable Saks, then Morgan, and even Sidd. Her ruminations brought back the anger, confusion, and doubt she'd been trying to suppress. What if they had been right all along? Had she seen what she wanted to see and been outwitted by a devious psychopath playing the role of a frightened victim?

Madrigal greeted her warmly. She looked more robust and less frail. She no longer wore a headscarf. In its place were tufts of soft hair that held promises of hope and resiliency.

"Hello Agent Kitts. Nice to see you again. Please come in and have a seat. I don't know how much I can tell you today, but I will let you know if there are things I don't have Raevyn's permission to share."

Kitts was struck by the warmth and simplicity of her office. Nothing pretentious. She noticed Madrigal's diploma from Case Western School of Social Work hanging on the wall. The Monet prints brought to mind her living room in Aurora, Colorado, where she had watercolors on one wall and military commendations on the other. On Madrigal's desk sat a single book next to her planner. When the therapist got up to adjust the blinds, Nicola squinted to read the title: *From the Shadows of the Mind: Trauma & the Symbols that Transform Them,* by H. T. Lukas. There was something familiar about the author's name, but she couldn't place it.

"So, how can I help you, Agent Kitts?"

"I get the whole patient confidentiality thing, but can you tell me how she's doing?"

"Well, generally speaking, better, but she's got a long road ahead with all she's been through."

"What has she told you about what happened at Calvert Cliffs?"

"I'm afraid I can't really say too much about that. Is she still a suspect, after everything that's happened to her?"

Now it was Kitts's turn. "Not to be coy here, Ma'am, but I can't get too much into the weeds on that one. Lemme just say that they're not quite done with her and have doubts about her credibility."

"Hmm, is that right? That's unfortunate. As you know, she's been through a horrendous ordeal."

"Yeah. I still can't totally wrap my head around all the pieces, twists, and turns. I know you can't say much, but do you think she's still on edge about her brother; thinking he might still be out there, that is?"

Idina gave no response.

"I know you can't say much more, but let me ask it this way: Are *you* personally afraid he's still out there, especially now that they've stopped patrolling your place?"

Idina paused. "Let's just say I may get a German Shepard."

"Okay, I get that. I do. So, just to finish up . . . and I'm not fishing here, but...."

"Yes, go on, Agent Kitts. I realize you've got a final report to write. Shoot."

"It's like this. Can someone like Raevyn *really* get better? I mean, after all she's been through. Some folks have pet theories about what's going on in her mind, but I don't know. Above my pay grade. I'm just saying that maybe she has some trouble knowing what's true and what's not, telling the truth, and all that. Either way, it seems like that girl *has* been through too much to come back from."

"That's been said about many of us.... I understand there are lots of questions about her. I don't know what happened at the bay house. None of us can be sure about that or what happened in her home growing up. But it's hard for me to believe that she did all this to herself. I'll leave it at that. Let's just say I wouldn't be working with her if I didn't think I could help. Hope is important for all of us who have walked in the shadows—hope and having someone who believes in us. I've never thought Raevyn was a saint or simply an innocent victim. She has not always been truthful. Few of us always are. Some more than others, but most of us are caught up in an invisible web of confusing, contradictory, and conflicted feelings and wishes that sometimes drive us in opposite directions."

"Yeah, I can see that. But honestly, I don't know how she, or anybody like her, could ever figure it out enough to get to the other side. Take me, for example."

Madrigal leaned forward. "Go on."

"Well, I look at someone like Raevyn, who, as I understand it, had everything going for her, but no one *really* knew her. Maybe she didn't even know herself. It's like she didn't feel she could ever let her guard down and go to anyone for help. Know what I mean?"

"I do. The curse of perfectionism or . . . thinking that strength and toughness mean never having doubts or being scared."

"Boy, that's the truth. Sounds like a page out of my life to be perfectly honest. I've walked that path since I was a kid. I grew up around two ex-Marines, my pops and grandad, and they drilled that kind of shit into me. Sorry. A tour in Afghanistan and a life in law enforcement kind of sealed the deal."

"You saw combat?"

"I saw my fair share of killing and dying. Plenty of scared people just trying to survive."

"Living through that must have affected you a great deal, but I imagine you've found ways to cope, just like our Raevyn or anyone else who's faced life and death situations."

"Yeah, but I don't know if my ways were all that healthy, to be honest. I drink too much and manage to keep people at arm's length, acting all tough and shit, sorry. I know this guy, actually. I've known him for about 10 years. His name is Carmine. Now *there's* someone you could do a case study on. But he's been . . . well, a friend. Might be my only one if I'm telling the truth. He came to see me a couple of weeks ago after I lost my pet bird. Sounds stupid, right? But Carmine told me he thought I was sleepwalking through my life and all this other crazy sh– stuff like that, and what I needed to do was wake up. He gave me an eagle feather. Said it would help me see better." She shrugged. "I don't know. He even said he thought I was living in a cage, picking at myself, same as my bird was. He does say some crazy-sounding shit."

"Sounds like a good friend, indeed. I could be wrong, and forgive me if I'm overstepping, but maybe you're wondering if what Carmine said is true."

Nicola paused and studied the pictures Idina had on her wall, particularly one of a small child and an older woman in a garden. "Maybe, maybe not. This'll surprise you, but I actually went to Smith School of Social Work. Got my MSW and was starting on a PhD. I always had this fascination with the 'whys,' you know, what causes troubled people to do what they do. Anyway, seems like ancient history since I've returned to law enforcement."

"I had no idea you have an MSW. How could I since we've never really talked? I'm also intensely interested in the whys, so if I may ask, what made you leave Smith?"

"Well, hell . . . that's a story that would usually require a bottle of

Irish whisky. Let's just say that some of what you called my coping ten-
dencies got in the way."

"Such as? I'm interested if you'd care to say."

Nicola took a deep breath, looked down at her hands, and felt the
sharp edge of her fingernails dig into her palms. "I've got this thing that
keeps getting me in trouble. Older married men . . . bosses, you know.
Happened at Smith, with a professor, no less. And I just went through
something like that here. Seems like it kinda keeps happening. Same
chorus, different verse. It's like, when the engine light on your dash-
board comes on, how many miles are you gonna drive pretending it's
not there? I just don't know."

"Hmm. Do you understand your attraction to these men and your
choosing to ignore the signals?"

"Think you probably already figured that one out, right? I mean,
the part about keeping folks at arm's length. What better way to have
my cake and eat it too than to start a romance with someone who'll
never be able to get that close? I can feel like I'm all special and everything and manage the risks of it going too far. Worked pretty well, 'til
it didn't. So, I left Smith 'cause everyone was whispering about me and
him. Figured it was easier to pack up and leave."

"But Smith is only one school. I'm wondering why you didn't pursue your PhD elsewhere."

"Right, you'd think. But to be truthful, and I don't think I've ever
said this before, the whole mental health thing got a little too close. I
figured to be open to other people's pain, I had to be in touch with
my own. My pops had this annoying saying he brought back from
'Nam that I can't get out of my brain: 'Don't mean nuthin.' He'd say,
if everything is really nuthin,' then ain't nuthin' can hurt you. That's
the way he talked. The whole social work thing started feeling a little
too real, and that felt risky. Realized I'd rather be dodging bullets than
looking too closely at what's inside of myself. Besides, I tried all that
shit before. You know, waking up and facing myself—the therapy show.

Back before I left the sheriff's department in Colorado for Smith, I was in the VA with a bunch of sorry-ass folks like me. I actually thought it made a difference at first, 'til it didn't. My old rubber band just snapped back. I like it that way. Staying on edge with policing or working with the bureau is what keeps me sharp."

"Like you're back in Afghanistan."

"Exactamento! Bingo, you win the prize. It's what I do."

"And you're okay with that?"

"I . . . don't know. I survived that way. You know, being sharp, trusting my instincts—what I see, what I know. But...."

"But?"

"But I'm beginning to wonder if those instincts are right. I probably shouldn't say this, but I thought I saw Finch walking on the beach that day in the Cliffs."

Madrigal nodded. "I know."

"He stopped and looked up at me when I was standing next to Raevyn. The problem is that no one else saw him. No one except for Raevyn, and everyone thinks she's nuts. Now, I don't know what I saw. The shadow of a rock? Maybe. My imagination? Who knows. Seeing what I wanted to see? Thing is, I know what I saw but don't know if what I saw was real. Kinda gets you questioning. See, I've always survived by being *certain*, knowing and being sure of what was out there, who I was, and what I wanted. It's what gave me my edge and kept me alive. Now, I just don't know if I can trust myself. I'm not sure what to believe. Truth is, I'm not even sure what I want anymore. Thought I knew. It all made sense—the mission, the action, the rush—but now I'm not so sure. Like what if everything I thought I wanted just ends up fading like the man on the beach?"

"I know about the figure on the beach, but must ask again . . . are you comfortable with all this—shutting out your feelings, keeping others at arm's length, trying not to look at things too closely, and now, not trusting yourself to make the right decisions? I can hear how uncomfortable this uncertainty is for you. So, I'm curious, Nicola. Are you okay with this life of yours?"

"Yeah . . . I mean no. But what am I gonna do? Start therapy? Don't let the whole Smith social work thing fool you. The way I figure, some people can do the therapy gig, and others like me would have no earthly idea how to open that vault, even if I wanted to." Her voice softened as she gazed down at her shoes. "I can't see me doing that. I don't think I've got it in me. Honestly, I wouldn't know how to even get started."

Idina stared out her window. In the stillness, she heard the gentle cooing of a pair of mourning doves and noticed that the leaves were beginning to change their colors. She smiled, turned back, and whispered,

"I'm not so sure, Nicola . . .I think you just did."

Epilogue

Six Months Later . . .

The man sat quietly in the waiting room. It was dimly lit and displayed a shabby shrink décor with an eclectic mix of modern and ancient furniture. He sat in one of the overstuffed faux leather chairs. He glanced at a dusty end table with a teetering stack of magazines. Many were tattered and yellowed with time. He noticed pictures of the seashore on each wall, signaling a safe harbor for those about to enter.

He thought back to the first time they met, wondering if she would remember, let alone recognize him after all these years. He sat patiently looking at his watch, noting she was running late, much as he remembered. He heard movement inside her office and listened as her footsteps drew near.

A woman in her mid-fifties, maybe older, opened the door. She gave him a formal smile and greeted him professionally. She looked different, but not so much that he wouldn't have known it was she. Prominent roots of gray betrayed her dyed red hair. Her glasses, no longer the signature black horn rims, were now sleeker, but the lenses were decorated with the smudges he remembered so well. Age had not been kind to her.

"Hello, I'm Dr. Sondra Metzenger. Why don't you come into my office, and we can get started? Please hang your coat and hat on the rack. I'm curious to hear about the changes you're interested in making. You mentioned something about your habits."

"Why thank you, Doctor." He stood, slipped off his raincoat, hung it on the coat rack, and carefully placed a maroon fedora on top. He turned back to her and said, "There's a great deal to catch you up on,

Doctor."

She looked puzzled. "I'm not sure I follow you."

"Oh, but Doctor, you soon will. We have much to discuss. It's about the treatments for my *disgusting* habits and *unfortunate* disease."

She squinted and stared at the man.

The quiet man stared back.

Her voice quavered, "I-I'm afraid . . . I don't understand. Do I know you? Mr. uh—"

The quiet man whispered, "It's Wart. Mr. Wart, remember? You see, Doctor, there are accounts to be settled. I'm ready now and quite eager to begin."

Author Notes

Good fiction strikes a balance between the real and the imagined. In my stories, I also strive to balance a mental health drama with a mystery or, in this case, a crime story. Despite my efforts to find balance, I may sometimes stray too far in one direction or the other. I try to make my characters and their struggles believable and relatable. This is especially the case with their mental health battles. I'm also intrigued by blending mental health fiction with a good mystery. But in writing about a crime drama, I'm aware that *Whispers* takes liberties with the realities of law enforcement procedures. This may especially be true in my depiction of the personnel and workings of the FBI BAU—what the agents and profilers really do and how they conduct their investigations. As a psychologist, I leaned heavily on the psychological reality of my characters' experiences but realize the ways I've depicted the law enforcement professionals, and the procedural aspects of their work may sometimes be more fanciful than real. Although the BAU profilers and agents did not fly around the country in their leer jet, the amount of time spent in meetings debating psychological theories was more likely a leap into fiction.

In writing mental health fiction, I attempt to present the complexities and poignant realities of individuals suffering from mental illnesses. I am interested in writing about characters, whether patients, healers, or protectors, who struggle with mental illnesses, become caught up in a mystery, and ultimately find hope in healing relationships. In creating such characters and their dilemmas, I wish to humanize them as they become embroiled in extraordinary events that carry ambiguity and uncertainty. Ultimately, I want to create characters who are more than a collection of symptoms or diagnoses. Like all of us, they are complex people doing their best to cope.

Actual books cited include:

- *Mindhunter* by John Douglas and Mark Olshaker (1995, 2017), Gallery Books
- *The Drama of the Gifted Child* by Alice Miller (1979), Labyrinth Books
- *The Mask of Sanity* by Harvey M. Cleckley (1941, 1982), Mosby
- *When Nietzsche Wept* by Irwin D. Yalom (2007)
- *The Juniper Tree* by the Grimm Brothers (1812)
- *Kiss the Girls* by James Patterson (1995)

All other books mentioned are fictional. Treatment centers such as Austen Riggs, Menninger, and McLean are real. Oak Harbor is fictional. Calvert Cliffs is real, but a residential community overlooking the shoreline called *The Cliffs* is not.

About The Author

J. Herman Kleiger is a renowned author of three novels and six professional books on the Rorschach test, psychosis, and bipolar disorders. He is a senior psychologist and psychoanalyst based in Maryland, known for his deep understanding of human psychology.

For more information or to contact the author, visit: JHermanKleiger.com

If you enjoyed *Whispers*, be sure to check out *Tears Are Only Water* and *The 11th Inkblot*—both available on Amazon.

Acknowledgments

This book inhabited my mind for the last two years, and I'm grateful to those who have lovingly and patiently listened to my ruminations about the story. I'm most thankful to my wife, Nannette Bowman, who always makes herself available to read and listen to endless drafts and share her feedback. Her work as my primary editor was enormously valuable. Her sharp eye and gift for language helped bring the characters to life. I couldn't have done this without you, Noni!

Family love and support provide quiet sustenance. I am fortunate to have had parents who loved me. Thank you, Mom and Dad. I am infinitely grateful to my son, Nike, for his love and for honoring me by being such a good man and adoring father. My multi-talented daughter Katie is an inspiration. I've learned how to be an artist from her. My daily life is enriched by having Jodie and Nicole, my loving, immensely talented stepdaughters, whom I cannot thank enough. Thanks to my son-in-law Tom for his goodness and steady presence in my life. I'm grateful to my daughter-in-law Colleen for her deep well of goodness and love, and Katie's constancy is now multiplied by having her soon-to-be husband, a wonderful man named "Lucky," in my life too. My sister Margy and brother-in-law Larry are the dearest of souls who are always there for me. Brother-in-law Greg, a fellow writer and friend, has been a wonder. And my gifts are magnified by my granddaughters! Thank you, Brooke, Maxie, Riley, Sloane, and welcome to Zoë! I treasure you and am immensely proud to be your Popi. To quote Greg, I'm truly blessed and grateful. Oh Lucky Man!

I'm incredibly thankful to my first readers, Larry and Margy

Bookman, for their careful reading and feedback. Thank you, Margy and Larry.

Several others took the time to read earlier versions of my manuscript and offer thoughtful comments about the story. Thanks to Rick Waugaman, Sam Goldberg, Barton Evans, and my daughter Katie Kleiger for their insights and editorial suggestions. The story grew under their tutelage. Katie was immeasurably helpful when I became stuck and needed a fresh perspective. Several other readers willingly gave their valuable time to provide early reviews of the book. I want to acknowledge Debra Bolton, Jeff Berman, Laura Wright, Susan Kraus, Steve Lerner, and others who agreed to read and review *Whispers*.

Thanks to Professor Bolton, who introduced me to Dr. Marianne Korten, who helped with the mathematical equations in the book.

Charlie Levin, Lily Drew, Neil Szigethy, Jenny Garrity, and the rest of the Munn Press team are a joy. I'm grateful to the cover designer for such exquisite artwork. Charlie and his teams' creativity and technical expertise turn a rough manuscript into a polished book. Thank you all!

All my writing efforts eventually lead back to Rachel Thompson, friend and social media guru. I can't thank you, Rachel enough for your help and encouragement.

Finally, I'm grateful to long-term friends and colleagues who have supported me and tolerated with good humor my obsession for writing fiction. Thanks to Ali, the Topeka Men's Group, Jed, Bart, Gavin, and Odile, to name but a few. I am also grateful for friends in the international Rorschach community.

Finally, finally, I couldn't write about people's inner lives and struggles to become whole without having had a legion of wonderful and sage teachers, therapists, and patients as my guides. I'm grateful for your wisdom, tolerance, and love.

Made in the USA
Middletown, DE
27 April 2025

74731189R00165